Heart of a Runaway Girl

TREVOR WILTZEN

Heart of a Runaway Girl
Trevor Wiltzen

Published by:
Trevor Wiltzen
PO Box 22528 Southbrook
Edmonton, AB, Canada, T6W063

Cover Design: Trevor Wiltzen

ISBN-13: 978-1-7774-2121-2

DEDICATED TO FAMILY AND FRIENDS

CHAPTER 1

Wednesday, September 3, 1986

M abel adjusted the nameplate pinned near her heart. She took out her notepad, flipped it to a blank page, then put it back in her apron pocket. Her fingernails weren't perfect. They hadn't been for years, but she kept a nice color on them. She smelled the steam off the coffee and knew the pot was fresh, just like her customers wanted. She turned to face her diner with the coffee pot in hand.

Starting through the aisles, she topped up cups with flair and left her customers smiling. Most were either guests at her motel, miners and construction workers servicing the new mine, truck drivers stopping in, or the local folks who didn't have someone at home to brew them a fine coffee or fix them a good meal. Most had already finished their dinners, except for two kids in the back booth, who hadn't ordered anything. They kept up with the coffee, though, and she was tempted to bring them something to eat anyway. They were too skinny.

The girl in the booth had face piercings and a tattoo spelling H-O-P-E on the backs of her fingers. She was barely eighteen if that. Likely came from a good family as her clothing looked new, though stained and rumpled. She was dressed in black, which matched her dyed hair and dark lipstick.

The local man across from her was familiar to Mabel. A former tree planter out of California, he was known to sell weed in Blue River, and maybe some harder drugs as well — or so the whispers went. Winston was his name, though Mabel didn't think it suited him.

Neither looked at her as she refilled their cups. The girl stared out the rain-streaked window as if to avoid looking at the young man opposite her, while his gaze was directed straight at the girl. He was angry, for sure. They'd been having an intense conversation for over an hour — occasionally, a voice had been raised and then muted like a gusting fall storm. They'd been practically face-to-face while they talked but now couldn't be sitting further apart. Their argument hadn't solved anything, Mabel thought. Most arguments lead nowhere good. The young man glanced up at Mabel, looking embarrassed and frustrated, and gave her a 'Why are you still here?' look. But in that glance, Mabel could see he was afraid. Afraid for the girl and maybe for what she might do next. Oh, you poor dears, she thought. You're too young for this.

"Do you need anything?" Mabel asked.

The girl turned away further. The boy — Mabel had

downgraded him from a man — said, "We're fine," drawing a huff from the girl. Mabel stayed for a moment, hand on her hips, coffeepot held tight, looking at them. They were too young for wisdom, too old for innocence, and it pained her. But this wasn't the time for a motherly sermon. These kids wouldn't listen any more than hers would in a mood like this.

"Well, tell me when you need anything, dears," she said and waited for just a touch longer in the hopes they would.

When they didn't, she swung around, eyes glistening, and hoped life wouldn't make an example of these two. If she had known, she would have turned around, swept them up, brought them to one of the motel's rooms, or — better yet — to her home out back. She had lived there for all her forty-one years. After her parents had passed in her early twenties, she'd taken over the diner, the motel, and the house with its beautiful wraparound porch.

At least some of it: a bank up in Seattle owned the rest. This town, Blue River, didn't have a bank — too small and practically a castoff from the highway. Farmers, sawmill operators, and miners called it home as well as extremists who called it a kingdom, a sorry lot of folks, mostly lonely men and women with nothing in their pockets or would-be-patriarchs who wanted a secluded place to raise their children. Not that Blue River was particularly good to its young. Most wanted to leave, and Mabel couldn't blame them. Any kid with ambition seemed to go. It had gotten so bad some folks said the only decent things tourists cared to see were Mabel's highway motel and diner, and her.

The compliment was nice, sort of, but she wasn't too affected by it. Between the roofs that needed new shingles or the few extra pounds around her curves, she certainly wasn't out to impress anyone anymore; her cooking alone was good enough to bring folks in. Though she had hired a cook now, cutting into her earnings some, as did the wages of her other waitresses and the motel cleaners. Altogether, she kept five locals fully employed. Something she was proud of. Her dad never thought a girl could manage a business, and it made her smile that she'd proven him wrong before he died. Her mother, more of a timid soul while he was still alive, had blossomed into a stronger woman after his passing, though she hadn't lasted much longer for this Earth either. Not that dad was mean or anything or that they made a bad home. It was just the times.

As for her, life wasn't turning out as she'd once hoped. Practically divorced, struggling to stay afloat, at least she had two growing boys she dearly loved. The eldest, Hector, was a ten-year-old future hell-raiser like his father, even if the boy couldn't stand his dad anymore, while Fred was two years younger and a real sweetheart. But her littlest one took on a lot of her pain, being so sensitive and all — and that hurt.

She reached the next table and filled another cup. The old trucker's face lit up as she gave a sweet smile. He spooned the sugar in and said, "Thank you, Mabel. This coffee is just fine."

"Oh, Luv, just come back on your return trip. That's all the thanks I need." She patted his shoulder and walked away. And knowing he'd be giving her a quick once-over, she put a little extra swing to her step to brighten his day.

Her charm, swagger, and a little bawdy humor were the only gifts she'd give her male customers. Still married, she was loyal to a flaw. Her poor fool of a husband, Bill, having stopped drinking, was at least smart enough to keep trying to win her back, the rare times he was back in town. And if he weren't so tough on our boys, she thought, maybe they could be a family again. But he just wouldn't learn. Even with the gray hair and wrinkles on his youthful frame, he was still more boy than man, and she didn't need another child to raise.

Reaching the counter, she picked up a cloth, gave the smooth surface a quick shine, then surveyed her world, with its green-and-white vinyl seats and dated décor. She hadn't changed a thing since her father built it in the late fifties, and it made her wonder if she weren't meant for these Nancy Reagan times. But as long as her clients left her diner with a smile, no matter how life treated them, it was fine with her. This world needed a little more love in it. And maybe, she thought, her life did as well.

She looked at the kids in the far booth and frowned. Now, why are those kids fighting, she asked herself. Evil is as evil does, as the Preacher used to say on Sundays when he was alive. So don't let that devil in. He preys on the weak — and you don't know how vulnerable you are.

CHAPTER 2

Thursday, September 4

The next day, Mabel knew the dinner rush was dying when the remaining truckers peeled themselves off their seats to get back on the road, and the few locals who had come in to play backgammon were packing up, laughing and ribbing each other. The locals nodded to Blue River's Sheriff, bearded and heavy-set, who had just arrived, opening the door for them and tipping his hat as they left.

Sheriff Dan tossed his hat and notebook onto the diner's long counter, hitched up his pants, and eased onto his favorite stool with a grunt.

Mabel came by with his usual coffee. "Not like you to be out this late," she said. "Shouldn't you be home with your hunting show on?"

The Sheriff used a napkin to wipe his forehead,

sweating despite the air conditioning. "That's exactly where I should be," he said before a short coughing fit took him. He pounded it out of his chest while scooping heaps of sugar into his coffee, spilling some on the counter.

"You want some pie too?"

The Sheriff stopped pounding his chest with a last grunt. "Mabel," he said, leaning back. "That sounds about right."

"You got it."

Customers like Dan often treated her more like a therapist or a bartender, and she knew more about some folks than they would tell their kin. But something was amiss with Dan tonight — she worried it was about her eldest son again — so she added an extra scoop of ice cream on his pie to make him feel good and slid it over.

Dan took a big bite and started talking with his mouth full, spitting crumbs over his beard and onto the table. "Just saw somethin' I wish I could forget."

"Accident?"

Deadly accidents were not uncommon here, the highway a long stretch leading from nowhere to nowhere fast. Beautiful by day, where the dark forest had been swept clear by winter avalanches, revealing spectacular views of mountains, blue rivers, and big sky; sinister at night while looking out a car window at the forest's blackness, with only the tips of its tallest trees cutting into the starry sky to give it form.

The Sheriff shook his head, looking rattled. "Those are bad enough. But no. This was much, much worse."

Mabel was relieved: Dan wouldn't be talking like this if

it were Hector. And though he wasn't the best sheriff by far — in fact, he wasn't too far off from the worst — he helped her family when he could. It wasn't that he was a bad man; he just never learned to be much more than a disappointment to his disappointing parents. Blue River was full of Dans. The wilderness, a breeding ground for weed farmers and end-of-the-world preachers, allowed fringe families to live without fear of Johnny Law and Bob Government. Sheriff Dan knew this, too, so he didn't try too hard to enforce the law. Mostly, he didn't want to get shot for trying. So, he let things slide, and the community knew if he put someone behind bars, it was because he couldn't do anything else.

"You going to tell me about it, Dan?"

"Actually, Mabel. I came here specific to talk to you."

"Oh really?" she asked, her voice cracking. "What's my boy been up to now?"

"No, no, not him. Don't worry," the Sheriff said, flipping open his notebook and resting it on the counter as he polished off a bite. This time he spoke after he swallowed, and she was grateful. "I just want to know if a young girl passed through here. Sixteen, maybe eighteen, years old. Black hair, tattoo on her hand—" He stopped as Mabel pulled back, concerned.

"I know the one. She sat back there."

The Sheriff glanced to where she pointed and then leaned in closer. "Anyone with her at the time?"

"That tree planting boy who sells pot — Winston."

"The black fella." His eyes turned cold.

Mabel gave him a fierce look for a warning. "The *boy*."

"You care about all them strays, Mabel, but they can

turn on you. If that fella did those things—"

"What do you mean? What happened to the girl?"

"She's dead."

"Oh, dear," Mabel said. "What happened?"

"Murdered."

"Murdered?!" At Dan's shushing motion, she lowered her voice. "How? What?"

"Them things that were done to that girl." Dan shook his head; he'd started sweating again. "Made my heart turn cold."

Kevin, the twenty-year-old cook, came out of the kitchen to start mopping the floors. With his long hair, handlebar mustache, and tattoos covering most of his body, he was a candidate for trouble himself, and Mabel had made a special effort to get him on the right track. Dan turned quiet and picked up his fork to eat.

When he finished, Mabel said, "Winston's not that type of boy."

Dan put his fork down and wiped his mouth with a napkin. "I don't know what type he is. But I'm going to talk to him. Maybe take him in."

Mabel was taken aback. "Those two kids were a couple, I could see that."

"That's good to know," Dan said, clicking his pen to write her words down in his notebook. "Most murders are committed by someone known to the victim. Someone dies, you look to kin and partners first. Can't see how anyone could have done what was done." Dan glanced up as he wrote. "Were they fighting?"

"Well, yes…" Mabel paused as the Sheriff kept writing and nodding. "No, it's not like that. They were talking for, I don't know, an hour, maybe more. Yes, they'd occasionally raise their voices, but then they'd pipe down again. Dan! Stop writing and look at me. That Winston looked like he cared about her. And more like he was scared for her."

Dan shrugged and clicked his pen closed. "Maybe he thought that girl was going to turn him in or something. Or maybe he was on the drugs, harder than the weed he normally sells. Who knows? This is good, Mabel. I thought this was going to be hard, but it looks like we got our man." Dan flipped his notebook closed.

"You can't say that! They were talking, yes. But that was yesterday. When did it happen?"

"Coroner said last night. Her body was dumped inside the sawmill when there was no shift." He started to get up. "State Police are at the crime scene, so I've got to call this in, maybe beat 'em to it. Get this done quick. It was pretty horrific. The brute beat her, abused her." Then he glanced around and lowered his voice to a whisper. "And likely raped her."

Dan grimaced, then leaned into the radio mic attached to his vest, and called Buster, his volunteer deputy, giving Mabel a moment to think about all she had learned and said. After he was done, she got started.

"Remember, he's innocent until proven guilty."

"Not if Larson's boys get to him first."

Mabel gasped. "Larson's an animal!" Larson was the local drug kingpin who lorded over Blue River like it was his personal domain and acted as the true arbiter of what laws could be broken in town.

"He's good to this community, Mabel."

"What a thing to say! He's only good to white people."

"It's true," the Sheriff said, ignoring her comment.

"He's a racist pig. And so are all those that follow him."

"Better me bringing the boy in than him then, huh?"

"Just don't let that man near him."

"I hear ya," he said, and then stopped. Looked at her. Then slowly said his thoughts aloud, "My man Buster saw the boy in the park earlier today, living in the trailer on Ted's property. But Buster would let Larson know, them being friendly and all. You're right again. I better get on this quick before there's company."

Mabel made one last plea. "Wouldn't the boy have run if he did it? Why would he have stuck around?"

"Don't care." The Sheriff tipped his hat. "Thanks. Didn't think this would pan out so easy, but thanks to you, this could be over quick."

"But—" Mabel protested, but Dan was already lumbering out the door.

The police cruiser lights flashed on outside, and the blue and red washed over the diner tables and booths as he backed out and then drove off into the night to pick up Winston.

The far empty booth caught her attention, and she blamed herself for letting the girl go last night — clearly, trouble had caught up to her, and now she was dead. And the boy? If Dan were to have his way, Winston would be going to prison tonight.

Tears started to flow down her cheeks, and she let them; the staff were used to her tearing up at least once a

11

day out of kindness — but tonight the intensity of Mabel's grief brought Kevin over.

"You okay, Mabel? What did the Sheriff want?"

Mabel didn't answer. She just pulled him in and gave him a long, deep hug, wishing she could protect all the children in the world.

CHAPTER 3

Mabel dried her eyes, sent Kevin to finish the cleanup, and looked around the empty diner. She had another hour till closing. If Buster knew where to find Winston, Larson wouldn't be too far behind. Buster hung out with that White Nationalist bunch — racists, in Mabel's eyes, though they acted like it was a badge of honor. Too many in Blue River had accepted Larson at the start of his reign several years back, which had given Larson time to recruit more supporters. Now, Larson was the big boss, and the small folks were starting to learn the truth. Too late, Mabel thought. Only a matter of time before he took things too far.

Mabel clenched her jaw. While it wasn't her place to get mixed in with the law, the boy needed protection, and Sheriff Dan would only uphold the law so far. His view on what was illegal mirrored the town's, which turned a blind eye to so many things, including bruises on girlfriends and wives, who, in the rare instances they were asked, blamed themselves for getting injured in preposterous ways. While Mabel urged them to leave, time and again, things would settle down, and they'd go back home and not a few months later show up with bruises again. But it wasn't just the violence, it was the emotional abuse, or the financial, or the keeping of the women away from kin and friends, that made Mabel mad. But a black man doing anything wrong in this town was an entirely different thing.

Maybe Winston could have done it, she thought — a crime of passion, like they say in the thriller books — but something told her no, and she trusted her intuition.

She took off her apron, closed up the till, and asked Kevin to lock the doors. Her boys, along with her niece, Kerry, were all hanging out at Consuela's — Mabel's friend in town. The Sheriff's office wasn't too far off. She could do a simple drive by to make sure Winston was safe, then pick up her kids.

She preferred driving into town at night anyways. Night hid all the wild overgrown trees and parched brown lawns, ancient homes in disrepair, and front yards filled with abandoned toys, car parts, or broken furniture. During the day, one might hear the shouts of children playing and dogs barking playfully, but more often than not, these days it was an eerie silence. And that bothered her. Family homes should be loud and boisterous places. They shouldn't be silent, as if all the children and animals had witnessed trauma and were too scared to make noise.

Mabel took out a cigarette and let it hang between her lips, unlit. A reminder of her carefree days with Bill, cruising in his black Mustang after her high school classes, and smoking like rebels, or so it seemed back then, when they were still dating. Her with an older man like him. All before they had got married and Bill had that life-altering contract of the mine stolen from him — before it had broken him and turned him mean, before he'd gotten hard on the kids and she'd kicked him out.

As she rounded the corner leading to the Sheriff's storefront office, a mob of trucks was gathered outside. She swore softly — must be Larson and his gang already. She was right to have come.

Five trucks in a semi-circle highlighted the storefront with their headlights aimed at the glass door. Ten to fifteen men surrounded Sheriff Dan, who had his hand shielding his eyes, blinded by the light. The few holding beers had shaved heads common to Larson's men and were goading on the rest. All fun to them, she thought. Terrifying for Winston if locked inside.

Mabel parked and got out and heard Dan shouting, frightening her. "Now, now, this is a state affair! I told ya, it's not just up to me."

Mabel recognized Frank Hudgens, who shouted back, "Give us the boy, Dan. We can take care of this right now!"

"I told ya. It ain't a local matter no more. I got the State Police involved!"

"Larson is going to get right pissed if you don't let us in!"

So, Larson isn't here yet, Mabel thought. Thank God

— maybe there's something I can do. And without thinking of the risks, she barged right through the group of men to reach the Sheriff.

"Mabel! You shouldn't be here," Dan said, looking shocked to see her in the scrum.

Mabel leaned in close, getting jostled. "What do you need?"

"Call the Staties." He handed her a card. "This is dispatch's number. Ask for Jesse—" Frank made for the door, and Dan shouted, "Hey! Get back!"

Mabel fought her way out of the mess but got shoved roughly by the town's gas station owner. "Hey, watch it Ken!" she shouted, but Ken, caught up by the frenzy, didn't recognize her — and that scared her.

"No one's going inside!" Dan shouted. "I seen the girl, too, and I'm with you, boys. But not like this. I got our man, and justice is going to be done."

"Won't be justice without a rope!"

Mabel rounded the corner fast and fumbled a quarter into the payphone to call police dispatch. She had to plead with the lady dispatcher, who took her time transferring her to Jesse's police radio frequency.

Finally, a man answered like he was speaking into a handset attached to his police vest. "Go ahead."

Mabel had to shout over the awful din. "Oh, thank heavens. Is this Jesse?"

"Hello, Dispatch? I can't hear you."

She shouted louder. "Is this Jesse? From the State Police?"

"Who is this?" The voice sounded annoyed.

Wanting to be taken seriously, she fibbed. "I work for

Sheriff Dan in Blue River. We got an incident going on at the local office."

The man sounded wearier now. "What incident? I'm busy with the crime scene."

Mabel tried to think of the right words to sound official. "We had apprehended the suspect Winston Washington, and he is at the Sheriff's office now. But we got a—" She didn't know what to call it. "A mob out here."

"Ah, crap," he said, and then after a beat, spoke again. "I didn't know Dan had a suspect already."

"He's in custody now."

"Good news and bad news, I guess. Who did you say the suspect is?"

"Winston Washington. But we're wasting time. The guys have got Dan surrounded! I think they're going to bust into the office and get the boy." She glanced around the corner and could see the Sheriff had one hand pressed against the door, and the other white-knuckled around his holstered gun. She doubted he would unholster it — he never had done so on the job before, but it was getting serious if Dan thought he might.

"Okay," Jesse said. "I got another car here. Give me a second."

She could hear him speaking to someone else, and then he came back on the line. "I got Kenny coming right away. I'll close up here. Be another five."

"Please hurry," she said, hanging up.

Mabel poked her head around the corner. The men were furious, and several had started to yank the resisting Sheriff from the door. Larson's men were laughing in back. A few more had shown up but still no Larson. She had her chance: now or never.

With hands shaking, she steeled herself before she stepped in front of the blazing headlights of a truck and screamed, "Police!" — meaning to shout that the police were coming, but fear cutting her words short.

Only a few men turned.

She screamed again, much louder this time, "Police! Break it up!"

The guys in the back gave in, shoved the ones in front, and then turned to look at her as one. Mabel, backlit by the truck's headlights, might only have been a dark form to these men, but she didn't know that. Her knees shook. Sheriff Dan was on the mob's far side, held back by several men, but no one was near her. She wanted to run, but she stood her ground and shouted. "Disperse now, or you'll be arrested!"

"W-h-ho are you?" Frank Hudgens called out, his voice cracking.

"You should be ashamed of yourselves!" Mabel cried out. "Harassing the Sheriff and interfering with the law."

"Is that you, Mabel?" came an incredulous voice from the mob.

"Yes, it's me. I am on the right side of the law, and you ain't! Move on now. You got no rights being here."

"Shee-it," one of them said to Frank. "You done got scared by a girl."

A few of the boys laughed and the mob tension broke.

Just in time, a siren wailed in the distance, and then a blue-and-white cruiser's lights flashed around a bend. The cruiser siren blasted again, two short bursts of its horn as it pulled up, and a few men jumped. The starch seemed to be taken out of the lot, and Mabel suspected they were one man short of a brave bunch — just a few Larson thugs, drunk farmers, and townsfolk from Blue River again.

Sheriff Dan finally got his voice back. "Come on, boys! Get home now!"

A few of the boys at the edge of the crowd broke up and moved to their cars. Mabel could hear Larson's name in their whispered conversations. The police cruiser blasted its horn again, and then an officer's voice came onto the loudspeaker, saying, "Go home. Disperse." But the officer didn't get out of his car.

Mabel stood there, arms crossed tightly, as the men walked past, shooting dark looks at her. Frank Hudgens, the loudest of the lot, nudged her none too gently as he walked away and then growled back at the Sheriff. "Larson won't like this. He'll want to talk to you."

Sheriff Dan scowled back, but underneath, he looked scared too, maybe more so than Mabel — and that took her back some.

When the rest of the trucks had pulled away, the State Police officer emerged from his cruiser and joined them. Mabel could see why he had held back, a scrawny-looking young man, not much older than a high school graduate, wearing an oversized police outfit.

Kenny's voice trembled as he asked, "What went on here?"

"Trouble," the Sheriff said, gruffly. "A whole world of trouble."

"Gosh. You stopped that whole group on your own?"

Dan tipped his hat. "I put the fear of God in 'em I did."

"And you got a suspect in custody already?"

Dan stepped past Mabel to poke the boy's chest. "Boy, sure did. This is Blue River. My town.

Mabel stood there, already forgotten, as Dan gave the young State Trooper orders. And with the second patrol car arriving, Mabel suspected there were enough officers now to hold off Larson if he ever came around. She headed off to pick up her kids, not too bothered that Dan hadn't acknowledged what she had done; women just weren't thanked for doing what was considered man's work in Blue River. But she knew if Larson had been here, the night would have turned out different. The law didn't rule this town. It was Larson.

By the time she parked under the warm lights of Consuela's porch, her rising pride had replaced her fear. Who knew she could turn back a mob? Not much more than a pack of schoolboys fighting, she thought, with a tension-releasing giggle. She wanted to tell her kids right away, but after Kerry stormed past and wouldn't talk to her for some reason and the boys started to fight, she focused on getting them home. Her night then became the usual exhausting routine of wrangling children who didn't want to sleep. She got Hector settled, and Kerry sorted, then she lay down beside Fred. But Fred woke up shortly afterward, screaming about monsters in a dream, and she had to stroke his back to soothe him again, and all his talk of monsters brought back thoughts about the motives of the men tonight and then about the dead girl and Winston. While caressing Fred's soft, fine hair, she stared wide-eyed into darkness, thinking about murder.

CHAPTER 4

Friday, September 5

Outside the kitchen window, the early morning sky was awash with pinks and blues and tinting the dark forest hues of greens and browns. Mabel had only had about five hours of sleep before getting the kids ready for the first day of the new school year. She plated bacon and eggs, placed them in front of her kids at the table, and rested her hands upon Hector's shoulders like a general watching her troops.

Hector wriggled out of her grasp, morose and angry, and kept his eyes on his food. Like his younger brother, he was a sensitive boy; yet unlike him, he buried his emotions deep inside until he acted them out. Though he had brightened up some after she kicked Bill out, it pained her that Bill was not here, especially now, with Hector hanging out more with those older Hudgens boys.

She didn't know what they were getting up to, and Hector wasn't telling, and that worried her.

Kerry had just finished her eggs, so Mabel edged over and scooped more on her plate, which Kerry shoveled in like a tomboy. The poor thing, forced to be here for her final year of high school after her parents tragically passed, hated everything about Blue River. And when she wasn't sad, she yelled, with little in-between. Such a challenge.

Then, there was her sweet, little Fred, who, like a bird, pecked at his bacon and eggs, existing more on dew than on real food. A people-pleaser, he knew she wanted him to eat, so he did. While the other two kids were wearing street clothes, he was still wearing his Star Wars pajamas.

Fred caught her staring and returned a big smile.

"Hey, Freddie, guess what?"

"What, ma?"

"Momma saved the Sheriff last night," she said, catching everyone's attention.

"Wow! You did?"

"Yep. I did. A whole gang was outside the county office before I picked you up from Consuela's. Fifteen men, all surrounding Sheriff Dan, and he was standing up to them alone — until I arrived — cause they wanted to punish a poor boy that was in jail."

"What did he do?"

"The boy?" Mabel asked rhetorically, stalling to hide the real reason. "He uh… they think he did something bad, but I don't think so."

Hector and Kerry joined in. "Did he steal something? Or was it drugs? Did he sell drugs?"

Mabel frowned. Frank Hudgens had been supplying Winston with marijuana, and she often wondered how much her son knew about it.

"It doesn't matter what they think he did, and besides, I think he's innocent. But those men wanted to drag that boy out of the county office and do who knows what, with only Sheriff Dan and me to stop them. A tight spot, I can tell you. And they were sure mad at Dan, all yelling and cussing at him, and my knees were knocking, I can tell you that. But I stood up for Dan and yelled at 'em like I would to you naughty boys. I told them to straighten up and get back home! And they did."

"Go, Mom!" Fred shouted. "You kicked their butts."

Her boys sparkled with pride, and Kerry did too, and Mabel soaked it all in.

"Well," she added. "I won't lie that I weren't also scared, but I done it. I just stood up to them, and that was enough." Her face fell as she saw the time. "Oh, dear. Okay, kids, chop, chop. We gotta go."

"Ugh, school," Hector said and then lumbered off to get his book bag until Fred raced past him, and Hector took it on as a race, and they ran up the stairs screaming, while Kerry just quietly went on her way.

Mabel slipped sandwiches into their bags as the bus pulled up. "Boys! Kerry! The bus is here!" she called up, and just as quickly, the kids raced down and then past her out the door.

She shouted, "Be careful! I love you!"

Fred turned back and yelled, "Love ya!" and blew her a kiss while Kerry ignored her, as did Hector getting into the bus. There were only about thirty kids in the whole school, and the pickings for friends were slim. Hector usually sat in the back with the older Hudgens boys while Fred stayed in the middle with Bertie Peterson's younger six-year-old twins. Kerry, alone in front, just stared out the window as the old, rusted-out bus made its way back onto the highway.

Mabel wrapped her shawl tightly around her shoulders and watched the bus round the corner. Then she walked back towards the house, seeing those shingles looking all ratty in this morning light. Going to need replacing in the next year or two, she thought, a big cost she could ill-afford. While she sure wasn't going to be rich anytime soon, at least the money she made from the motel and diner met her basic needs, especially now with the new mine opening up. It had brought in lots of construction workers, and the motel was full — new for her — as the construction company had booked her place on contract for months. Most of the workers treated her motel like a home, which was fine with her — long as they didn't make things too dirty. She liked a clean place, and she wasn't shy about kicking anyone out who didn't respect her rules, and they seemed to appreciate her more for it.

But all this thinking about business made her reconsider her checklist for the day. With the cleaner sick, she'd work a morning shift at the diner until Sally showed up at two PM, after which she'd spend the rest of the afternoon cleaning motel rooms. Once the kids got home, she'd be back in the kitchen. After dinner, she'd make the boys do their homework and get 'em straight to bed by nine PM. Likely sleep with Fred, the poor dear afraid of the dark, and then wake up at four-thirty AM and do it over again.

Mabel blew the hair out of her eyes — that sounded like a lot, even to her. But with the soothing scent of pines from the forest behind lifting her mood and the morning sunshine blossoming around her, she reconsidered. If she were candid with herself, she actually loved living in the country and wouldn't change many things.

"Well, Mabel," she said out loud. "The diner won't open without you."

CHAPTER 5

At the two PM shift change, Mabel cashed out the till as Sally Prescott was putting on her apron. Sally leaned over the counter and whispered like a conspirator: "I heard about last night."

Mabel started, not expecting word to have got out. "Yes, I had to help Sheriff Dan last night. There was trouble."

"Trouble?" Sally quickly lowered her voice again. "I heard there was a murder."

A pang of guilt caused Mabel to glance over at the booth where the young girl had been two days back. Sally went on. "Some stray from out of town I hear killed dead by that Winston boy, no less."

"Now, we don't know it was him," Mabel admonished. "Innocent till proven guilty, right?"

"Not in this town."

Mabel deflated. "That's why I went to the county office."

"With all those angry men there? Weren't you scared?"

"Terrified, Luv."

After a long pause, Sally asked, "And?"

"Well…" Mabel said, reluctant to say more but reconsidering since Sally was so eager. "I'll just say this then. I went there around eight last night, and those men were sure angry as sin, with poor Dan all backed up almost to the door."

Sally asked breathless, "What did you do?"

"Well… I take a deep breath in and then walk right through them."

"No!"

"Yes. I walk right through that angry mob and straight up to Dan. I could see fear in his eyes, that's for sure. But when he sees me he slips me the Staties' number and says, 'You go call them for me, Mabel.' So, I goes and slip out the back just as they really started shouting at him."

Sally touched Mabel's arm. "No way!"

"Oh, believe it," Mabel said, starting to get into it. "They were furious. I turn the corner to get to the payphone and call the Deputy — Jesse was his name; I figure him an older fella, the way he sounds — and he says, 'Thanks, ma'am, for all your help. I'll send over a car right away.' So, I peeps around the corner again, and there was Dan holding onto his gun—"

"No!"

"It was still holstered. But he was holding it nonetheless, and I know now I better step in darn quick.

28

So I shout—"

"You shouted?"

"Yep, like their mothers would've. And then like one, they all turn to face me."

Sally used both hands to cover a gasp.

"Yep. All those angry men turn and stare at me at once, and, oh boy, did my knees knock! But I treated them like they were my boys and used my disappointed mother voice on them. And girl, did they wilt!"

Both laughed, and then as Mabel calmed some, she wiped her eyes. "Now that I think about it, those men folded like boys pretty quick."

"I heard Larson wasn't there," Sally said, turning serious.

Mabel's humor left her too. "No, he wasn't, and I'm sure glad he wasn't. I'm not sure if I could have stopped it."

"Wow," Sally said. "I don't think I could have done what you did."

"Oh, come now, sure you could."

"No, I couldn't," Sally said, firm on that point. "But I have to say this, this morning, Eugenia Hudgens was over at my house picking up some farm eggs, and she says that maybe you shouldn't have gone and done that." Sally moved Mabel further aside and lowered her voice. "Now, Eugenia said to keep this quiet, but Larson heard about what you did and wasn't too happy about it. He's furious with his boys for not grabbing Winston, and now that them Staties have whisked him off to jail in Seattle," She paused to make her point and then let her voice fall to the barest of whispers. "He didn't say anything kindly about you, Mabel."

Mabel rubbed her arms and looked at Sally, who was scared for her. She didn't like Larson one bit, but she didn't want to be on his bad side, especially with Hector mixed in with the Hudgens boys.

Mabel reached out to touch Sally's arm. "It's okay. No need to worry about me. I can take care of myself."

"Well, watch yourself," Sally said. "You know this town. Sometimes it's not safe here."

CHAPTER 6

Sunday, September 7

Two days later, Mabel was finishing up her evening shift. A few construction workers staying in the motel were playing cards at one table, while a big, burly trucker at the counter was laying into a plate of steak and eggs. He was a regular who didn't say much and usually just piled into his food and left. Some people just weren't talkers.

The bell above the door chimed. "Welcome," she said, out of habit, before looking over. Her breezy smile fell. It was Frank Hudgens. Frank had never come into her diner before, and he sure wasn't welcome. Mabel suspected he beat Eugenia, his wife, and wondered if this were about Eugenia's warning about Larson. Even if that all weren't enough, Frank's role in the lynch mob made her debate whether to kick him out.

Frank trudged over, leaving a trail of mud on her newly swept floors.

"Hello, Frank," Mabel said from her side of the counter, closest to the burly trucker. "We're a family establishment, so we take our hats off here."

Frank ignored her by picking something from his teeth. "Ain't stayin' long. Here to talk to you, Mabel."

"Oh?"

Frank glanced at the stranger busy with his food and, knowing he wasn't local, paid him no mind. "Need to talk to you, personal like."

"Well, talk then," Mabel said, folding her arms.

"You coming closer, or do I need to shout?"

"You don't need to shout. I can hear ya fine."

Frank grumbled, came over, and sat down on a stool. He still hadn't taken off his hat. "Saw you at the county jail the other night."

"Saw you, too," Mabel said.

"You know, Larson ain't happy about what happened."

Mabel shifted her stance — no one in town wanted to be on Larson's bad side — but she kept quiet as Frank kept on. "He said I should talk to you."

"Go on then."

"He said you need to be careful."

"I'm always careful, Frank."

Frank lowered his voice. "Listen to me. Larson wanted me to talk to you because your boy knows mine." Mabel hated that but said nothing. "You probably heard what that Winston boy did to that girl. Terrible things. So, he said for you not to interfere. That the ni—"

"Don't you dare talk like that in here, Frank."

Frank's eyes narrowed. "That black fella then," he said. "He should have been punished local. He's a low-end drug dealer. A no-good punk."

"That's funny. He gets his drugs from Larson."

"Watch what you say!" Frank hushed her, glanced around, and then said sternly, "Larson doesn't deal with drugs."

Mabel huffed. Everyone knew Larson had the largest private marijuana fields in Blue River and supplied Winston and many others.

"That's what I mean. Don't mess with his business," Frank said.

"You're here. In mine."

"That's right," Frank said. "And you might see more of me. Or my friends. Maybe even Larson will want to stop by to get some dinner."

Mabel didn't like that one bit. "We're a family place. Larson isn't welcome."

"Don't matter," he said before his face twisted into a crass smile. "A whole lot of our boys might want to get something made sweet from you, and often. Breakfast, lunch, dinner, no matter. You being a divorcee and all. You'd probably like some male company to take care of this place."

Mabel shuddered; she worked hard for this place and didn't want thugs tearing it down. "Does Eugenia know you're here?"

Frank frowned, hitched his pants, and stood up. "You don't get it. You interfere in his business, he'll interfere with yours. Watch yourself. Or you'll hear from me and my boys."

He moved to leave, but the trucker pushed off his stool and blocked Frank's way. "What did you say?" he said.

"I wasn't talking to you."

"You threatened Mabel. You deal with me."

"I-I didn't threaten nobody."

The trucker took a step forward, and Frank took a step back. Even the construction workers at the middle table stopped playing cards to watch. "I-I ain't looking for trouble. I got no beef with you."

"Then apologize to the lady."

"I don't need to, I done nothing wrong," Frank said, getting angry. But the trucker loomed over him.

Mabel blinked, surprised, and stood by, watching Frank shrivel. She wondered how far she should let her customer take it, but she was kind of proud of him, too. But Frank broke fast. "Sorry," he said, but not at Mabel.

"Take your hat off like she asked," the trucker said. "And apologize like you mean it."

Frank was furious, breathing heavily. Yet he took off his hat and glared at Mabel. "Sorry," he said petulantly.

The trucker said, "Good." Then let Frank pass.

Frank opened the door, half-turned, and shouted, "Larson will hear about this," then bolted into the night. Mabel shook her head, unimpressed.

The trucker sat down, picked up his fork to finish his meal, and said, "He weren't treating you right. I hate guys like that."

Mabel touched the top of the man's hand until he looked up into her blue eyes.

"Thank you."

The trucker looked pleased but only grunted. "He shouldn't have said that. About you, or the boy."

"You have a nice smile," she said. "You should show it more."

The trucker blushed, unsure of what to do or say.

She made it easy for him. "Let me get you some pie to touch up your dinner. On the house."

He thought about that, then nodded and bent over his plate to hide his pleasure and finish his meal. As she moved away to give him space, she glanced over at the construction workers watching her. She gave them a nod to tell them everything was okay, and they returned to their game.

Heading back for the pie, she felt strangely safe among these rough, out-of-town men. Proud that she could offer a home-cooked meal and a bit of comfort to lonely men away from wives or girlfriends or just on their own.

But when she glanced back at the far empty booth where almost a week ago the girl and Winston had been arguing, her sense of ease vanished.

CHAPTER 7

Monday, September 8

Six hours into a long afternoon shift, Mabel took a quick break to check on the kids who'd just gotten home from school. With the diner packed for the dinner rush, she didn't have much time.

Kerry was lounging on the couch, headphones on, listening to music on her Walkman. Mabel hesitated, unsure of what mood her niece was in before sitting down and putting her hand on her knee to get her attention. Kerry moved her knee away.

Mabel insisted, so Kerry moved the headphone off one ear. As the music blasted out, she gave Mabel the 'What do you want now?' look that teen girls do so well.

"Just checking in, honey."

Kerry rolled her eyes, making an elaborate show of turning off the music and removing the headphones.

Mabel checked her irritation since Kerry had made it clear she was leaving Blue River as soon as she turned eighteen. That worried Mabel, not wanting to see her end up with a wrong crowd wherever she went. She hoped Kerry could feel at home here.

"You want to know my day?" Kerry asked, clearly irritated. "What? So you care now?"

"Of course I care, dear."

"Oh. Really? Like you care about me. Or your kids."

Mabel bit back a harsher response. "Come on. I've had a hard day, and I just want to see how my niece is doing, that's all. Do you need anything?"

"You ask if I need anything, but you've been gone all day. You think I need something? Did you check on your kids? Do you even know what's going on with them?"

"No. What?"

"You don't even know. What a mother. You spend hours away from home. Your kids are practically raising themselves. At least my mom didn't do that. She stayed at home, but you! You're always gone — at the motel, at the diner. I feel sorry for Hector and Fred. This isn't a home. It's a motel — for them."

"I have to work. I can't just—"

"Do you even know what's going on? Your son's upstairs with a black eye, and you're asking me about my day? Talk to your kid and stop interfering with my life."

Mabel stood up. "Which son? Who has the black eye?"

"Go find out yourself," Kerry said and went to put on her headphones again, but Mabel stopped her.

In a tone harsher than she intended, Mabel said, "You can get mad at me all you want. But don't you dare tell me how to raise my kids. You're part of my family now, and I want respect in this house. Which boy? Who was it?"

Kerry's eye's widened like she'd taken it too far. "Hector. It's Hector. He's upstairs in his room." Then she put on her headphones, conscious Mabel was still there.

Mabel didn't want to leave the situation like this, but she needed to find what had happened to Hector. "Thank you for telling me," Mabel said, not knowing if Kerry could hear her through the headphones but wanting to set an example of polite manners in this house. Then she went upstairs to Hector's room and knocked on the closed door.

"Go away!" Hector shouted.

Mabel put her head against the door — oh dear Lord, another angry child, she thought. Exhausted from work, she didn't know if she had the patience to keep this up, so she prayed for motherly strength and then opened the door.

"I said, stay out!"

Hector was at his desk. His clothes were torn and dirty, and he kept one side of his face hidden from view.

Mabel's heart melted. She crossed the room to look at his black eye and ripped clothes.

"I said, get away, Mom!"

She ignored his protest and folded him into her arms, and for a second Hector leaned in too before he squirmed out of her grasp.

"What's wrong, son? Who did this to you?"

Hector turned away, wiping tears from his eyes as he

sat down on the edge of his bed. She sat down beside him and asked again: "Honey, who did this?"

"Who did this?! You did!"

"What are you talking about? I love you."

Hector screamed at her. "This is all your fault. You had to go and stick up for that… that n—!"

The word slashed Mabel like a knife, and she slapped Hector in the face. "Don't you ever talk like that!"

Hector froze in shock before he started crying hysterically.

Mabel's anger melted into despair and self-loathing; she abhorred violence, and though it hadn't been a hard slap, it was a slap nonetheless. "Oh, Hector, I'm so sorry," she said, embracing him. "But promise me, promise me that you'll never use that word in this house, okay?"

He cried for a full minute before he calmed down enough to nod his assent, breathing hard.

"Tell me what happened."

Through a shuddering sob, Hector said, "It was Jacob and Isaiah. They done it."

Mabel turned ice cold, and her anger only grew, as Hector explained. "Jacob and Isaiah told me I loved that—" Hector stopped himself. "That I loved that Winston kid. That you were someone that cared less about her own kind and worried too much about… the other kids."

"Black kids," she said it for him.

"Yeah. They said you supported a murderer. And they said I did too. I tried telling them, ma, and stood up for you, but they just laughed at me and held me down and hit me over and over again."

"Oh, Hector," Mabel said, her anger mixing with shame as she pressed her cheek into his hair. "I'm proud of you for trying to stand up to them. I am. But you need to know that we are all human, right? Isaiah and Jacob and their father are just uneducated racists. Just like that bad man, Larson. And, yes, I don't really know if Winston is a murderer or not, but they were going to do something awful to the boy that night if they got their hands on him. Maybe hurt him. And that's not right, dear. That's not justice. If Winston hurt that girl, then he'll go to prison. If not, he goes free. Larson and his crew can't decide that. Not because that boy is black."

"It wasn't Larson, mom! I told you. It was Jacob and Isaiah."

She knew it wasn't. Not really. She knew where those boys got their hate. "Oh, son," she said. "This is bigger than that."

"You don't know them. They're my friends."

"You can find better friends."

"They're the only friends I got. There's no kids my age!"

"I know, son." Mabel sighed. "I know how small this town is. It's just… they're just like their father. And he is a bad man."

"No, he isn't, mom. He's nice, and he gives us stuff."

"What?!"

Hector looked like he regretted saying too much and shut down.

Mabel held onto both his arms and looked him in the eyes. "What does he give you?"

Hector tried to squirm away to no avail. Finally, he answered: "Beer."

Mabel closed her eyes and hung her head. "What else?"

"Bullets for their .22s. That sort of thing. He takes us to the firing range."

Mabel cursed inwardly. Clearly, her son desperately needed a father figure to look up to — but not Frank Hudgens. Please, God, not him, she thought. "Son," she said. "Frank is a bad man."

"No, he isn't." Hector pulled away further. "What about Dad? He hit me."

"That won't happen again, dear. No one is going to hit you in this house anymore."

"But you just did! Dad did! Isaiah and Jacob hit me, and their dad hits them too. When does it stop?"

Mabel winced, feeling like a terrible mom. Maybe Kerry was right; she was working too hard and not seeing her kids and not really knowing what her son's days were like and not doing enough to teach them right from wrong. She needed to be better.

"It starts today. It does. You shouldn't be seeing those Hudgens boys."

"Then who do I play with, Mom?!"

"Your brother."

"Fred?!" Hector said. "He's a baby. He still wears jammies and has a stuffed animal. It's always about Fred. Goody-two-shoes Fred. And what am I? I'm just a stupid loser."

"Don't think that. Is that what's bothering you?"

"You got rid of Dad because of me." Hector sniffled.

"Oh, no son. I kicked him out because of what he was becoming. Your father is dealing with personal things related to that new mine. You know he discovered it and his old partner kept him out of that. That's why the drinking started. That's why—"

"I *know* all that, Mom, but it doesn't help. Kids made fun of me all summer for not having a Dad. They made fun of me because of you." Hector was getting worked up again, and she could see that hysterical tears weren't far behind. "I got no one here, but Isaiah and Jacob. And now they hate me, too. I hate this family!" He stormed out of the room and down the stairs.

Mabel sat for a moment, defeated, and was about to follow when she heard the front door slam.

Dammit, Mabel thought, and then raced downstairs and out the front door. She called out to Hector, but he was gone. Worried now that he might go back to the Hudgens', she came back inside to get her car keys.

Kerry was still on the couch but had her headphones off and mouth agape. For a second, it looked like she would make a biting remark but then thought better of it.

Mabel felt like she was going to regret asking but did anyways. "I need your help. Can you come?"

Kerry thought about it for a moment. "Can I drive?"

Mabel gave in, too desperate to argue, and said, "Sure." Then tossed her the keys.

CHAPTER 8

Kerry drove down the access road trailing a forest path that Hector might have taken to the Hudgens' acreage at the end of town. On the edge of her seat, Mabel scanned the forest, but the sun filtering through the dappled foliage and pine branches created ever-changing tints and hues of the emerging fall colors that made it hard to search for her missing son. Harder still were her shifting emotions, from guilt and shame to anxiousness and anger, for having slapped her son, for having allowed him to hang with those Hudgens boys in the first place. I'm no better a parent than Bill was, she thought, and that hurt.

Kerry asked, "What was that all about?"

Mabel didn't answer right away. Not happy with Kerry either these past few weeks, she certainly didn't need any more attitude. But maybe it was time to reach out.

"Hector and I had a fight."

"I heard that."

Mabel gave her a look. "The Hudgens' boys hit him."

Kerry winced. "Those boys are pigs. You should see them at school, picking on all the younger kids. Well—" She paused. "Except Fred. Hector makes sure they don't touch him."

Mabel closed her eyes and sent up a prayer of thanks that she must be doing something right. Then promptly teared up again for having slapped him.

"Hey, uh." Kerry looked over. "It's not your fault."

Mabel wiped the tears away.

"Really," Kerry said. "You're only doing your best."

Mabel waited, ashamed, expecting a biting comment to follow. When none came, she looked over and for the first time saw a young woman instead of a hurt, angry teen.

"You remind me of your mother," Mabel said at last. "When we were young, we used to tell each other everything."

"Did she tell you about my dad? About what he did?"

It was the first time Kerry had asked a question about her father, and Mabel did not know what to say at first. In the end, she went with the truth. "Yes," she said finally. "We talked a lot after your father passed. Every night after work, we talked about her illness, about your dad, you, a lot of things."

"So, you know he—"

Killed himself, Mabel thought, finishing Kerry's sentence. "Yes, of course, dear. It was tragic."

"Did my mother tell you why he did it?"

Mabel nodded. For the insurance, she thought.

Kerry's eyes misted over, but she kept her gaze on the road.

"He loved you dearly, you know."

Kerry shook her head, starting to sob. "I don't think so."

"He did. He did love you. Oh Luv, I wish I could convince you of that." Mabel's heart turned over, but her intuition told her more. "I don't even pretend to know what it's like for you. I don't. And I know this might sound strange, but I asked a friend before you came who went through a similar loss so young. And one of the things she told me was that she had suffered terrible survivor's guilt after her mother had passed. That she didn't know why she was still alive, and her mother had died. She felt guilty for being alive."

Kerry sobbed harder and had to pull over to the side of the road, and Mabel knew she was on the right track and pressed on. "She told me it's natural to feel guilt when someone passes, honey. It's part of the process."

"Why did he leave me?! What did I do to him?!"

Mabel reached out to touch her arm. "Oh, dear, it wasn't about you. He was in pain. He didn't think through what it would mean."

"He hurt us!"

"I know. But he was trying to do the right thing, I think. But I agree it was wrong. He shouldn't have. But he was having such a hard time coping."

"He, he never told us. Why didn't he ever tell us what was happening?"

"Sometimes…" Mabel started and then paused, realizing she didn't have an answer. "I don't know. Your mother and I never understood it. All she knew was that John loved you both. But the bankruptcy caused by Owen, his business partner, followed by your mom's illness, broke something inside him. Didn't your mom ever tell you this? About his depression?"

Kerry shook her head, wiping away tears. "We never really talked."

Mothers and daughters, thought Mabel. They could be so similar, just like sisters.

"She blamed herself too, you know, your mom," Mabel said. "She felt she should have known. Should have seen something. And she wanted to talk to you, but she just… just never knew how."

Kerry swallowed and then spoke in a low voice. "I hated him. For the longest time."

"Oh, Luv," Mabel said. "I can only imagine. But he tried being a good father."

"Does it ever get easier?"

Mabel was tempted to lie but didn't. "No," she said, finally. "It's just hard in different ways. You gain the strength to deal with something, and life becomes easier for a time, but then something else comes up, it always does. Then you have to learn to adjust and do your best again. You end up making mistakes — lots of them. I know I do," she said, thinking of Hector and realizing she needed to forgive herself, and him, and move on.

There was silence between them for a few minutes, each lost to their own thoughts.

Then Kerry wiped her tear-stained face, put the car

back in gear, and spoke first. "Let's go find Hector, yeah?"

Not long after, Kerry turned into the drive of the Hudgens' farm. Frank was out on his porch, rocking his chair, his shirt open, gut out, and chewing on some tobacco.

Mabel burned hot at the sight of him, got out, and made her way to the porch, Kerry just a few feet behind.

"Is my son here?"

"Don't know, don't care. You lose him?"

"Where're your boys at then? I'll ask them."

Frank rolled the chew in his mouth to one side. "You thought about what I said?"

"Your boys hit my son, Frank."

Frank's mouth curled into a smile. "Your son probably gave them some sass. Boys fight. Happens."

"I don't like it that you're teaching him filth about black kids."

Frank sneered. "Oh, boy! You think you're better than me. But you ain't."

"I don't want my son around here."

Frank spit out some chew and then wadded in another load. "Don't care for him either. But he needs a father figure. Divorced families like yours ain't good for kids."

"I'm not divorced."

"Absentee father then," Frank said, then turned crass again. "Maybe you're looking for a real man now?"

"How dare you! You pig."

"You and your trucker boyfriend at the diner better watch out." Frank spat again. "If you're on my land, it's my rules. Hector, too. If he comes here, he's fair game."

"You hurt my son, and I'll—" she said, sputtering, too enraged to finish the threat.

"You'll what?" Frank sneered. "You need a man in a home to look after boys, that's for sure. Maybe I take Hector in for you?"

"I'll kill you, Frank. You hurt him, and I'll kill you."

Frank sat up quickly and jabbed his finger at Mabel. "Watch it. Don't you come here and threaten me."

"You come to my place, Frank. I'm coming to yours."

Frank stood up like he was aiming for a fight, but Mabel stepped forward and stood her ground, undaunted, willing to protect her children. Perhaps sensing this, Frank hesitated, then yelled: "Git off my property! I don't want you here again." He spit some chew near Mabel's feet, and it splattered on her pants. "I said, git."

"You afraid of a woman, Frank?"

Frank waved her off, scowling. "Larson will hear about this!" Then he stormed off into his house and slammed the door.

Mabel's eyes burned holes through the door before Kerry finally broke the silence. "Maybe Hector went somewhere else? Back home, maybe?"

Mabel breathed out some anger and nodded, and then finally backed off. "Let's try home."

Kerry climbed behind the wheel, and Mabel got into the passenger seat. "You sure told him off," Kerry said with the hint of a smile. "I thought he almost peed himself when you said you'd kill him."

"He did look pretty scared," Mabel acknowledged.

"Terrified," Kerry giggled. "You're a tough momma bear."

"I like that. Momma Bear." Mabel started to smile. "That's just how I felt: no one harms my family. Fred, Hector, you — no one."

"I pity da fool," Kerry wisecracked, mimicking that Mr. T fellow from the television show. Then she laughed, started the car, and drove off the acreage.

Mabel looked out the front window and eased into her seat. What a day, she thought. Worst fight with Hector. Best day with Kerry.

Parenting teens is a nightmare.

CHAPTER 9

Hector was sitting on their porch steps. With legs pressed tight to his chest, he did not look up when Mabel and Kerry got out of the car and came to the porch. Kerry wisely gave them space without Mabel having to ask.

Mabel sat down beside her son. They sat on the porch silently, with the rich scent of pines and forest moss surrounding them like a blanket and making her feel calm. The deep woods across the highway had the odd red or yellow poplar leaf scattered amongst the greenery like embers about to spread a blaze of color over the land. She put her arm around his shoulders, and he let her, though his scowl remained deep and ugly, and only his eyes betrayed vulnerable emotions until he finally spoke.

"I'm *sorry*," he said, likely expecting that was what she

wanted to hear.

She didn't like his tone. But he had started, and that was enough. She pulled him in closer, to soften him some more, but his guard was still up, expecting a lecture. She kissed him on top of the head, unsure how to begin, except to return his gesture. "I'm sorry too."

He blinked in surprise and looked up, thirsting for more.

Mabel cleared her throat. "Violence is wrong, my son, especially in a home, in a loving family. I hit you, and I regret that, deeply. And I want you to know, really know, that I won't do that again. I promise."

He cleared his throat, raw with emotion. "Why do you care?"

"I will always care about you, my son. I love you."

"No, I mean… why do you care about what I said — that word. About black kids. Everyone says it."

Mabel sighed. "Just because people say it here doesn't mean it's right."

"But you say cuss words. Why is this different?"

"It just is."

"Black people say that word."

She nodded her head, not quite having an answer for him. "I know. It's just… not right for us to say it. Didn't Mr. Clemens teach you this in school? About slavery and where those words come from?"

Hector shrugged. "Last year, but it was only a page or two, I think. The civil war fixed it or something."

Mabel frowned, disappointed. "No. That's not right. It's not over. The civil rights marches were just after high school for me, but no one in this town marched. No one spoke up about it then, and now I think that was wrong. Their silence did us all a disservice." She paused. "I am ashamed to say it, but the first time I really understood what black folks might be going through was by watching *Roots*."

"What's that?"

A little embarrassed, Mabel said, "A mini-series on TV. It showed me what life was like for black people in our country. Like that Kunte Kinte character, but for real. How mostly white people put them in chains, beat them, starved them. Families separated, torn apart, forced into a life they did not want for generations. It was terrible, and it happened right here in our land. That's where that bad word comes from and why it hurts so."

Hector winced, and then looked down at his shoes. After a long moment, he asked, "Where are all the black kids? There ain't many."

"There are lots in our country. Many folks are black or Hispanic or minorities."

"But not here."

"No," Mabel conceded. "Not many."

"Why is that? They don't like this place?"

Mabel looked down at the gravel. Thinking about all the times she had witnessed someone in town making black people feel unwanted or not being allowed to feel like they belonged. Not even a week ago, Ken, the gas station owner, had denigrated a black couple in his store. He said it to one of his co-workers but not to her, so she didn't feel part of it. The couple had heard it too and were affected by it as she had been. Then the shock of the moment passed, and there was no time to signal to the couple that she didn't think like Ken. "I don't think they feel welcome," she said at last.

"Can we make them feel welcome?"

"Of course, son. We don't have to be like those mean racists in town."

"But you just said that people who stay silent are being bad too, right?"

"Well, yes, but ..." Mabel said, hesitant, not sure where he was going with this.

Then his words sunk in.

She flushed and did know what to say.

Hector's eyes burned into her, waiting for an answer, and she felt ashamed that she had no answer. Except that maybe Frank was right — she wasn't as innocent as she had thought. She looked into her son's eyes, deep wells of thought and innocence, looking to her for a clear answer, but she had no answer to give, only platitudes which seemed meaningless without actions. She drew her boy in and hugged him tightly for comfort. After a moment, she wiped fresh tears from her eyes and said, "I guess I don't have the answers, son. I don't know what it's like to feel racism. But you're right about the silence. Silence allows racism to flourish." She looked down at the hard gravel drive and then back to her son and brushed the hairs from his face. "But there's more we can do, my son. I can see that now too. Maybe we can do it together? Both you and I?"

Hector nodded.

"You are so wise," Mabel said.

She hugged him, and he squirmed before settling. Then they looked off at the forest together, and after a long moment of silence, he finally came around and agreed to stay away from the Hudgens kids and play more with Fred. It was a start.

CHAPTER 10

Tuesday, September 9

After a customer left, Mabel wiped the diner's counter, swept the tip into the communal staff jar, and then brought the dirty dishes back into the kitchen. The cook was fixing a special turkey order. Its heavenly smell brought back pleasant holiday memories with Bill and the kids.

She came out of the kitchen, humming a holiday jingle. She saw the empty coffee pot, got the water, poured it into the machine, did a little hip shake, and then scooped up the black grains and added them to the filter. As she pressed the brew to start, two new out-of-towners, a middle-aged couple, came in and settled into the far booth. Their exhausted, strained faces screamed 'stressed-out parents,' and she smiled grimly to herself, knowing what that was like. Not even a day after her long talks with Hector, she still couldn't make sense of it all. Then, after the boys went to bed, she and Kerry had a long talk too, and things got a little more personal and a little more real. Kerry asked many questions about her parents, and Mabel shared insights about their hopes and fears, gleaned from past conversations with her sister. It seemed to be helping Kerry's grief, and Mabel hoped it would last.

The buzzer sounded on the coffee machine, jarring her out of her reverie. She picked up the pot, swept up the menus and made her way over. Mabel reached the couple's table and said with a restrained smile, "Welcome." Then poured coffee right away. "On the house, of course. My coffee here is always fresh, free, and fast — especially for parents."

"Thank you," the woman replied softly.

Mabel had to strain to hear it, so low it caught her off guard, but she simply smiled in return, and set down the menus and asked, "What can I get you? We have the best home cooking on I-67."

The man cleared his throat. "Just coffee, please. We're passing through."

"Oh, what brings you to Blue River, Luv?" Mabel asked, wondering if she guessed right about them being parents. "Not too many families come up here this time of..." The woman started crying softly, startling Mabel. "Oh, my, I'm sorry, is everything okay?"

The man spoke for his wife. "No, it's—" He glanced painfully at her. "It's just that we are looking for where our daughter..." He cleared his throat roughly and then grimaced and shook his head like he couldn't continue.

Mabel understood immediately. "Oh, my dears, are you the parents of the girl that..." But she couldn't say it either.

The husband nodded, choking up. "Our daughter, Karen, yes."

"Oh my God," Mabel said softly. She set down the coffee pot and reached out to touch his shoulder. "I'm so sorry for your loss."

He swallowed hard, tearing up as well, and then looked away and tried to compose himself.

"I've been thinking about you so much," Mabel said. "I saw your girl." They both looked up, wiping their eyes. "And she was even sitting right here. In this booth."

"Right here?" the mother asked in a whisper.

"Yes," Mabel said in awe. "Right where you are. How did you know?"

"I didn't. It just felt right."

Mabel smiled at her. "Because you're a mom. We mothers know these things. But wait here one second, I want to set you two up nicely." She hurried into the kitchen to dish up three pieces of pie with big scoops of ice cream, then asked the cook to watch the diner and went back to the table, set down plates, and squeezed into the booth beside the husband. "Please join me. On the house."

"Uh, thank you... and your name is?"

"Mabel, my love."

"My name's Jack. Jack Thompson. And this is my wife, Isabelle."

"What lovely names," Mabel said. "Please, go ahead and eat with me."

Jack took a big bite, Isabelle only a small one. She looked thin and worn out, and Mabel thought she probably hadn't eaten much since her daughter's death.

"She looks like you. Both of you," Mabel said.

"Our daughter Karen?" the woman asked, her voice more than a whisper now but still soft.

Mabel breathed the girl's name in and thought about that day in the diner a little less than a week ago. "She had black hair and black eyeliner. And she had a tattoo on her hand."

The father spoke up. "What was it?"

Mabel asked gently, "When did you last see your daughter?"

Jack and Isabelle shared a pained look before saying, "I'm ashamed to say it, but more than two months back. She, uh, she ran away. We looked, but…" He grimaced, overwhelmed, and then hung his head.

Isabelle reached out to touch her husband's hand, and then she picked up the story. "It was the drugs." She looked at Mabel. "She had gotten into the drugs."

"I am sorry to hear that. This place — Blue River — is known for it. We have a bad drug problem."

Isabelle asked, "What was the tattoo?"

"It spelled 'hope', written on her knuckles where she could always see it."

The father started, shocked at first, and then Isabelle encouraged him, and he rolled up his sleeve to show the tattoo on his wrist. HOPE, it spelled too. Isabelle said to Jack, "Maybe she was on the right path."

He nodded, then explained to Mabel, "I uh… I had gotten into trouble when I was young too. I was reckless.

A biker. Before I met Isabelle." Isabelle smiled at him encouragingly. "And she changed my ways. I was addicted to heroin, and I had done some bad things, but Isabelle, she, well, she stuck with me. So, I got this tattoo on my wrist to remind me that I needed to be better, a better person, and get on with my life. I had told Karen that story. Maybe she had met someone as well — someone to help her through a terrible time. Drugs had almost killed me then and now that it affected my daughter too, I…" His voice faded, and then he banged a fist on the table in anger, and Isabelle hung her head. "I'm sorry," he said finally.

Mabel reached out to touch his arm until he looked at her. "It's all right," she said. "This is a safe place."

"I've been angry ever since I heard the news about that man, about how he—" He glanced at his wife, "killed her."

Mabel didn't know what to say. She didn't think Winston had done it, but this wasn't the time to bring that up. She felt terrible.

Isabelle broke the silence. "You said you saw her? When?"

Both parents' eyes bore into hers. She realized she was possibly the last person to have seen the girl alive — except for the murderer and Winston — and somehow, she thought that carried a lot of weight. "I did. A week ago. She was sitting here like I said. And Winston—" the parents flinched at the name "—was with her." She paused. "It looked like he loved her, the boy."

"Then how could he have done that?"

"I don't know," Mabel said. "The boy has been saying

59

he's innocent, I've been told."

"But they arrested him."

"I know," Mabel said, not wanting to contradict them. "It's just what I saw. They were here that day for a little more than an hour. Yes, the conversation, at times, was heated. But I got the impression that Winston was worried about Karen. Worried about something related to her, that's for sure. And your daughter, she seemed to be the one in control of the conversation. It's like she knew what path she was going to take, and he was scared for her."

Isabelle and Jack looked at each other, and Isabelle smiled slightly. "That sounds like Karen. She knew what she wanted, and boys, it seemed, would do what she said. She was a Daddy's girl."

Jack fought back a sob, so Mabel touched his shoulder until he got himself settled. But he looked broken, almost beyond repair.

"She obviously looked up to you," Mabel said to Jack. "With the tattoo and all. It's like she was going back to you."

Jack whispered, "I didn't know she did that. She musta done it after she left."

He looked over at his wife, as did Mabel. Isabelle now seemed the stronger of the two, prim and proper, yet displaying an inner strength, and Mabel wondered why she hadn't seen it at first.

"We loved her, you see," Isabelle explained. "But she was headstrong like me. I don't know what I could've done different, yet every day, I wonder."

"We," Jack said gently.

"What *we* could have done," Isabelle corrected herself. "But I don't know. It was terrible when she had run away and now, with her death and how she died." Her voice trailed off, then she swallowed and continued. "Every day, I ask God why she left us, why he allowed Karen to die. And I don't have the answers. I don't. But I blame myself. Maybe I was too hard on her, but I don't know. I relive all our moments together and wonder what I could have done different, how I could have been a better mother. I made so many mistakes." She blinked back tears and looked at Mabel and gave a soft, pained smile. "But there's nothing more I can do now." She reached down then and touched the vinyl cushions of the booth and caressed the fabric. "It's nice to know my daughter came here. That she had some comfort before her death."

Mabel's gaze dropped to the melting ice cream pooling on her plate, and she felt she had failed Karen and her parents.

"It's time," Isabelle said to her husband. "We should go." Isabelle and Jack stood up, but Mabel didn't want them to leave. She held Isabelle's hand and said, "I'm sorry."

Isabelle replied, "There's nothing you could have done."

"I could see she was in trouble. That the two of them were worried," said Mabel, fighting back tears.

"Her path was written," the mother said. "So is ours." Then Isabelle opened her arms to Mabel, and Mabel stood up to hug her, and then Mabel hugged Jack, and nothing more was said.

Isabelle guided her husband out.

The bell on the door chimed twice.

Mabel stood there unable to stem the tears for several minutes, watching the couple leave. Then their car disappeared down the highway.

"So help me God," she said to herself. "I will find who did this to your daughter. I will give you the answers you seek. To give you peace."

CHAPTER 11

Wednesday, September 10

Mabel was entertaining a group of construction workers finishing up their breakfast. After setting up a dirty joke, she finished with, "'So the waitress asks, 'What do you want, luv?' The customer responds: 'If you wash your hands, I'll have the steak.'"

Two of the guys broke out laughing, while the third, the youngest, looked embarrassed like he shouldn't be laughing too.

"Oh, you're new here, honey. It's fine."

The youngest relaxed and chuckled.

"All you boys good here?" Mabel asked the group. "You need any seconds?"

"That'll be thirds for me, Mabel," one of them said. "But I'm good." Everyone nodded assent.

"Well, that's good, boys. I like to see my customers

well-fed, especially at the start of a shift." She poured their coffees. "Take your time. You got forty-five minutes till shift change. Enjoy your coffees."

"Mighty fine," said Carlos, the foreman, looking into her eyes and taking a sip. "We'll settle up shortly."

"Oh," she added, waving him off. "Remember, second helpings and the coffee are free, but leave a nice tip for the cook. He's a young boy who needs it."

"Hope you get to enjoy some too," the youngest worker said, giving her what he hoped was a winning smile.

"Honey," she replied, swiping her notebook at him. "I *own* the place." Then she flashed her smile to each and made her way around the counter.

As she wrote up their bill, Sarah, one of her motel cleaners, walked in through the side hallway connecting the motel to the diner. Mabel was surprised to see her. Being a timid woman, Sarah avoided crowded places like the diner. And while Mabel thought all women were pretty, even she thought a doctor should remove the wart on Sarah's cheek, and a stylist should give her a professional perm. Sarah used a home kit, which left her hair dry and frizzled. Mabel encouraged her to treat herself, but Sarah only said, "Pete don't like it when I spend money on things. Besides, who am I trying to impress?"

What a shame, Mabel thought. Like most Blue River women, the poor dear was more a husband's wife than her own woman.

"What can I do for you, Luv?"

"Can I talk to you please?"

Mabel had to lean in to hear with all the diner conversation behind her. "Of course," she replied, wiping her hands on her apron and following Sarah into the hallway decorated with black-and-white photos of Blue River's past: frontier loggers cutting down trees; the first sawmill men running logs through the mill; the old town mayor driving a sleek Chevrolet Bel Air at the highway inauguration; color photos of the construction workers building the mine.

Sarah asked, "Is there anything wrong with Room Seven?"

Mabel tried to recall who the tenant was. Sally had signed him in: a new worker who'd been here only two weeks, and since he hadn't eaten at the diner yet, Mabel hadn't seen much of him either, which was kind of strange, her motel such a tight community and all. "No. Why?"

"Well, nothing's changed."

"I don't understand, dear."

"Well, I cleaned the room last week. And then I come back today, and nothing's changed. All his gear is where it was left."

"Is he just neat?"

"No ma'am. I make sure all the rooms are just right, with the right creases in the sheets, fresh soap in the dish, and a new roll in every bathroom, like you want, but nothing was touched."

"Hmm, that is strange," said Mabel. "Let me see."

With the unpaid bill in hand, she glanced back. The men had settled in again, drinking coffee and chatting. She had time. It wasn't far, anyway. Room Seven in her two-level, L-shaped motel was the closest room to the diner on the main level, facing the highway. The short hallway they were in led past the motel desk and right to Room Seven outside.

Mabel led the way, took out her motel master key, and entered. The early morning light cast her profile deep into the darkened room, so she flipped on the main switch to see better, and it was just as Sarah had described. Spotless, except for the man's dirty duffel bag and soiled clothes slung over the chair and in the closet. Mabel wiped her finger along the kitchenette countertop, and then showed Sarah a bit of dust.

"I haven't cleaned anything yet, ma'am," Sarah said, a little defensive. "Why clean a room as clean as this?"

Mabel nodded. She opened the fridge and found rotten food and a milk cartoon going bad. She said, "At least we can empty the fridge. I don't want food spoiling."

"Yes, ma'am."

Mabel went to the bathroom, and again, it was as Sarah had described.

"Something else was funny here last week."

Sarah was the type who needed prodding, so Mabel asked, "What's that?"

"There was blood."

"Blood?!"

"Yes ma'am, on the counter here and in the sink. Not enough to cause a mess, but more than just a shaving nick if you know what I mean."

The sink was spotless now, Sarah being good at her job. Mabel said, "That is strange. When did you do it last?"

"Last Thursday. Beatrice was home with a sick kid, as you know, which is why I come in, being casual and all."

Mabel nodded. The day after, the poor girl, Karen, had been murdered. She went back into the main room and casually looked through the man's things, not wanting to snoop but wanting to figure this out. An empty knife scabbard was on the duffel bag. It was covered in dried mud and broken pine needles, like his work boots, sitting on a mat by the door. Mabel turned to Sarah and said, "Okay, thank you, dear. It was right to tell me."

"Maybe he went home on a shift change and left his things?"

Mabel shook her head. "They take all their gear. The company doesn't want to pay for an empty room, and they're usually pretty good about telling me." She thought about it some more. "Hmmm, I know they just extended shifts again to meet a deadline, and the men are busy," she said, tapping her fingers against her leg. "Okay. You're right. No need to clean here. Go finish up with the other rooms. I'll ask Carlos what's going on here." She patted Sarah's shoulder as she left.

Mabel came back into the diner as Carlos and his crew were getting organized to leave. He flashed his best smile as she waved him over.

"Afraid I was going to dine and dash?" Carlos teased her. A motel resident as well, he regularly signed off on the entire crew's tab staying at the motel and was probably sweet on her too, but she paid that no mind.

"No worries," Mabel said, handing him the bill. Then as he bent over the counter to initial it, she asked, "Hey, what's going on with the newbie in Room Seven? I didn't sign him in, it was Sally who done it. His name is Bill Jordan."

"Oh yeah. Guy got injured on his own time and had to go to the hospital. Stupid."

"Oh dear, is he all right?"

"I don't know, some sort of hand injury and some minor scrapes, I guess. I needed that guy, and he cost me some time. But it's probably a good thing in the long run. He was only here a week and didn't really fit in. Always buggered off at night and didn't hang with the boys."

"How many days ago was that?" Mabel asked, not asking what day of the week, since for the construction crews, days were described as numbers to match how many days passed since they'd been on shift. Most crews worked twenty-one days on, seven off, for months on end.

"Oh, about seven days back. Six or seven, I think. It's been a hard haul making up for a lost man."

Seven days was the night of the murder, she thought. She didn't like that one bit. "Can you check for me? What day it was? I don't want to charge the company a room when no one's using it." Not why she wanted to know, but she didn't want to throw out shade just yet.

"Yeah, sure. Anything else?"

"All his stuff is still in his room."

"Ugh, typical greenhorn," Carlos growled. "I'll get someone to clear it out. We'll ship it back to him as I don't think I want him here."

Mabel touched his arm. "No need. I can do it."

He brightened noticeably at the touch. "That makes

my life easier. Thanks. And sorry about not telling you. I should've, but like I said, it's been really busy, short a man."

"No worries, dear," Mabel smiled.

Carlos left, and her smile faded as she considered what was at stake. While she was good at reading people, the short time Bill Jordan had stayed at her motel meant she never really got a good look at him to know what he was capable of — including murder.

CHAPTER 12

Thursday, September 11

The Sheriff belched as he sat down on the stool, pounded his fist against his chest to knock out a second one, and then tossed his files onto the diner counter.

"Tough day?" Mabel asked, pouring him a coffee.

"This damn paperwork is too much." He slid his bulk over to grab the sugar. "Let me tell ya—" he opened the folder "—I thought scooping the Staties on this was a good thing, but now *they're* laughing. All this paper-pushing ain't worth it. Serves me right I guess, trying too hard."

Mabel peeked at some photos mostly hidden under the forms but couldn't make much out, so she prompted, "Is this the Winston case? I never did hear the details."

"Pretty bad," he said absently as he bent over the

forms to get to work.

"I got time. I ain't that busy tonight."

Dan glanced around. "Place looks full to me."

Mabel whipped her cloth at him in a playful way. "Sally's got it covered, I don't have much to do." Which was no accident. Dan came here every Thursday to do his paperwork, so Mabel had scheduled Sally on purpose to give herself time to ask Dan some questions.

"So?" she drawled out after a pause. "If you already caught him, why all this paperwork?"

"Procedure."

Mabel waited for more, but Dan kept working.

"So where is he now?"

"The black fella?" Dan asked absently.

"Winston Washington," she corrected with a frown.

"Oh, up in Seattle's King County Jail. Buster's boy, Sam, works up there as you know."

"Any visitors?"

Dan stopped writing, a little annoyed at being interrupted again. "For the Washington kid?"

She tried to sound breezy. "Yes. I mean, how does someone get a visitor in jail anyway?"

"Easy. Anyone can see anyone. You sign up for visitor's hours, wait a bit, and they bring the cons out in a room." He bent over his work again.

"So, anyone can visit?"

"Yes, Mabel." Dan looked up, irritated. "Even you could visit him if you want."

"Now, why would I do that?" Mabel said, laughing it off — but that was precisely what she wanted to do. And to make it seem like it wasn't a big deal, she moved to the end of the counter to clean up some dishes. But Dan often left before eight PM to watch his hunting show, so to ask her questions, she needed another way to get his attention quick. She went back to the kitchen for a fresh pie, then came out and walked the pie past Dan, who sniffed at the aroma, but didn't stop working. She frowned — that didn't work. So, she dragged over the pie display to clean it. Then used errant sweeps of the cloth over the pie to send its aroma Dan's way.

The irritating noise and delicious smell finally drew Dan's focus onto the pie. He asked, "Got some for me?"

"You betcha," Mabel said. She hid her smile, cutting him a big piece and then adding ice cream. "A little extra," she said with a wink and then slid it in front of him.

The Sheriff grunted, "Well, that's all right." He pushed the papers aside and started eating.

Mabel took a moment to casually use her cloth to push the papers around to see the pictures.

"Oh, dear God," she said as she saw the first photo. The girl was white-faced, covered in blood, with her clothes half off.

"Sorry, Mabel. Shouldn't have it out like this." Dan went to cover it up, but she stopped him with the cloth.

"Mind if I look?"

"You really want to?"

She nodded.

"All right then," he said.

She picked up a graphic photo, initially more fascinated than disgusted by it. Her eyes zeroed in on the details.

Dan pointed out a few things with his fork. "She was raped you see." Mabel winced. "Then these cut marks. Looks like she been tortured some. But here?" He took another bite of pie and then used his fork to point out another photo. "She fought back. Gave him hell, is what the coroner said."

"Any fingerprints?"

"One. No match on anyone with a record," Dan said. "Coroner also found a few different protein markers in the—" He looked around and then pointed towards his crotch with his fork. "—men's samples. Inside her." Then he spoke louder again. "He can't say for sure, but he thinks they're samples from two different men."

"The coroner said she fought like hell?"

He nodded, chewing.

"Did Winston have any scratches or bruises from the fight?"

Dan shuffled through the papers to find the right sheet and then swept it over to her with his fork. "Inconclusive," he said and kept eating.

Mabel picked it up and tried to read it. "What does that mean? Did he have scratches or not?"

He shrugged. "Staties wrote that one."

"But you brought him in."

"Didn't look."

"So, you're missing something here."

"What I'm missing is more ice cream," Dan said, smiling through a mouthful.

Mabel hid her frustration by going to get him another scoop. She came back, slid it over, and started again.

"You said she was raped. By who?"

"By Winston," he said, his tone implying "obviously."

"He was her boyfriend. You said there was evidence from two men."

He shrugged. "Not my job. I found him. I brought him in." Mabel glared hard at him for his indifference. "What? You still on the innocent kid thing?"

"How does Winston explain what happened?"

He shrugged. "Witness statement, I guess."

"Which is?"

"It's all there," he said, pointing his fork at the files and then looking at his watch.

Mabel knew he'd be heading off soon, so she grabbed the remote and turned on the diner's television. "You want to watch your show?"

"You never let me watch it here."

"Change of heart. I'm bored."

He glanced around at the truckers and out-of-towners. "You sure your customers won't mind? They skin them animals at the end."

She covered her disgust with a painful smile. "No, no, watch it. I can even get you a beer."

"Wow," Dan said. "That's mighty fine."

She clicked the remote to find the channel with *The American Sportsman.* "Here, and I'll also hold these for you on this side of the counter," Mabel said, sweeping up the file folder as she handed him a beer. "You can pick them up when the show's over. Saves you from having to fuss over them."

"Mighty fine," Dan said, lifting his cold brew and settling in closer to the television.

She waited till he was distracted and then pulled the

files closer and dove right into it. She stopped at a large photo showing the whole crime scene. Karen — she couldn't think of that young girl as just a body — was sprawled out on the sawmill floor, covered in blood from stab wounds in the chest.

She searched for the witness statement next and then found the photocopied version of it.

Winston wrote that after leaving the diner, he and Karen had smoked a joint in his car but got into another argument before Karen stormed off. A man inside a black truck parked nearby had waved her over. Winston didn't see the driver but watched her get in, and that was the last he'd seen her. After that, he went home to his trailer and smoked more weed before passing out. He didn't really have an alibi.

Mabel tapped her fingers against the counter. How did Karen end up in the sawmill of all places? The killer must have known the site. Did Winston? Larson was rumored to own a piece of the sawmill, and his gang supplied the local drug dealers, including Winston. Even though Larson was a racist, he was an equal opportunity distributor to various gangs: black, white, Asian, Latino. Quite the humanist if it meant better profits, she thought sarcastically.

Her mind turned to the black truck. Who drove it? It had been dark, and the truck could have been any sort of color. It didn't help that pretty much everyone in town had a truck, but Winston had written that the truck was black and looked new, which narrowed things down a little. While most locals and the mine's construction crews had beaters, Larson's gang bought new, as their drug money fueled most of the town's purchases. But there were more suspects than just his gang members, like her motel guest, Bill Jordan.

Mabel looked through the rest of the police files. The assigned detectives didn't ask Winston if he was familiar with the sawmill and didn't search long for the truck. At least they highlighted the second semen sample as indicating a possible unknown suspect, but after interviewing Winston and then the Thompson family, had simply hypothesized that she had been trading sex for drugs. Mabel frowned — that didn't sound right.

She went back to Winston's statement. He wrote he had been worried about Karen and that she felt she was being watched. By who? Mabel wondered. And why didn't he stop her from getting into that truck? That seems weird.

She closed the file folder slowly and thought about what she had learned. If only—

"You got another beer?" the Sheriff asked, jiggling his empty can, which startled her into dropping the folder and scattering papers onto the counter.

Dan gathered them together. "I better keep those," he said. "Ain't supposed to have them lying around."

"No, no, I'll look after them," Mabel protested, handing him another Bud to keep him occupied.

"No worries, I got 'em." Dan tucked the folder under his arm and hoisted his beer in a gesture of thanks. "Got me a show to watch." Then walked back to the TV.

Mabel swore under her breath — she wanted those files. And now she'd have to suffer through that stupid hunting show.

Unless... she considered with a growing smile: Sally hated those types of shows, and if Mabel spelled her off, after one look Sally would shut that TV off in ten seconds flat.

CHAPTER 13

Friday, September 12

The next day after lunch, as Mabel was busy clearing dirty dishes off the counter, Carlos came up.

He asked with a winning smile, "Hey, do you have Bill Jordan's things? I can get them out of your hair and shipped back to his place."

"Oh sure, Luv," she said, then paused, worried she could be giving away clues. "On second thought, hand me that address, and I can ship it for you."

"You don't have to do that," Carlos said, but he gladly handed it over anyway. A busy man, he had enough on his plate, managing a large crew of men.

Mabel took a look — Tacoma. Not too far away. She smiled at Carlos. "No worries. My wholesaler is nearby, and I got a regular run going today and could even drop it off to save you some charges."

"Oh, it's on the company. No need to put yourself out."

"I'm fine, a little thing."

"Well, thanks. I'll make sure my boss knows about this." He smiled again. "That's mighty fine of you."

"You're busy, and I'm here to help. I want all you boys to have a nice stay."

Carlos thanked her and headed off, whistling down the motel hallway back to his room.

Mabel looked at the address, thinking of what she might do. Kevin, the cook, typically did all the weekly pickups on Fridays. But not this time.

She went into the kitchen. "Kevin?" He glanced over his shoulder as he put a burger patty on the hot grill. "You have the list for Shelby's?" Shelby's Wholesaler was their food supplier. He nodded. "I'll be going in today. Sally's on in an hour. That okay?"

"I don't mind, I can do it for you," Kevin said, ever helpful.

"That's okay, I got this."

He saluted with one hand while holding the spatula down on a sizzling patty with the other. Mabel really liked that boy: he had a good work ethic, was always helping out, and had started dating a girl too. Not long ago, that lanky young man, covered in tattoos, had been a candidate for prison. Kevin had gotten into a fistfight with a Larson crony at a beach party on Long Lake, and Dan was about to send him to jail to appease Larson when Mabel had an idea. Knowing how good Kevin's mother was in the kitchen, she'd offered to take him in as a cook. To everyone else's surprise, and in particular to

Kevin's, he'd loved the job, and with him out of sight in the kitchen, Larson soon lost interest.

With the day getting on, Mabel grabbed the car keys from the office and then asked Sally to mind the diner. Bill Jordan's gear was heavy, and she had trouble carrying it over to the trunk of her station wagon. Dropping it in, she wiped the sweat off her forehead, and then took off her apron, draped it on the back seat, and got into the front.

After twenty minutes of driving, doubts started creeping in — she was no detective. When she reached the address in Tacoma, she felt pretty foolish. Wanting to get this over with, she lugged the gear out and hauled it to the townhouse door, on the edge of Tacoma's rundown industrial district, then knocked.

The door opened a sliver.

"Hi, I'm—" Mabel paused upon seeing a distraught young woman with tear-stained cheeks. "Dear? Are you all right?"

The girl wiped her cheeks, embarrassed. "What do you want?"

"I'm Mabel Davison, from the motel and diner. In Blue River."

The girl shrugged.

"Where Bill Jordan was working?"

"Oh," she said, perking up. "Are you with the construction company?"

"No dear, I own the motel. Bill left all his things in the room. I'm just dropping them off."

"Oh, okay," she said, numbly, and opened the door wider. Mabel helped her drag the gear into a sparsely furnished room.

The woman, more like a girl of nineteen, stood awkwardly, rubbing her arm. Then she noticed Mabel's downward glance and quickly rolled down her sleeve to cover a slight bruise, looking deeply embarrassed.

Mabel wanted to stay now and ask questions, so she said, "It's been a long drive. Do you mind if I get a glass of water?"

The girl nodded and then went off to the kitchen. She seemed a meek sort, and Mabel followed her in. There was nothing of a woman's touch in this place, but Mabel took a guess. "Are you Bill's girlfriend?"

The girl nodded as she poured. She seemed to want to cry again but only handed over the glass.

Mabel reached out to take it, and the girl jumped at the touch. "What's wrong, dear?"

She looked pained and just shook her head.

"Come here, girl," Mabel said and guided her to sit at the kitchen table. Mabel reached out to hold her hands, and this time the girl did not pull away but would not look into Mabel's eyes. "What's wrong, Luv? Are you okay?"

She shook her head and was silent for a solid minute until she finally said, "Bill and I got into a fight. Again." She seemed to collapse in on herself and said nothing further.

"Oh dear, I am sorry to hear that," Mabel said, struggling to find a way to reach this girl. "I didn't catch your name."

"It's Susan."

"Susan? What a pretty name," Mabel said, trying to

tease out a smile. "You are a very pretty girl, too, Susan — that name fits you."

Susan tried to smile but failed miserably.

Mabel frowned and cut right to it, but as softly as she could. "Did he hurt you?"

Susan flinched. "It's my fault, really. We got into a fight is all."

"It's never anyone's fault to get hurt. Especially not in an argument. What was it about?"

Susan sighed and shook her head. She didn't speak for a long moment, but once she did, it flooded out. "Bill... he, uh... he and I've been struggling, for a while. He's been off work for ages. Then he got the construction job. That was supposed to change things. But after less than a week, he uh, he's back home again, getting all cut up and scratched from some stupid backcountry climb he was doing, and now he don't have a job again." She grabbed a tissue and blew her nose. Then she broke down and sobbed. "I don't know. I thought he was the one for me. But he's struggling and angry all the time, and I don't know what I'm doing here. I should just go home."

"What sort of cuts? Where?"

"Scratches here," she said, pointing them out on her face and arms. "And a bad cut on his hand, here." She pointed to her left hand. "He took a fall, he said. Then with the bushwhacking he did to get out, he got scratched up some. Since it wasn't on the worksite when it happened, he needed to go the hospital out here, which just adds to the bills. I met him there and took him home."

"What time was that, dear?"

"Last Wednesday night."

A chill went down Mabel's spine. She sprang into action. "Listen to me," she said, grasping Susan's arm. "A girl got murdered out in Blue River that night. Apparently, she tried to fight off her attacker. Scratched him up good. Seems to me that Bill got those scratches at the same time. So, you think he was telling you the truth about some climbing accident, or maybe he got that from the girl?" The girl's jaw dropped, and her eyes widened, and her reaction told Mabel everything. "I don't know what your boyfriend did or not, but it's possible, right? Him squeezing your arm too like that? Getting angry a lot, like you said?" Susan nodded, scared now. "Do you have some kin to go to? Or some friends?"

Susan nodded. "My parents." She looked around. "I wasn't planning on staying anyways. I wanted to leave, but I…" Then she looked down and sobbed again. "It's been so hard. This isn't what I want." Mabel brought her in for a long hug until her crying subsided, and then the girl looked up, frightened. "Do you think he done it? Really I mean?"

Mabel moved the stray hairs from Susan's face and said, "I don't know. But I'm not taking any chances. Let me ask a question to be sure. What time did you meet him at the hospital?"

"I think ten PM or ten-thirty, I'm not sure, but no later than that."

Mabel felt a chill again. The timing was tight. Karen had left her diner around eight PM. If Bill had murdered Karen, he'd only have had about an hour or less to drive out to Tacoma. He'd have to be speeding, but if he were involved in a killing, she thought, he'd be fleeing as fast as the devil could drive him.

"Susan," she said, getting up. "I want you to listen to me very carefully. I want you out of this house. Don't come back here, no matter what. You said you have parents here, right?" She nodded. "Go straight there. Tell them Bill hasn't been good to you and that you're moving on, okay?" She nodded again. "Now, get your things and come meet me at the door." Susan got up, shaken and frightened, and then went into the bedroom. She only had a few spare clothes, and it didn't take her long to come out holding them.

Mabel had grown terribly anxious, expecting Bill Jordan to burst in any minute. She grasped Susan's arm and started to lead her out. "Let's get you out of here this minute, okay? But first, I'll need you to report this to the authorities. We'll go straight to the police rather than your parents, and you're going to tell them that Bill arrived at the hospital at ten or ten-thirty at the latest, like you said? Okay?"

She nodded, scared, but then said, "That's when I arrived, yeah."

Mabel opened the door ajar and peeked out, the street clear of danger. "Yes, when he did, Luv," she said. They were almost free.

"No, uh, he had already been treated. He was there a few hours, at least."

Mabel stopped, confused. "That can't be right. The girl hadn't even arrived at my diner by then. Think. Are you sure? How do you know he arrived so early? You said you saw him after ten."

"Yeah, but he'd already had his stitches in. He'd been there for hours, I'm certain."

Mabel's concern deflated. "You're certain?"

Susan nodded, scared, and wiped her nose. "Does that mean he still did it?"

Mabel hesitated, her adrenalin fading fast. In its place, she felt ill and a fool. "No," she said finally. "No, dear. I don't think so."

"So, I'm not in danger?"

"Maybe not."

"Oh," Susan said, lost and alone.

"I can still take you to your parents," Mabel said. "I don't think you should stay here anyway."

Susan started to cry again. "I just don't know what to do."

Mabel's heart melted for her. "I'm sorry I scared you." Then she put an arm around her shoulders to build up the girl's courage. "It's probably for the best. You're not happy here."

Susan nodded. "Let's go then," she said in a whisper.

Mabel led her out and waited for her to lock the door. When Susan did, she paused, not knowing what to do with her key, but then simply dropped it in the mailbox. When the key clanked hitting bottom, a weight seemed to lift from her shoulders, and she stood straighter. She breathed in the fresh air and then turned around, holding her spare clothes with one hand.

Mabel waited, watching her, as Susan started to come alive.

Mabel reached out to hold her hand.

Susan grasped it tight and then gave a soft smile to

Mabel, who returned it in measure. "Are you going to be all right?" Mabel asked gently.

Susan nodded, and a touch of hope appeared in her eyes. "Thank you."

"Oh, don't mind me. I'm just a silly woman who asks too many questions," Mabel said, leading her to the car.

"Are you really just a waitress?"

Mabel laughed embarrassedly. "Just a waitress, dear. Really. But the girl that was murdered is personal to me. You see, she was a customer and I… I saw that trouble was catching up to her fast. But I didn't do anything. I let her go without stopping her." Mabel paused. "I don't know what I could have done, but whatever God's plan was, she left. And she got murdered. And her boyfriend is suspected of being the killer."

"But you don't think he did it?"

Mabel thought about that some more. "No," she said finally. "I don't." Then she guided Susan to the passenger side before walking around the car, but Susan just stood there, waiting.

"Why?" Susan asked.

"I can read people. I have a gift," Mabel said, getting in. Susan did too.

"A gift?"

Mabel started the ignition and then sat back. "Yes, I know it sounds strange, hon. But it's something special in me. I can't explain it. It's in the eyes, for me. When I look into them, it's… it's like I can read a person's soul if you get me." Mabel breathed out and then gave an enigmatic smile. "I can't explain it more than that."

"What do my eyes tell you?"

Mabel looked into her red-tinged, watery blue eyes and didn't see a weak girl. "You are strong. You will get over this."

Susan swallowed and then looked out the front window and reflected. "I think I... lost myself in this relationship. At first, it was good, and he made me feel special. But, after a time, I don't think he liked me for me, you know?" She looked over. "I thought I wasn't good enough for him."

"Oh, luv," Mabel said, reaching out to touch her hand. "It's him who's not good enough to see who you really are. You can do better."

The barest hint of a sparkle appeared in Susan's eyes, and a slow smile grew upon her lips. Mabel smiled in return. Then put the car into gear, stepped on the gas, and got her out of there.

CHAPTER 14

Friday, September 19

Mabel rarely took personal time off, so when she asked both Sally to cover a shift and Consuela to look after her kids, it became quite a sensation. Mabel ignored staff chatter and let them think whatever they wanted: she didn't want anyone to know she was visiting a jail to see Winston Washington.

A loud electronic buzzer sounded before the jail gate opened, and a guard beckoned her into the security area. Out of place and nervous, she waited with the other visitors, who looked to be a mix of wives, kids, girlfriends, and some rough-looking folks. Her sleep had been affected, so she wore extra concealer to hide the puffiness under her eyes. It was almost too much to expect that Winston wasn't guilty — but her intuition told her otherwise.

A guard stepped into the room and barked out the rules: don't touch the inmates, don't hand them anything, abide by the time limits, follow all instructions. Then he let family and friends in one by one, and by the time Mabel was allowed in, the seats were filling up. Winston was sitting by himself, watching the visitors come in. Mabel doubted he remembered her, but he had agreed to a visit, so that was a start.

Mabel approached with a welcoming smile. "Hi, Winston. Can I sit down?"

"You the gal who signed up?"

She nodded.

"It's your hour."

She sat down, and he sized her up.

"Hey, wait a minute, you're the owner of the diner. In that shithole Blue River." She nodded. "You like prison dudes or something?"

Mabel's smile fell. His rude comment made her focus on his brown eyes, which showed anger, pain, stress, skepticism, but nothing she would call evil, not like looking into Larson's eyes. The man in front of her was nothing more than a boy who'd grown up maybe too fast in some ways, too slow in others, and with what happened to Karen, had probably been damaged for the rest of his life. Was he guilty of a crime? Sure. He was a drug dealer. But murder? That's what she was here to find out.

"I wanted—" She paused to settle her nerves "—to find out if you had worked at the sawmill."

Winston's head cocked back in disbelief. "You drove all this way to ask that?"

"No, no." Mabel became flustered, looking for the right words. "Karen, um, she was found—"

"Yeah, in the sawmill," he said, getting a little angry. "That's what the pigs said. You with them?"

"No, I…" Mabel hesitated again. "I met Karen's parents, that's why."

Winston gave her a "what did that matter" look and the callousness took her aback. Clearly no saint, she thought. She pressed him, wanting to know if he was innocent or not, and if not, she would leave. "Did you work at the sawmill?"

Winston gaped at her. "Lady. I never even been in a sawmill. I sell drugs. You think I deal, and cut lumber too? Come on, do you see me as a nine-to-five woodcutter chopping sticks with an ax, with these hands? I sleep till noon, and I sell weed, and sometimes I smoke it. Jesus."

Mabel's hunch was confirmed, and she excitedly pressed on. "You told police that Karen got into another vehicle. A black truck?"

"What's it to you?" he asked, crossing his arms. "I thought you said you weren't with the police."

"I'm not. But this is important, Winston. You're facing murder charges, and you told police about a black truck."

"I don't get this. Most of your kind in Blue River would lynch me for my skin. You one of Larson's gang then? You looking for payment? I told them I don't have it. How could I? I'm in jail."

"So Larson sells to you?"

"Lady. Larson sells to everyone."

"But why? He's a racist pig."

"He's a racist pig who likes green more than he hates black."

Ah. She nodded, understanding. "Who was in the truck then?"

"How do I know?" Winston said, looking exasperated. "It was dark. I couldn't see the motherfucker in that truck."

"You said Karen was worried. That she was being followed."

He glanced away like this was a waste of time and said, "I told the police already."

"Tell me, please. I'm here to help."

"I don't know you, Lady. And it's not like Karen was my girlfriend or anything. I'd picked her up in Seattle outside a bar, and we'd shacked up for a few weeks. She was just a weed rat looking for a score."

"I don't believe that. I saw you two that night. You cared about her, Winston."

A look of pain washed over him, and he tried to hide it by shifting in his seat and brushing her off with a shrug. "She was just a white girl, you know? Didn't have a white girl before."

"No. You *cared* about her."

Winston sighed and looked down.

A long silence followed before he whispered without looking over. "So?"

"I could tell you were worried about her. It looked like you were trying to talk her out of something."

He cleared his throat roughly and nodded. "She wanted to go home, back to her family. But I... I knew I couldn't exist in her white bread, suburban world. She wanted to go to university. I haven't even finished high school. I'm just some fuckin' loser who deals weed for a racist."

"No. You are a smart man, Winston."

Winston looked back, not wanting to let the compliment in, but he did. "She liked that about me. That I'm a good reader. Well-read, I mean—" he corrected himself and smiled. "She saw through my bullshit too. That's why I, uh, I… loved her. I know that sounds stupid. But it's the truth."

"Why did she leave you that night?"

"She wanted out. To go home. But I told her I wasn't going with her. That I was staying in Blue River."

"So, she got mad."

He took a moment then nodded.

Mabel then asked as gently as she could, "So why didn't you go after her?"

Winston flinched, and all that was left of the tough guy act disappeared; like that night at the diner, he looked more like a boy in a man's clothes than the murderer the police had branded him. He crossed his arms to hold in his emotions but failed, and though he hid his tears from the others, he did not from her. After a time, he said in a hoarse whisper, "I'll never forgive myself for that."

"The police said she did tricks for drugs."

"They would have."

"Did she?"

He scoffed and then added, only a little embarrassed, "She wouldn't even go to bed with me for the first while, so I know she wouldn't be turning tricks for anyone else."

"When did she get the tattoo?"

"It was new. About two weeks. She wanted one like her dad's."

"Was she trying to turn her life around?"

He looked down at his hands and nodded. "She'd done heroin before. Meth. But with me, only weed." He sighed. "Look. She was trying to do right. Get back on track. I was trying to help her. I wanted her to dump my ass."

"But she didn't."

He slowly shook his head and then became absorbed by his own thoughts.

Mabel glanced at the time; she didn't have much left. Without knowing of a delicate way to ask the next question, she just asked it directly. "Did you two have sex that day?"

Winston's eyes locked back on hers, and Mabel felt nervous again from his anger. "No. Not for a few days," His voice started rising. "The police told me about that. God damn, that fucker. Raping my girl." He clenched his fists. "If you find whoever did that to her, you tell me, and I'll kill 'em. For free. You hear me?!"

The guards started to break up the other conversations, so she quickly moved to her last questions, desperate to get it all. "The truck," she said. "Is there anything about the truck that you noticed? Did Karen say anything about a man following her? Or anyone she might have known at my motel?"

The talk of the rape had clearly thrown him, and he forcibly wiped the last of the tears off his face.

The guards got closer, and she pleaded, "Winston! I'll help get you free. But tell me who was following her.

What did Karen say?"

"You really think I'm gonna get free?!" Winston snapped at her. "Look around you. I'm just another black guy in this shithole. None of us black men are going free. You white chicks, you think you're the saviors, but you're not, you're the ones who put us here."

The guard was beside Winston and told him to get up. Winston brushed him off but got to his feet anyways. He said nothing to Mabel, and while she stood up to give him a hug and offer some final comforting words, he just turned his back on her and left through the rear gate.

Mabel crossed her arms to hold in her emotions and let herself be escorted out. It was not until she got back to her car that she broke down sobbing.

CHAPTER 15

Wednesday, September 24

Mabel was telling a dirty joke to a customer at the counter when Sally came up and quietly waited, smiling politely, until the customer laughed at the punch line and left and Mabel could focus on her.

"What's up, Luv?"

Sally pointed backward and said, "That Bill Jordan character. You know the one. High-tailed it after a week and left the room a mess. Wants to talk to you."

"Oh," Mabel said, her sense of humor vanishing as she looked past Sally to the scowling young man with the strong, wiry build of a climber. "He looks none too happy," Mabel added, touching Sally's arm as she passed.

"You need any backup?" Sally asked.

Mabel glanced back with a confident smile and said, "For this little pup?"

Bill Jordan folded his arms across his chest. The bandages on one hand were clear to see and the thin scratches on his face looked almost healed.

"What is it?" she asked, not feeling like giving him a luv or a hon, as she normally would, thinking about Susan, and how he had treated her. She was half-tempted to give him the door already.

He was fuming and came right out with it. "Did you come to *my* place and talk to *my* girl?"

"You mean drop off your things that you left here?" Mabel said, giving his tone right back.

"Um, okay. Yeah *that,* I mean."

"You're going to thank me for doing it?"

He tried holding her stern gaze until Mabel gave a look that said "Are you going to do the right thing here?" He gave in. "Okay, fine. Thanks for that, for bringing my things. You see, I, uh, I got injured. Had to go to the hospital." He uncrossed his arms to point out the bandage, which she had already noticed, and then awkwardly let his arms swing down to his side. The starch seemed to be taken out of him some, but he came out with it. "Susan said you thought I'd *murdered* someone."

Mabel almost smiled at his forthrightness. Because if two weeks back, she had looked into such perplexed, self-conscious eyes the brief time he had moved into the motel, she would have known he was no killer. "Yes, I felt bad for that. I told her, in the end, it wasn't you. You see, there's a—" She didn't know how to say it, so just came out with it. "There's a potential suspect who was driving a black truck. Plus, the victim, Karen, had fought off her attacker."

"I read about that. I thought they caught someone."

"So it appears."

He looked puzzled, giving her a once-over. "You some detective too?"

Mabel laughed this time. "Oh God, no. I'm probably someone who's sticking her nose into something she shouldn't. I own this motel and diner, and I'm a waitress. That's pretty much what I do. I only think our justice system isn't all that just in this instance." Bill Jordan didn't seem to understand, but she had no interest in explaining herself further. "So why are you here?"

"Susan. She, uh, she left me." Bill's face fell. "Told me after you came and talked to her that she, um, got the courage to leave me. Now she's at her parents and won't see me and I don't know what to do. I miss her and I want her back."

"Then why did you hurt her?"

"Now that was a mistake. I didn't mean to, uh... We were arguing. I didn't mean to get rough."

"That's no excuse."

"No." Bill deflated. "No, I guess you're right."

"So why come to me?"

"Could you, uh... talk to her?"

"You want *me* to ask her to go back *to you*?"

"Maybe, yeah. If you could."

Oh dear God no, Mabel thought. You poor, misguided boy. "Sorry," she said at last. "That's on you. I wouldn't even let you back in my motel knowing how you treated her."

A passing customer overheard what Mabel said so he guided her aside and said, "I know I did bad. I'm ashamed of it. But I want her back and I don't know what to do anymore."

Mabel didn't feel any inclination to be generous to this boy. She said, "If you want her back, be a better man." She waited, expecting him to protest, but he kept listening, eager to hear what she had to say. "You don't treat women that way," Mabel went on, scolding him. "If she's the one, then you support her, build her up, you don't tear her down. The poor thing was frazzled, crying, at the end of her wits. She'd already wanted to leave you with the lousy way you'd been making her feel lately, so don't come here expecting me to rescue you from your own stupidity. If you want her back, change. Learn to be a better man, treat her better. It's on you. Only you."

Bill looked like a deer caught in the headlights. After a moment, he blinked rapidly, like what she had just said filtered in, and he nodded without speaking.

She continued, "You got a lot of work to do. Not just with her. She said you needed this construction job, but you went off like a fool going climbing and getting injured. First thing you do is you need to get your head on straight. I doubt Carlos, your foreman, wants you back, but you could try there. Then leave her alone for a bit. Get your life in order." Mabel didn't know why she was giving him advice.

Bill seemed to come out of his daze and whatever anger and swagger he had before was gone. He just breathed out slowly like a valve letting out steam and finally nodded. He said, "I guess you're right."

"You damn straight I'm right. Get it together. Then maybe, just maybe, if you let her be and, more important, let her be the woman she is, you might, *might*, have a chance. She's a good girl, a great girl actually, and any man would be lucky to have her."

He nodded, scared now. Probably worried she'd fall for another man, Mabel thought. If he gets jealous, he's lost. "Now don't be worrying about who's she's with. You worry about being a better man. A better man doesn't get jealous. He lets the woman be herself and loves her for who she is, not who he wants her to be." She thought of her own Bill — her husband — and though she'd kicked him out too, she still loved him. This young pup had nothing on her Bill though.

While Bill Jordan was busy absorbing what she had said, she looked around her diner and could see a few customers with empty glasses of water and one couple needing menus. Enough time had been wasted with Bill Jordan. "Looks like you got some work cut out for you," she said. "But I'm going to have to get back to work here. You gonna be all right?"

Bill blinked himself back into alertness and stepped back, contrite. "Yeah, sure. No problem. And uh, thanks. Not just for collecting my stuff, but for the talk. Yeah." He nodded, sincere. "I really appreciate it."

Taken aback by his change, she examined him more closely, wondering if he was just fooling her, like he didn't really mean it. But he actually looked sincere. So, a bit of her hardness eased, and though she wasn't going to go completely soft on him, she softened a little. "Like I said, hon. Focus on yourself. Let her do the same. Then maybe, just maybe, you'll get back together."

He nodded. "Again. Thank you."

Mabel nodded, satisfied, then touched his arm as she passed him to go attend her customers. The door chime rang twice behind her, signaling that Bill had left. After she gave the couple menus, she spied the young man getting into a dark blue truck, and then back it away and head off up the highway. Mabel wondered if she'd ever see him again. For his sake, she hoped he learned something here.

But for her, she was back to square one. Winston was still in jail and no one else seemed to be looking out for the boy but her. Sheriff Dan certainly wasn't. But it was clear from all this, she was no detective. A waitress at heart, that's what she'd stay, so she might as well see if she could light a fire under Dan, the one man with a badge in this town, to do his job. She'd share what she'd learned from Winston and hoped that would be a start.

Then she looked down at the couple and flashed a welcoming smile. "What'll it be, dears? I got the best cooking in Washington State and you two look hungry, and not just for each other."

The couple blushed; she was right on both counts.

CHAPTER 16

Friday, September 26

Mabel expected Dan at the diner to do his weekly paperwork, but when he didn't show, she went to see him the next morning. She found him with his feet on the desk, hands behind his head, chewing gum and staring at the ceiling of his storefront office. He didn't seem to care that she'd caught him loafing, slowly easing himself back into a sitting position.

"Good day, Mabel," he said. "I ain't seen Hector if you're looking."

Mabel flushed, embarrassed that Dan's first thought was to ease her mind that Hector might not be in trouble. "No, I..." she said, pulling out a muffin from her shoulder bag. "I made some of these last night, expecting you to come by. Thought I'd drop off one."

Dan reached for it and took a big bite. "Thanks," he

said, smiling through a mouthful of crumbs.

She waited for him to swallow so he wouldn't spit out the crumbs and then asked as innocently as she could, "So? How is your case going?"

"What case?"

Mabel gave him an "Are you serious?" look. "The murder of Karen Thompson."

"Oh. That." He shrugged. "Like I said, that's mostly a Staties thing." Dan took a last big bite of the muffin then licked his fingers. "Why? You still poking around this thing?"

Mabel played it innocent. "Why do you ask, Luv?"

"I heard from Buster. His boy said you visited the jail."

Mabel frowned, folding her arms. "Well, I don't think he did it, Dan."

"The law might disagree with you there. He's going to be arraigned Tuesday."

"A what? What does reined mean?"

"No, no, it's arraigned. A-R-R-A-I something something." He flicked his hand like he didn't care and then scratched his beard. "It means he either pleads guilty or not and if not, the judge fixes him a trial date. If he has no money for an attorney, court appoints him one. Standard procedure."

"Would she be any good? This court-appointed lawyer?"

The Sheriff smiled a little. "Likely a he. Hopefully, it's Arronson. He's okay. Prosecutors like him."

"That doesn't sound so good for Winston."

"It is to the system. Leave it be."

"No. I won't *let* it be. Because yes, I did go see Winston at the jail, and he told me he never went to the sawmill before," Mabel said, raising her eyebrows like she had proven her point. "The killer would have had to have known that place, which Winston didn't, so why would Winston go there to murder? Makes no sense."

"Maybe he sold weed to a guy there once. Who knows?"

"Well then, what about the second semen sample?"

Dan winced, shifting in his seat. "Ugh, Mabel. I'm not used to you saying those words."

"Winston loved her."

"Well, then he shouldn't have killed her."

"How can you be so sure?"

He shrugged. "Most killers are kin or jilted lovers."

"Yes, but the police say she was doing tricks, and she wasn't."

"How do you know what the police said?!" Mabel froze, wondering if he knew she read his report. "Did Winston tell you?"

Mabel raised her eyebrows, not wanting to admit she read that from Dan's files last Thursday.

Dan pointed his finger at her. "Don't you be listening to that boy. He'd say anything to get out of jail. Probably even said he's innocent."

"Dan! There are problems with this case. What about that black truck?"

"It's a black truck. You see lots of trucks come in and out of your parking lot, don't ya? Besides, Staties chased that lead and got nothing."

"How?! What did they do? Did they drive around Blue

River to see who owns a black truck?"

Dan scoffed. "To find one truck? Ain't how it's done. Anyone with a record would show up in the system."

"Well... what if they don't have a record?"

The Sheriff shrugged.

"That's what I mean. Karen was turning her life around. She had a tattoo on her hands that spelled 'hope.'"

"So, you're calling the vic Karen now," Dan said and raised his eyebrows like he'd made his point. "Got a tattoo of my mother's face on my arm. Don't mean I'm going to marry her."

Mabel bit her lips to keep it serious. "The victim got a tattoo like her dad had when he had turned sober when he was her age. She was getting sober, too, and turning her life around. Winston knew it and was helping her."

"Okay, you're going to have to stop this," Dan said, raising his palm to soothe her. "He's in jail. He's going to trial. Let the justice system handle it."

"Will it? How many in prison are black? Or other minorities? He has a point."

"You do the crime, you do the time."

"That sounds like Larson talking."

"Well, Larson owns a lot around here."

"Are you with him now?"

"Now hold on, Mabel. You saw that mob the night the boy was here and how I protected him. I do my job when I have to. I stood up to Larson, and now he's right pissed at me. This is a tough town for one policeman."

"I know, Dan. But we can't let them win."

"Who?"

"The racists."

"They're community folk, most of them. You can't blame them for wanting to protect the community."

"They farm drugs."

"Look. I get it. But if I tried arresting folks for being racist or farming drugs around here, practically the whole town would be in jail. Maybe this new mine will change things, but right now, I can't change it."

"You're the law."

He nodded but said nothing more.

Mabel sighed. "So, nothing's changing then."

"You can go to the arraignment," Dan said, trying to mollify her now. "Go see justice in action. That might settle your thoughts."

CHAPTER 17

Tuesday, September 30

Mabel took another afternoon off, and her staff almost had a gossiping fit. After she tamped that down, she asked Kerry to watch the boys, and even though their relationship had been improving, Kerry refused — until Mabel agreed to let Kerry drive to Lisa's for dinner. And since Mabel expected to be back by the time Sally, covering her shift, had to leave at five-thirty PM for an appointment, the timing worked out for all.

But once Mabel made it to the back of the courtroom, she learned to her dismay cases earlier on the docket had taken extra time, which backed everything up. Now she'd be lucky to be out of here by four PM, and with that hour-and-a-half drive back to Blue River, she was cutting it close for everyone.

It was then a vast relief when the bailiff finally led

Winston Washington into the courtroom around 4:05 PM.

The bailiff called the court to order, and the judge read out the criminal charge against Winston. Then the judge asked Winston if he had an attorney.

He shook his head no, looking lost and alone. Mabel's heart bled for him.

"Please speak for the record," said the judge.

"Excuse me?"

"Answer yes or no."

"No."

"Do you need the assistance of a court-appointed attorney?"

"Sorry, what?"

"Are you hard of hearing?"

"No. I mean, yes. Yes, I need a lawyer."

The judge glared at him before looking down at the papers on his desk. "Note for the record that was a yes and that I will appoint attorney Stevenson—"

A voice from the gallery called out, "Stevenson's on vacation."

The judge frowned. "Then Gibson."

"Sick," said the same voice.

"Jamison? Akbar?"

"Both quit."

The judge took off his glasses, clearly irritated. "You're available, right, Arronson?"

The same voice responded, "Yes, Your Honor."

"Then, you're it."

The person stood up, and Mabel got her first look at Winston's attorney. He was in his forties, with a round paunch, sloppy tie, and wrinkled jacket. He moved over to his client and whispered something to Winston.

"How does your client plead?"

Arronson whispered to Winston, and Winston muttered something back.

"What did he say?" the judge asked harshly. "Speak up."

"I said, what does it matter what I plead?" Winston said as Arronson replied, "Nothing, Your Honor."

The judge glared at Arronson. "Advise your client to answer properly."

Winston muttered, "You're going to find me guilty, anyway."

The judge pointed his finger at Winston but looked at Arronson. "Is that his plea? Guilty? Make my day easier, please."

Arronson conferred with Winston, the two going back and forth for a few minutes until, finally, Arronson gestured at Winston to speak to the judge. Arronson looked down at his notes.

"Not guilty then," Winston said, in a petulant tone.

The judge looked up. "Pardon?"

"Whatever gives me the better deal."

"That's something you work out with the prosecutor," the judge replied, sounding unimpressed. He turned to Arronson. "Do I understand that your client is pleading not guilty, for now?"

Arronson stopped rubbing his forehead and glanced up from his notes. He said, "Yes, Your Honor. He is pleading not guilty."

"Okay," the judge said. "I'm going to set bail."

Arronson spoke up as if he didn't expect a positive

response. "I request he be allowed out on his own recognizance."

"Denied."

Arronson nodded resignedly.

The judge continued, "Since it's a murder charge and the defendant has an existing criminal record and is considered a flight risk, bail is set at one hundred thousand. I'm assuming we can skip the pre-trial, Mr. Arronson?"

Arronson whispered something to Winston, who just shrugged. Arronson nodded to the judge.

"It would be good if we can get this matter settled," the judge said, looking between the prosecutor and Arronson. The two looked at each other, and Arronson nodded to the prosecutor, and then the prosecutor nodded to the judge.

Mabel frowned.

"Good," the judge said. "Trial date set for—" he referred to his calendar "—November 14th. Let's move on. Bailiff?"

Arronson said a few last words to his client before Winston departed with the bailiff.

Arronson stuffed his briefcase with his files and notes and made his way over to the prosecutor. They exchanged a few words and then shook hands. Mabel frowned again and stood up. As the pudgy attorney went to leave the courtroom, she followed him out. In the lobby, she called his name. "Mr. Arronson? Mr. Arronson!"

Arronson looked back, startled to be addressed out of court. "Yes?" he said, looking like he was trying to figure out who Mabel was.

"I have concerns about the Winston Washington case."

He adjusted his glasses up the bridge of his nose. "We haven't met. Are you a detective on the case? I haven't read the full file yet."

Mabel had worn her most professional skirt suit — the only one she had — but she was tongue-tied about how to answer and not give herself away. Before she could speak, however, Arronson continued. "What is it, Detective?"

So be it, Mabel thought. I didn't tell a lie. "Two things," she said, newfound confidence in her voice. "The unknown man with the black truck, and the second, unidentified semen sample."

He didn't bat an eye. "Are they linked?"

"Uh, what?"

"Do you have reason to believe the man in the truck raped her?"

"Oh, I'm, uh, no, I mean yes, I'm looking into it."

"Okay, but I haven't read the files yet. Do you have a card?"

"A card?" she asked, not wanting to say no, as she fumbled with her purse.

"Forget it," Arronson said. "Here's mine."

She read it: Lavi Arronson, Attorney-at-Law and Public Defender.

"If you have any follow up, call me, right?"

She nodded, still looking at the card, amazed that she had access to Winston's lawyer.

"That's it?" Arronson asked.

She nodded, and he left.

Mabel put his card to her chest, laughed, and then quickly glanced around to see if anyone was looking. She glided down the hallway as if on air until she spied a clock on the wall. Ten minutes before five. Oh no, she thought, dropping back down to reality. She raced to the payphones, put in a quarter, and called home. It rang five times before Kerry finally answered.

"Hiya, Luv. I need—"

"Why aren't you home yet?"

"Good news. I'm done here and—"

"When are you coming *home*?"

"It'll take me about an hour and a half."

"What?!" Kerry shrieked. "I told Lisa that I was coming over to her house!"

"I know, honey. Things just took longer—"

"You won't be back till six-thirty!"

"Kerry! Enough!" Mabel raised her voice and then glanced around, embarrassed. She calmed herself down and said, "I know I'm late. I will be there as soon as I can. I'm sorry you'll be late to see Lisa, but you will get to see her. Now, can you tell Sally—"

"Ughhh. Hurry up," Kerry said and hung up.

Mabel bit back a swear. She put in another quarter and dialed the diner. A sudden headache caused her to rub her forehead. It rang several times before Kevin answered. She waited a little longer until Sally came on the line. "Mabel?"

"Yes, Sally. I'm at the courthouse and coming back now."

A pause. "How long?"

"I'm sorry. Things went late, and, um, I'll be there at six-thirty." Mabel cringed, knowing that she was forcing Sally to stay late too. Several seconds went by in silence.

"Okay, Mabel." Sally sounded disappointed.

"I'm sorry, Luv. I'll be there as fast as I can."

"Drive safe."

"I will," Mabel said and hung up the phone.

Her initial euphoria of helping Winston morphed into disappointment. And while promising she'd make it up to Kerry and Sally, in all honesty, she didn't know when with how busy she was, and that troubled her. This situation was taking up whatever little time she had, and life was such a struggle as is.

CHAPTER 18

Thursday, October 2

O rder up," Kevin called out. For the past two days, Mabel had worked double shifts to make it up to Sally.

She limped over to drop off dirty dishes and then picked up four lunches to take to a table full of construction workers, setting down an extra bottle of ketchup before they had to ask. With the mine's central administration building almost built, the crews hadn't set up their eating hall yet, so traffic to the diner was heavy. She knew it wouldn't last but wanted to make sure the crews were well-fed and happy, hoping some would come back after the hall was built. And while Sally had forgiven her for being late two nights back, Kerry hadn't. The teen had been extra moody since then, and Mabel had had enough. Mabel had been about to confront her coming out of her bedroom that morning but caught her drying off tears, which melted Mabel's heart. Still, the girl managed to leave the house with much unsaid; Mabel would just have to wait her out.

"Order up," Kevin repeated.

Mabel's feet ached, and she hobbled back to the kitchen, where Kevin told her they needed more potatoes.

Mabel wiped her forehead while scanning the diner. "Can we wait till tonight?"

Kevin shook his head. "Got more lunch orders to fill."

She checked the time, just past one PM, as Kevin pressed her. "Can't cook fries without potatoes."

"Okay," she said, blowing the hair out of her face. "I can make a run into town and pick up what they've got."

She served the next batch of meals before taking off her apron and rushing out the door to her car.

At the town grocer, she bought most of the potatoes in stock. The price was much higher than at her Tacoma supplier, but it was important for the business. Big portions were part of her diner's charm, her customers appreciated it, and it usually meant more tips for her staff, so she didn't mind the added cost.

She loaded her car and headed out.

Checking her watch, she'd been gone about fifteen minutes, fast for a run that usually took twenty or twenty-five. Kevin would be pleased.

Then she saw it — a black pickup pulling into the sawmill's parking lot. She slammed on the brakes, almost skidding past the turnoff. Dozens of vehicles were in the lot, with more than a few new dark pickups, the sawmill being an economic powerhouse in the community, paying good wages to men who liked their toys.

Mabel rechecked her watch — she had time, so she drove around writing down black trucks' license plates in her waitressing notebook. By the time she finished, her mood had improved. But she was late, a good twenty minutes. Kevin was beside himself in the dining area, and she got an earful from a couple of impatient customers. She soothed them with her usual charm, but they didn't leave much of a tip for Kevin and Sally, so she padded the tip jar out of her pocket to keep the staff happy.

Mabel leaned against the counter, exhausted. She had six more hours here, then about two more hours cleaning motel rooms. The only bright side of today was having the truck plate numbers. Now she just needed the Sheriff to look them up.

She picked up the phone, and after the fourth ring, a gruff voice said, "Sheriff's office."

Mabel tried to sound chipper, though she didn't feel it. "Hiya, Dan!"

"What's up?" Dan said. "You don't sound like anyone's in trouble."

"No. All good," Mabel said. "Got a question for you."

"Shoot."

"I need to know the owners of some vehicles from their license plate numbers."

"Why? Folks skippin' out on their meals?"

"Something like that."

"Okay, fire away."

Mabel smiled to herself and started to list off a few plate numbers.

"Wait," said the Sheriff. "You mean to tell me all these customers didn't pay?"

"Well…" Mabel hesitated. "Not exactly. These are license plates of black trucks at the mill."

Silence.

"Dan?"

"Ugh," Dan protested. "I can't run those. They didn't do nothing wrong."

"Isn't that what you do for investigations?"

"This isn't an investigation. I can't just run plates if there was no crime."

"There was a murder."

"And the killer is in jail."

"It's not like that. He's innocent."

Dan sighed. "You need to drop this."

"If you could just run me the numbers I can—"

"I can't." Dan's voice was firm. "It's illegal."

Mabel didn't respond as she felt like crying.

"Mabel?"

"Yes?"

"Drop it."

She breathed out before she said finally, "I hear ya." Then she hung up.

"Order up," Kevin called out.

Mabel dragged herself from the phone and hobbled over to collect the finished order. She carried it over to the construction workers and left them their meal. She didn't give them a smile or a bit of pep talk. She just went back to her place behind the counter and felt sorry for herself. This was a terrible day.

CHAPTER 19

Friday, October 3

O ff you go," Mabel said to her kids while clearing away breakfast plates the next morning. Fred jumped up and ran off to finish getting ready for school while Hector grumbled and trailed behind. Feeling blue and short-tempered since talking to the Sheriff, Mabel didn't think she could help Winston at all, and it was making her surly. Kerry had seemed to pick up on this, periodically eying Mabel throughout the morning routine and remaining in her seat. "You done?" Mabel asked, a note of impatience in her voice. "I have to clear the plates."

"What's wrong?" Kerry asked as Mabel started the wash-up.

Mabel paused for a second. "Nothing you would understand."

"Try me."

Mabel half-turned. "I thought you were mad."

Kerry blushed. "I was. I'm not anymore."

"You want something?"

Kerry shook her head and blushed again. "I just want to say I'm sorry. I *was* mad… but at my parents. You were the only one I could take it out on. So… sorry."

Stunned out of her bad mood, Mabel came over to hold the young girl's hand. "My love, you've gone through so much."

"So have you."

"It's okay. I don't mind."

"You're always giving, but you don't do anything for yourself."

Mabel was about to say no, but then realized the truth of it. She gave Kerry a slight, tired smile. "It *is* hard," Mabel admitted. "Being a single mom."

"And owning the diner," Kerry said.

"That, too."

"And the motel."

Mabel shrugged. "It's my life. I wouldn't change a thing."

"So, what's bothering you then?"

Mabel sighed, unsure whether to tell Kerry the truth as strange as it was, but she also wanted to build trust with the girl, and maybe this was a way to do it. "I am trying to help that young boy, Winston."

Kerry's eyes widened. She opened her mouth to speak and then abruptly closed it again.

"Silly, huh?" Mabel asked, expecting a snide remark.

Kerry frowned and then shook her head. "That's not

what I was going to say."

"Then what?"

"I thought... well, I guess it doesn't matter what I thought. I'm glad you're doing something for you." Kerry scrunched up her face from a new thought, and "Even though, like, you're really helping someone else again?"

Mabel smiled tiredly. "It's what I do."

"So, have you found out anything?"

Mabel shook her head, discouraged. "I'm looking for an owner of a black truck. Winston said Karen — the young girl — got into a black truck. I found a few of them at the sawmill, but the Sheriff won't match plate numbers to the owners for me."

"So? What's stopping you?"

"I can't find out who *owns* them, dear. I'm stuck."

"Did you ask at the sawmill?"

"Why would I?"

"Remember? Consuela works there? You know, Lisa's mom?"

Of course, Mabel thought. Why didn't I think of that?

Kerry smiled as she read Mabel's expression. "Good thing I'm around, right?"

Mabel laughed and said, "It sure is. You're part of the family now."

Kerry appeared touched by the sentiment but kept right on. "You got time off this morning?"

"I'm free till two, surprising enough. I was going to take a nap."

"Screw naps," Kerry said. "Why don't you go to the mill and find out who owns those trucks?"

Mabel ignored the cussing and slowly smiled and said, "I think I will."

"And I'll come with you."

Mabel gave her a "Not on your life" look. "You have school."

Kerry put her hands to her hips. "A girl's gotta ask, honey," she said, mimicking Mabel's tone, and they both laughed.

Twenty minutes later, after Kerry and the boys had departed on the school bus, Mabel jumped into the car. She trailed the bus for the mile into town before veering off into the sawmill parking lot. The lot was full, and since the sawmill worked several shifts, the appearance of a whole new set of trucks set her back a little. She hadn't thought of that — the sheer number of people who worked there.

She parked in the visitors' lot and headed to the administration offices to see Lisa's mom, Consuela. Although Consuela had lived in Blue River for the past twenty years, she still had her Venezuelan accent and a bit of Mabel's sass, too. The two women got along well, though they didn't see much of each other due to Mabel's schedule, except when Mabel dropped off her kids for babysitting.

"Mabel." Consuela drawled out the syllables and then added in Spanish, "*Come, cava?*"

"I'm fine, Luv. How are you?"

"Perfect," Consuela purred. "Glorious day making a living."

Mabel loved her attitude as always and asked, "How're the kids?"

"Oh, you know, Lisa got accepted into beauty school."

"Congratulations! She got in."

"Yes, my little darling is almost all grown up. She will be moving away to Seattle for at least eight months next year. And you? How are your boys?"

"Fred is my little man, as per usual, and Hector, well, Hector keeps me on my toes," she replied with a laugh. "And Kerry is... adjusting. I'm trying to learn her moods, and though we're having some good moments, it's when she's quiet I worry most."

"That's a teen girl for you. You're just not used to having one. Lisa and I fight all the time, too — it's normal. So what can I do for you today?"

Mabel, in all her eagerness to get here, hadn't thought this part through. She wanted to tell Consuela the truth but didn't want to put her in a position, so she compromised and opted for a white lie. "I need your help. A customer left his wallet on the table, but there was no identification inside. Sally got the license number as he drove away and thinks he might work at the mill."

"Oh, no problem," Consuela replied. "I can put a note on the community board."

"Oh, um... no, I'd like to make sure he gets it right away. I would hate to lose my purse, you know? Do you have a list of staff plate numbers? I don't mind looking and have time."

Consuela reached into a filing cabinet and pulled out a binder. "Tell me the number, and I'll look it up for you."

That wouldn't work. Mabel wanted to match several plate numbers to names, and one plate wasn't enough. As the seconds passed and not knowing what to say, she paled, feeling caught in a lie.

Consuela picked up on her discomfort right away. "Oh, you look ill, dear. Can I get you a glass of water or something?"

"Actually, that would be nice."

Consuela got up and made her way to the kitchen, leaving the binder behind.

Mabel saw an opportunity and called out, "I'll just check quickly, no mind!" Then flipped open the binder. Fortunately for her, Consuela had listed the trucks and their owners alphabetically, so Mabel found a total of ten black trucks, five more than she knew of, and while keeping an eye on Consuela's return, scrawled out the owner's names into her waitressing notebook. Just as she finished, a hand fell on her shoulder. Mabel jumped in fright, causing Consuela to spill the glass of water onto the carpet.

"You're jumpy as a rabbit, dear!" Consuela said. "You sure you're all right?"

Mabel grabbed a box of tissues from the table and then dropped to her knees to mop up the mess — and pocket her notebook. "Oh fine, fine," she said.

"You got what you needed?"

"Yes," Mabel said, blushing from her guilt. "And sorry about all this—" Apologizing for more than the spilled water, though Consuela wouldn't know why. Mabel stood up abruptly, smiled awkwardly, and fled, imagining Consuela's inquisitive gaze burning the back of her neck all the way to her car.

CHAPTER 20

Monday, October 6

A few days later, the school bus pulled up, the kids piled out, and Mabel met them at the front door. While Fred walked into Mabel's open arms, Hector tried sneaking past, but she pulled him in for a hug too — he didn't resist too hard, even smiling when she kissed his hair — and then Mabel wrapped Kerry in for one last bear hug.

After the boys had kicked off their shoes and run upstairs, Mabel told Kerry, "I followed up on your idea." Kerry looked confused, so Mabel added, "About the mill. I talked to Lisa's mom."

"Oh, rad! How did it go?"

Mabel showed her the list. "I got ten names. Five I scratched off right away, and Sarah, one of my cleaners, said this one — Greg Waterton — is a family man near retirement, so he's out. These other four I'm following up with. So, can you do a favor for me and watch Hector and Fred for an hour?"

"Why-y?"

"Cause I'm going to tail them to their homes to see where they live."

"Oh, wow, badass." Kerry then paused a beat and smiled slyly. "So... what do I get for it?"

Mabel gave her a "Don't test me look" but gave in anyway. "The car. But when I get home."

Kerry pumped her fist in delight. "Yes," she said as she flopped down on the couch.

"And only to Lisa's," Mabel added.

Kerry shrugged, smiling, and then put on her headphones and dragged over her math textbook. Mabel didn't begrudge Kerry's time at Lisa's since Kerry's study ethic and grades were fantastic, and she hoped they would rub off on Hector somehow. Now, with the home being in somewhat good order, Mabel grabbed the car keys and left.

But upon arriving at the mill, Mabel had cut it almost too close to shift change, as trucks were already pulling in and out of its parking lot. She parked on one side of the highway in the direction of town to get a better view of license plates. Soon enough, a black Dodge Ram emerged from the lot. But it turned away from Mabel and though the plate number matched with one of her suspects — Don Sigmundson — she couldn't turn around in time, so had to wait for several more departing trucks before a black Ford pickup turned to her side of the highway. Its license plate matched to a Petar B. Having written only his first name in her rush before Consuela had come back that day, she had been extra curious about him, so she whooped in delight and then pulled out behind.

Her initial excitement ebbed slowly into anxiousness as Petar eventually turned off the highway onto a back road feeding scattered farms and acreages. As the only two vehicles on the road, she had to keep a fair distance between them except when he disappeared around blind corners when she had to speed up to catch him.

After Mabel had nearly lost him twice, Petar turned into wilder, more forested terrain on a twinned gravel road. Most properties in this area were hidden behind deep woods with only the odd KEEP OUT sign and barbed wire fence to prove someone lived in these wildlands. This region housed Blue River's most eccentric characters, folks who took pride in living off the land as lords of their domains. Most were notorious hunters who lured deer and moose into backyards and then shot them while perched on their porches drinking beer or smoking weed. Larson had several marijuana farms hidden out here, too, and most honest folks avoided this area.

When Petar drove into the last gravel driveway before the forest ridge beyond, Mabel held back until his truck disappeared inside. Then she slowly edged up and found no welcoming family name on the gate, just a NO TRESPASSING sign hanging on a rusted barbwire fence. She killed her engine and got out, the door chime momentarily breaking the unnerving quiet of the woods.

The gravel driveway leading deeper into the woods was rutted, narrow, and partly overgrown with errant branches of poplars and pines. Flies and mosquitos lurked in the underbrush. Mabel had seen her share of dump properties driving in, and she suspected this would be another. And though she was nervous and a little scared, she did not want to waste the long drive here without checking things out. She carefully walked into the man's forested land.

A creaky door shut in the distance. Mabel froze, heart thumping, ready to flee if anyone walked towards her, but the ferocious mosquitos and renewed silence convinced her to keep moving. As she rounded a bend, a house appeared through the foliage as she had imagined, a shack with a pine shingle roof covered in moss and fallen leaves and a weathered front porch with a pile of split wood on it. The shiny new black truck parked out front looked out of place on this dilapidated property. Two other beaten-down trucks were on the edge of the gravel drive, one likely used for parts, another splattered with mud.

Mabel briefly considered knocking on the front door and just talking to Petar, but folks out here did not take kindly to strangers, and it sure wasn't safe for a woman to be on a man's property alone, let alone a murder suspect's. She'd just take a quick peek into the truck's cab to see what she could see and get out.

She kept a nervous eye on the house — the shack's windows were grimy but revealed wooden shelves filled with jars, animal traps, and metal tools; it was a loner's house for sure and that fact brought her no comfort. She peeked into the truck's cab but didn't see much. She tested the door handle — it was unlocked — and opened it carefully.

The door springs creaked. She cringed and blindly

prayed, 'Dear Lord, don't let him see me,' as she fearfully peeked at the shack.

No movement — she slowly breathed out. Then she eased into the truck's cab, and while keeping watch on the shack's windows, searched the packed glove box, and found right away the man's registration, but it was torn and covered in dust like it had been unused for some time. After taking out her waitressing notebook, she jotted down his full name, Petar Brzila, noticing he had a California address and an expired five-year-old registration. That's odd, she thought.

She dug deeper into the stuffed glove box, crammed full of papers, screws, nails. "Oh my God!" she whispered as she pulled out a knife.

Its sharp edge glinted, but it was its serrated back that nauseated her. She could only imagine what that would do to a human body like Karen's — she shuddered.

Afraid of what Petar would he do to her if he found her on his property, she got out, keeping the knife as evidence.

A low, deep growl sounded behind her.

Her knees almost buckled as she peered back at a big, ugly boxer, about twenty feet away, blocking her exit. It growled and bared its teeth.

The dog launched, Mabel screamed and scrambled back into the truck. The knife fell outside as she shut and locked the door. The dog thudded into the side and then barked fiercely as she frantically tried to shush it.

The shack door burst open.

Petar stepped out.

A massive brute of a man, with a thick beard, thinning

hair on top, and deep-set angry eyes, he growled at the fearsome dog to shut it up, and it did, instantly.

He yelled at Mabel. "Who the hell are you?"

Karen's brutalized body flashed through her mind. "Don't hurt me!" she cried. "People are coming! I know the Sheriff!"

"What do ya mean?! You're trespassing!" He stamped down the stairs then reached out to yank the truck door open, but she had locked it. He tried several more times, getting angrier each time. "Open this door!"

She refused, terrified.

"Open it!"

Mabel glanced at the knife near the man's boots. Now the man had his weapon outside. The same knife he had used to kill Karen. Now all he had to do was get the keys and pull her out to murder her.

He banged his fist against the glass in frustration. "Open this door!"

After he kept banging and trying the lock over and over, Mabel clued in: maybe he doesn't have the keys! Maybe they were locked in here! Frantically, she searched under the seat, in the glove box, flipped the driver's side visor — a set of keys fell into her lap — and she nearly laughed.

Petar saw it too and banged his fist against the glass. "Don't you dare!"

She slipped the truck key into the ignition. The engine roared to life.

"I'm getting my gun!" he screamed as he ran back to the house.

Mabel put the truck in reverse and spun it around. She

took the corner fast, ignoring the branches clawing the finish. She reached the end of the driveway, hit the brakes, and jumped out, racing to her vehicle with the dog advancing fast. Mabel fumbled with her door handle before getting in, just in time. The dog threw himself at the glass, clawing, barking and salivating. Mabel tried the ignition key. It didn't fit. She grew frantic before realizing these were the truck keys, so she cracked the window a sliver and pushed the keys out, screaming as the dog tried to bite her fingertips.

Starting up her car, she backed up fast. She hit the gas, nearly swiping a tree before over-correcting and almost slamming into another. Then as her car bucked and bounced over the ruts, she straightened out and stepped on the gas, only slamming once on the brakes when she came up to a ninety-degree turn and nearly slid into a ditch. Looking over her shoulder, in the far distance, she could see the dog still chasing her.

Behind the dog was Petar with his rifle.

She completed the turn, stomped on the gas, and sped away fast. Then as soon as she pulled onto the highway, she made a beeline to the Sheriff's office.

Dan was inside watching TV as Mabel ran in, tears streaming down her face. He gaped at her and then got up fast for him and rushed to her side. "What the — Mabel! You look like the devil is after you."

Mabel was hyperventilating.

"Just breathe," said Dan.

She gulped, her throat dry and hurting. "I... I... f-found—"

"What happened?"

"I found him!"

"Found who?"

"The killer, Dan! I know who killed Karen!"

CHAPTER 21

A half-hour later, Mabel was in the passenger seat of the patrol car with Dan, retracing the roads that she had just driven in a state of terror. While Dan had originally been skeptical of Petar's guilt, her confidence convinced him to drive back to the property. She was adamant they get there as soon as possible, worried that Petar might try to hide the murder weapon and flee. Her emotions transformed from terror and panic to elation and pride. She had done it, she thought: she had found Karen's killer.

As they approached the thickly wooded entrance to the property, Mabel's fear returned, and her palms and forehead were sweaty. As her breathing quickened too, Dan looked over and said, "Just relax. You're safe with me."

Petar's black truck was no longer where she had left it. Good, she thought. The guilty always run.

Dan pulled into the gravel lane, driving carefully over the ruts while avoiding the overgrown tree branches that threatened to scratch the sides of his patrol car.

As the house emerged through the trees, the boxer leaped off the porch and ran to the car, barking furiously.

Dan whooped his siren, scaring the dog backward, but it didn't stop growling.

The screen door opened.

Petar stepped out, and Mabel gasped. He ordered the dog to the porch and then kicked it to make it sit.

"Okay, Mabel, I'll do the talking. You stay in the car," Dan said, opening his door and getting out. He raised a palm, signaling that he just wanted to talk, but kept his other hand near his holster. Petar remained on the porch but glanced at the rifle on the bench beside him, then back at the Sheriff.

Petar spied Mabel inside the police cruiser and yelled, "She was trespassing!"

"I'm only here to talk," Dan said, before shutting the patrol car door and walking over to the porch steps.

Mabel expected Dan to slap handcuffs on him right away. When they kept talking in normal voices — she was unable to hear the conversation with the door shut — she grew frustrated. Petar gestured toward Mabel and his truck. Dan pointed to Mabel and then the dog. Petar paled and looked shocked, and Mabel wondered if the Sheriff was asking about the murder. Petar pointed to the forest in the direction of town, looking more confident now, and the Sheriff raised his palm again. Mabel was confused. He wasn't arresting him. In fact, it looked like Dan was trying to soothe him!

After a few more minutes of gestures and talk, Petar swiped his arm angrily in Mabel's direction and then went into the house, bringing the dog with him. The shack's door slammed shut as Dan lumbered back to the cruiser.

"What are you doing?" she asked when he opened the door and got in. "Arrest that man!"

Dan gave her a frustrated glance but stayed silent. He put the car in reverse.

"Hold on. You've got to look for the murder weapon. It was right there, in the gravel. He must have picked it up!"

The Sheriff clenched his jaw as he started driving out.

"Dan!" Mabel said. "He's the murderer!"

"Mabel. He ain't no murderer."

"How can you say that?"

"He was working his shift."

"What do you mean?"

"He was working his shift the night that girl was murdered."

"The mill was shut down that night."

Dan frowned but didn't stop the car either. "I guess it was."

"He's going to flee if we leave him."

"If he runs, he's guilty," Dan said. "I'm fine with that. But I can't be taking in no innocent man, Mabel. Whether he was working his full shift or not, we'll find out soon enough. I'm gonna ask at the mill. It's not yet six, and the main office don't close before then. We got time to figure this out."

"He's going to flee," Mabel said, lifting her arms up in frustration, believing with all her heart that she had found the killer. But when Dan didn't stop, she added. "Fine. You do that. Then we'll find out the truth."

Dan glanced at her but was wise enough not to say anything more.

It was a silent drive back to town.

As they pulled into the mill a few minutes shy of the main office closing for the night, they parked. Both Mabel and Dan got out, but Mabel led the way in.

"Hiya," Consuela said, happy to see Mabel at first glance. As Mabel, clearly flustered, rushed over to the counter, Consuela's face showed her concern. "What happened?"

Mabel half-turned, standing tall, and gestured for the Sheriff to take over.

The Sheriff seemed a little sheepish under Mabel's gaze, but he went on. He said, "Hiya, Consuela."

Consuela looked between the two, clearly confused, and asked, "What can I do for you both?"

Dan cleared his throat and said, "I need to ask you about an employee."

"Petar Brzila," Mabel added.

"Petar?" Consuela asked, surprised. "Yes, he works here."

"We need to know if he worked a shift a month back."

"Petar? He works off and on. More of an on-call man."

Mabel gestured to Dan like this proved her point. But Dan ignored her. "If you don't mind, Consuela, can you check for me?"

"Sure, Sheriff," she said. "Is he in trouble?"

Mabel nodded, but Dan waved her off. "Now, we just want to see if he was working that night."

Consuela did so but was uncomfortable as she did it. She paged through the register and asked, "Which day?"

"September 3rd," both Dan and Mabel said.

Consuela scanned his record. "Uh, yes. Wednesday, September 3rd. The four to midnight shift. Oh! The night the poor girl was killed. Yes, we were closed due to a maintenance issue, but the manager took some of the men, including Petar, for a supply run near Edmonston. About four of them went."

"Wait, what?" Mabel said. "That's impossible."

"It's right here," Consuela said, putting the register on the counter and turning it so both could read it.

"Well, he could have just signed up for his shift and then left."

"But then he doesn't get paid, dear." Now it was Consuela who sounded confident. "If they leave their shift early, they lose pay. He'd have to ask Bob, his foreman, for permission. See Bob's signature here? Bob wouldn't have signed off a full shift if Petar didn't go. Bob doesn't pay men who don't work, especially on-call boys like Petar."

Dan leaned back, looking both vexed and relieved. He said his thanks to Consuela and gestured for Mabel to follow him out.

"Is he in trouble?" Consuela asked as they left.

Dan glanced at Mabel before looking back. "No. He ain't. Sorry to be bothering you."

Mabel berated Dan as they went outside. "Dan! How

do we know he went with the manager? It could have been faked. We should talk to him."

"You serious? Drop it! You almost got yourself killed back there." Dan was fuming but was trying hard to calm himself. He stopped at his cruiser door. "Look. Petar Brzila is not your man. I know Bob. Like Consuela said, he don't sign off on a shift if his men don't work." He sighed. "Get it through your head, Mabel. Petar isn't the one. That Winston boy is. And you certainly don't need me to tell ya that when you go trespassing on some folk's properties, you're going to wind up shot."

"But—"

"Enough! Stop this."

Mabel was about to argue back, having been so sure Petar was the killer a moment ago, but with all the adrenaline pumping in her system, her frustration simply dissolved into tears.

Dan let her cry for a moment and then softened his tone. "Look, I know you care about that Winston boy, and you think he is innocent. But you have to realize that you are doing more harm than good here." Mabel wiped her eyes, angry at herself for showing weakness. "I didn't tell you on the drive back, but I warned Petar not to come after you or I will hunt him down. You got no worries there. But you know Mabel, you can't make enemies like this. This is a small town. There are a lot of bad characters around. Trust me."

Mabel didn't answer, feeling defeated, and Dan must have noticed it as he continued, "Now. Enough of this. You're a good woman, Mabel. You just have that kind heart of yours that gets you into trouble is all."

She nodded, a little ashamed. "I'm sorry I got you involved."

"It's my job," Dan said. "Come on. I'll drive you back to my office so you can get your car."

Mabel nodded again and got in the cruiser. In the silence, she had some time to think.

Maybe Petar wasn't the killer, she thought, looking over at Dan. But that don't mean a killer ain't loose. And what happened today just proves it. Bad men live in this town just like Dan said, and if Petar isn't the murderer, then it's darn obvious someone else is.

She settled into her seat, confident again, and didn't tell Dan that she had three more suspects left on her list.

CHAPTER 22

Saturday, October 11

W hy did you want to come along?" Kerry asked Mabel as they drove down the highway. "I've driven to Lisa's house by myself lots of times. Don't you trust me?"

"I do, dear," Mabel said, and though her intent hadn't been to tell Kerry why, she felt compelled to now. "I want to apologize to Consuela."

"So that's why the pie." Kerry nodded towards it on Mabel's lap.

"Pumpkin is her favorite."

"So-o-o?" Kerry prompted, eager to know. "What's the apology about?"

Mabel sighed. "I told a lie."

"You? *Lied?* Wow. I didn't think you did that."

Mabel flushed. "I don't, normally, but I needed

information for the case."

"Oh, it's about a case? That's legit. Cool." A short pause. "So? What was the lie about?"

Mabel sighed. "I told Consuela a customer forgot his wallet and that I needed to match a license plate number to a name to find out who to give it back to."

"*Oh, Auntie!*" Kerry drawled out to dramatize her shock.

"I know. I feel really bad."

"No, stop. I'm teasing," Kerry said. "I think you're overreacting."

"That's what the Sheriff said."

"You told him about the lie?"

"No. About the case. He said I should drop it," Mabel said and looked off into the deep woods. Although she didn't want to frighten Kerry, Mabel needed to confide in someone, so she confessed, "I also made a mistake."

Kerry took her eyes off the road to look at Mabel. "What happened?"

"I followed one of the men from the sawmill to his home out near Sandy's Ridge."

"Oh. My. God." Kerry's jaw dropped. "Wait a minute. Blue River is like totally the boonies, but even I know you shouldn't go to that area — that's crazy."

"It gets worse," Mabel said. She launched into the full story from searching the truck for clues to her confrontation with Petar Brzila, ending with him holding a rifle as she sped off.

"Wow. That's dangerous," Kerry said quietly.

"It doesn't end there, Luv," Mabel added and then finished the story about returning with Sheriff Dan and

139

speaking with Consuela.

Kerry was shocked. "That man must be furious with you. Will he come after you?"

Mabel shook her head. "Sheriff Dan told him not to. That I was to be left alone."

Kerry pulled in front of Lisa's house and parked the car. She didn't get out but didn't look at Mabel either. "What about Fred and Hector?"

"What about them?"

"You could've got hurt. Maybe killed."

"Oh, I'm fine, dear. Don't worry. I'm safe."

"No. That's not what I meant," Kerry said, getting worked up. "I know what it's like to lose a parent. Trust me. I don't want the boys to go through that, too."

Mabel grasped Kerry's hand. "That's the sweetest thing. But it's all good now."

Kerry pulled her hand away and burst into tears.

"Oh, Luv," Mabel said. "I'm—" Fine, she was going to say, but stopped, clueing in that Kerry was more worried about what a mother's death might mean to Hector and Fred. And that rocked her. As a mother, she should have put her kids first and not the case. What would have happened if she had been killed? Her kids would have lost their mom, and now, with Bill gone, they needed their mom more than ever.

Shaken, Mabel teared up too and then reached over and wrapped Kerry in a big hug. After a few moments, Kerry stopped crying but stayed within Mabel's embrace. Mabel wiped the tears off the girl's cheeks until Kerry grabbed a tissue and moved away.

Mabel said, "You're a good girl, you know? Too wise

for your years."

Kerry dabbed at her wet eyes and offered a half-smile. "Lisa is probably watching and thinking we're dorks." Then smiled to show no offense.

"I love you," Mabel said.

"I love you too," Kerry said, nearly breaking into tears again.

Kerry got out of the car and ran up the steps and inside like it was her own home. Mabel walked up to the porch as Consuela came to the screen door, clearly surprised to see Mabel and not looking particularly welcoming either.

Mabel offered the pie. "It's pumpkin," she said. Then realized that was not enough. "I really just came to apologize. For my behavior. On Monday."

Consuela's gaze softened, and she opened the door. "Come join me for tea," she said, then led the way into the kitchen.

Mabel sat down and waited as Consuela took her time, fussed with the kettle, put down two mugs, added tea bags, and poured. When Consuela had finished, Mabel started.

"Consuela. I am so sorry I lied the other day. I feel terrible."

Consuela put her hand on Mabel's and then sat down opposite and said, "What happened?"

Mabel had trouble meeting her gaze. "I wasn't trying to find a customer's license plate like I said. I was…" She hesitated, realizing how strange this was going to sound and not wanting Consuela to dismiss her like Dan had. "I was trying to find who killed that girl in the mill."

"What?! And you think it was Petar? Oh my God."

"I thought so at the time. I followed him to his house."

Consuela put her hands to her mouth.

"Yes." Mabel winced, contrite. "It didn't go well."

"Dear, you had no need to do that. You could have asked me." She put her hand back on Mabel's and tightened her grip. "I was so shocked that a poor girl was murdered in this town and left to die in the place that I work. But I thought they found the killer? That black boy who deals Larson's drugs."

"They've charged him, but I think it was someone else."

"Shouldn't the Sheriff be following up on this?" Mabel gave Consuela a look that caused her to laugh. "Okay. I guess not, now that I think of it. Sheriff Dan is not the most investigative type. But," she countered. "The State Police interviewed our manager and some of the staff. The investigation lasted for a few days. The mill had to shut down some of its operations until it was over."

"Did they ask you about a black truck?"

"I wasn't interviewed. I don't know."

"Did they ask to see license plates?"

"No, no one asked, and only I take care of that."

Mabel nodded. "I think I'm onto something then. You have ten black trucks out of… how many employees?"

"153."

"Okay, so out of those ten, I have ruled out seven, which leaves three more."

"Who?"

Mabel hesitated. "You sure you want to know?"

Consuela leaned closer. "Of course."

Mabel relaxed as she pulled out her list and showed her, only a little embarrassed. "I was planning to follow them all to their homes as I don't know where they live."

Consuela tsked and shook her head. "No need, dear. I can find this out for you." She put on reading glasses and peered at the list. "We have a few bad characters at the mill. White supremacists. Abusers. Men that scare me. I agree with most of the names you've crossed out. I don't think it could be them. But wait... I see you crossed out Wade Concella?"

"I know the boy's mother. She cleans my motel sometimes. She does great work."

Consuela frowned. "Well, I wouldn't cross him off just yet. Put him as a maybe. And yep, this Lee Wallach feller works the cutter. He's one of Larson's boys for sure. White power tattoos on his arms. I don't like him. Now this other one. This Don Sigmundson. Yes. His girlfriend showed up at last summer's barbecue with a black eye. He is a Larson man and none of the office girls like him. He comes in and flirts with Annabelle, but she hates it. I don't like him at all. The last one, this Cole Smithson, is a casual."

"Do you know where they live?"

"Sure. I can get that for you."

"Isn't that against office rules?" Mabel asked, not wanting Consuela to get into trouble for disclosing confidential information.

"Oh shush. What you're doing is more important. Besides, without me, their office won't run half as good, and they know it. They need me. And now that I think of it, Don's girlfriend works down at the grocer." Consuela's excitement turned into a squeal. "Oh, we got lots to talk about, girl!"

The two women leaned in over cups of honey-flavored herbal tea and whispered a plan of action.

CHAPTER 23

Monday, October 13

Two days later, Mabel was waitressing the lunch shift when Consuela called. She'd been thinking about Mabel's list of subjects and couldn't get Wade Concella out of her mind. "Acting really funny lately, darling," she said. "And seemed kind of shifty at work these past few weeks." Then Consuela related how Wade had been late several times, and Bob, the foreman, had been upset with him. Then this morning they'd had a big shouting match. With Wade being only eighteen, fresh out of high school, Bob had told her that he thought the kid was just getting used to the realities of work, but Consuela wasn't so sure. She had whispered into the phone, "It could be guilt. From murder."

Wade had been given a forced day off to think about things and was likely at home now — he lived in a roadside trailer park owned by his parents, Sarah and Pete. Sarah was one of Mabel's casual motel cleaners, but Mabel didn't know her husband well. Pete hauled seed for the farms around the region and apparently was one of the main delivery men for Larson as well.

After hanging up, Mabel took off her apron and beckoned Sally over, and with the lunch rush almost over told her she'd need to step out for a bit. Then she was off driving the highway to visit Wade to ask him questions.

When she got close, a car aggressively tailgated her for a moment and then sped past. The driver, his head shaved like one of Larson's young recruits, slammed on the brakes like he'd missed his turn, forcing Mabel to do the same, and then sped up briefly before turning into Sarah and Pete's trailer park and parking in front of Wade's trailer, the last spot available, so Mabel had to park at the far end of the complex in a gravel turnabout.

With the driver being a Larson skinhead, Mabel stayed in her car, watching. The man banged on Wade's trailer door. After a few moments, Wade appeared, looking disheveled, though he had left his shift only an hour before. He was obviously expecting the man, as they exchanged something, which Mabel couldn't see. It was small enough to fit in one hand. Then the skinhead turned with a smile and headed down the steps and into his car to drive off.

Mabel watched the car leave and hoped Sarah's child wasn't involved in crime but seeing a skinhead here didn't help his cause. After a minute, she got out and walked up the porch steps. She knocked on the door politely. No response. She knocked again, this time harder, and still no response. Then she banged the door like the skinhead had until, finally, Wade opened it.

"Oh, hi!" Mabel exclaimed, shocked by his appearance. His pupils were wide as saucers, and he had trouble focusing on her. "My name is Mabel. I know your mother."

Wade tried focusing his gaze on her, but he swayed slightly. "M-y-y mother?" He slurred.

"Yes. Sarah — your mother." Mabel waited for a reaction. When he didn't say anything, she asked, "Are you all right?"

"All right?" he echoed, then smiled languorously and slumped against the doorframe, holding it with two hands like he was propping it up.

"Dear, are you sick? Do you need a doctor?"

He shook his head and giggled, and when Mabel tried to touch his arm, he cowered back, afraid.

Mabel took charge, guessing what this was. "Okay. I'm coming in. I'm here to help. What happened?" She scanned the room and spotted crumpled tin foil scarred with black burn marks in an ashtray on a table. She went over and sniffed it, wrinkling her nose at the smell, and then touched the tin foil, still hot. Oh my God, she thought, this is crack cocaine! *Nightline* had had a story on it, but she never thought she'd ever meet someone on it.

Wade, back leaning against the doorframe, was scratching his arms blissfully until Mabel came close, and he cowered again.

"I'm going to take you to your mother's right this instant."

Taking his arm, she marched him down the porch, but

Wade kept slipping and nearly falling, and she struggled to hold him up. She shouted towards the other trailers for help, but no one came out, so Mabel half-carried him to her car, which he collapsed against. After struggling to right him, she opened the door and guided him into the seat. He groaned intensely, holding his stomach with his eyes closed, and did nothing to help her. Concerned he was experiencing some sort of overdose, Mabel rushed over and into the driver's seat and drove off. She held onto his arm to soothe him until Wade whooped in delight with a sudden burst of energy that nearly scared the wits out of her. He started to beat the dash like it were drums, bobbing his head up and down and giggling.

Mabel raced to Sarah's farmhouse at the end of the property, noticing Pete's hauling truck at the side — so he was home too.

After pulling to a stop, Mabel told Wade to stay in the car, so Wade leaned back, sweaty and smiling, and started air-drumming against the roof. Mabel ran up the porch and pounded on the door.

After the door opened, Sarah exclaimed, surprised and a little concerned, "Mabel?! What brings you here? Are you okay?"

"Sarah! It's your boy. I think he's sick."

Sarah hesitated, her concern for Mabel shifting to deep embarrassment. She asked in a quiet voice, "Where is he?"

"My car. Come quick."

Pete showed up behind Sarah and said, "What's going on?"

Sarah half-turned, and said in a whisper, "Wade again.

In Mabel's car."

Pete scowled and pushed past Sarah. "Let me get him."

Mabel hung back as Pete stomped off. She turned to Sarah, who wouldn't look her in the eye. "Sarah, is he all right? He looks quite sick, and I think he needs to see a doctor."

Sarah just shook her head, ashamed.

A car door shutting caused Mabel to glance back. Pete had pulled Wade out none too gently and was hauling him back towards the house. Wade whelped in fear and pain as Pete pulled him up the porch steps, and then Pete pushed him on past Sarah and Mabel. Mabel wanted to stop Pete but didn't feel it was her place. She looked at Sarah to see what she should do, but Sarah simply let them pass and then pulled Mabel aside.

Sarah said, "I'm so sorry you saw this."

Mabel wasn't sure what to say. She was more upset about how Pete was treating his son. "You sure he's all right? He might need a doctor."

Sarah shook her head. "It's... He's been like this before. We don't know what to do."

"How long has he been on drugs?"

Sarah winced. "We don't know for sure, months most likely. It's this crack thing. He smoked weed before, but this... is different."

"I saw one of Larson's skinheads give him something at his trailer door, and I bet it was the drugs. It's a good thing I showed up, or I don't know how he'd be doing."

Pete's harsh yell inside the house caused Sarah to flinch, and she glanced at Mabel, crestfallen. Mabel could only imagine how hard this was for her.

"How… how did you find him?" Sarah asked.

Mabel paused, not sure how to answer that — that she suspected her son of murder. She picked her words carefully. "I wanted to find out where your son was the night that poor girl was killed up in the Sawmill."

"Why?" Sarah asked, looking terrified by the question.

Mabel, startled by such a reaction, tripped over her words. "I just… need to find out."

Sarah started to blink away tears but failed and hung her head, defeated, and said, without looking up, "How did you know? I'm ashamed he did those things."

Mabel's eyes widened in shock. "You *knew* about it?!"

Sarah nodded, crestfallen, and rubbed her arm, ashamed. "I couldn't believe what he did. I know it's not right."

"It's horrible!"

Sarah just wilted under Mabel's withering gaze.

Mabel added, wanting to expose this terrible crime once and for all, "We need to talk to the Sheriff about this."

Sarah looked up, surprised, and said, "The Sheriff knows."

"Dan knows?!" Mabel was floored. Dan knew who the real murderer was! And he pinned it on Winston instead?! How could he have kept it from her?

Sarah explained. "It was Dan who found him that day."

"At the murder scene!?" Mabel cried, clearly thrown, and feeling faint now, suspecting they were all involved in a cover-up.

Sarah blinked, surprised, and then explained, "What? No. On the beach. In town. Wade had overdosed that morning and tried to set the beach house on fire. The Sheriff was the one who brought him to us. That's when we first learned that Wade was... into drugs."

Mabel shook her head, confused. "Wait. What? Wade overdosed? During the day, not after the murder?"

Sarah looked confused. "What? No. We were in a Seattle treatment center that night. That's why I remembered it. We'd taken him in, and he was getting treated." She paused for a moment and then reached out to touch Mabel's arm. "Dan was good to us. He searched the trailer and threw out all of Wade's drugs. He didn't report us." She started to cry. "I'm so ashamed, Mabel. He's my son, a drug addict. It's terrible."

Mabel's emotions shifted from rage to relief to complete embarrassment that she'd suspected Sarah of a cover-up. As Sarah cried on, Mabel came out of her reverie and threw her remaining questions to the wind. She reached out and pulled Sarah in for a hug.

Sarah sobbed into Mabel's shoulder as tears now came to Mabel's eyes.

After a long cry, Sarah pulled away and said, wiping tears away, "I'm so ashamed, Mabel. I'll understand if you don't want me helping at your motel."

"Oh, no, dear," Mabel said. "It's me who's at fault. I thought, well... it really doesn't matter what I thought. Look, of course I want you to keep working at the motel. Don't worry. I understand what's happened here. My son gets into trouble too, and Dan is there for me as well. I understand. I do."

"Is he into drugs too?" Sarah asked, surprised.

"No. God no. But my oldest gets into trouble too, Luv, for breaking things."

"Drugs are so terrible," Sarah said, falling back into her sadness. "Make sure it never happens to your boys."

Mabel touched her arm. "I didn't know you were going through all of this."

Sarah shrugged, downcast.

"Is Dan doing anything more about it?" Mabel asked. "I saw the man who sold your son drugs. He's a skinhead. That's something."

Sarah flinched. "No. That's Bobby. He works with Larson. Pete knows him too."

"You know him? Well then, let's report him!"

"No!" Sarah said, pulling back from Mabel, surprising her. "No. It's... complicated."

"Why is it complicated? The man's dealing drugs. He should go to prison."

Sarah pulled back even more, scared now. "You can't tell on a Larson man. It's not how it's done."

"But Sarah, your boy. You have to stop these men from selling drugs to him."

Sarah grimaced and turned for the door. "I have to go see my son."

"Sarah!" Mabel said, stopping her from shutting the door all the way. "I'll report that drug dealer to Dan. I can get him to stop. I can do that for you."

"No!" Sarah said vehemently. "Don't!" Then she added more gently, "Pete will talk to them. Please. We're handling it."

"But Sarah...," Mabel pleaded, unable to find the right

words.

"Look around you," Sarah said, distraught. "Pete wouldn't have a job if it ain't for Larson. I can't…" She stopped and corrected herself: "We won't say anything about this. I hope you don't either. And I… I don't think I should do shifts at your motel anymore. I hope you understand."

"But Sarah! We can stop them from selling drugs to your son."

Sarah's resolve hardened into anger, and she turned cold. "You're lucky, Mabel. You are. You have your diner, and those crews and truckers of yours will support you. My family? We don't have a choice. We're not lucky like you. So don't say anything to anyone. Please, let us take care of our son, our way." Then she shut the door.

Mabel took a step back in shock and then slowly turned around, holding her arms in tight, and made her way to her car.

One thing was made clear today — Wade was not the killer — and while she was disappointed that her case was no further along, she was more horrified to learn what Sarah was facing at home.

Mabel looked back at the house and wished she could help make things right. Dan was clearly in the know about the drugs, and, if she were honest with herself, so was she.

But if Dan couldn't do anything to stop Larson, what could she do?

CHAPTER 24

Wednesday, October 15 to Thursday, October 16

The question of what to do about Larson haunted Mabel so much she hadn't gotten any sleep over the past two days. At least she could do something to help Sarah with her son, she thought. When the motel cleaners had their scheduled shift, Mabel dropped by to check on her. Bernice, a regular, was on and confirmed Sarah had quit.

Mabel felt so awful she headed home, baked Sarah's favorite pie, and then drove over to her place after lunch. Mabel rang the doorbell, and only Pete answered, and while he took the pie thankfully, he didn't call Sarah to the door. "Can I speak to her?" Mabel asked, but he looked uncomfortable and said she wasn't feeling well. She asked how Wade was doing, but Pete just thanked her again for the pie and said they were doing their best as a family and not to trouble them again.

Mabel left the porch wishing she could ease their shame somehow and thought about them for the rest of the day. She wrestled with telling Dan about the skinhead. While Sarah had made it clear that Dan already knew Larson's men were selling crack cocaine, Mabel felt compelled to do something. When Dan showed up at the diner Thursday night to do his paperwork, Mabel brought him some pie and then questioned him about Wade as he was eating. Dan wasn't in a good mood to begin with and he tried to explain that Larson was primarily into weed and that his boys were only selling crack on the side.

"And besides," Dan had said, "I'd already told Larson selling crack would lead to jail time, and he promised he would look into it."

"Yes, but—" Mabel had protested.

"Just stop! I keep telling you you're sticking your neck into matters that are not your business!" Dan said, glancing around the diner before moderating his tone some, as he had caught some stares. "I mean it."

"Well, I mean it too," Mabel said, not lowering her voice. "That Winston boy has got no one else looking out for him. And you know what? You only arrested him after I said those things, and I wish to God I hadn't. Look what's it done."

"It got the right man in jail is what I'm telling you."

Mabel breathed out, frustrated she wasn't getting through. "I feel just awful about this. Everyone thinks they got the right person because the man is black."

Dan gave her a stern look. "You don't know police work. Nine times out of ten, it's the boyfriend or husband. You don't need to be a detective to know that. And besides, you know I'm not like Frank or the boys. I don't see his color like them."

Mabel's mood softened, as did her voice. "No. But most of the town does. I saw that justice system you talked about, and it didn't seem all that fair to me."

Dan looked at her for a moment, and then he eased back over his plate and took a bite of pie. After he chewed some, he pointed his fork at her and added, "Just leave the law to me. I can handle it." Dan didn't seem to notice her mood changing back. "I like to take care of our people. If it weren't for me, some families would be visiting loved ones in jail rather than seeing them safe at home. I don't have to tell you those jails ain't safe." Then he planted his fork in the remains of the pie like it was some victory flag. "I'm here to protect us."

"And what about Winston? Isn't he part of us?"

Dan scoffed. "A drug dealer?"

"Isn't Larson one? And half this town?"

"I told you to stay out of this," Dan growled, getting worked up again.

"Well, I ain't stopping, I can tell you that."

Dan's eyes turned fierce. "I tell ya— You're going to break the peace!"

Mabel folded her arms to her chest. "Well, I don't think this is much of a peace if young kids are getting high and doing hard drugs, not just weed. People are suffering, and you ain't doing nothing to stop it!"

Dan paled like Mabel had slapped him in the face; she wondered if she had finally gotten through to him or had taken it too far.

When Dan finally cleared his throat and said, "I got my hunting show on. I'll be seeing you," she had her answer.

She watched him go until the door chime rang twice, and he was gone, with words unsaid between them. She dropped her gaze to his unfinished pie, thinking what a waste this night was. Then she picked it up and dumped it into the dirty dishes bin. Her tears came hard and fast, so she held onto the bin for support and kept her head down, not wanting anyone to see her crying.

The next morning, she had woken up early with Sarah's words repeating in her mind: "You have your diner, and those crews and truckers of yours will support you. My family? We don't have a choice. We're not lucky like you." It made her wonder: if Larson's money were the only thing keeping the bank from owning all her business instead of just part of it, would she be behaving differently? She certainly hoped so. But in all honesty, she didn't know what she would do in Sarah's shoes.

And she didn't want to be — no mother would. So she sat down beside Fred and Hector eating their breakfast the next morning before school.

"Hey, boys, I have something to ask."

Bleary-eyed and exhausted, only Fred looked up from his bacon and eggs to listen, so Mabel poked Hector's arm to get his attention.

"I want to talk to both you boys about drugs."

Fred's eyes widened, and even Hector stopped eating, curious. Kerry breezed in just then, grabbed her plate from the counter, and sat down. Then she noticed Fred and Hector's seriousness and asked, "What's up?"

Fred told her. "Momma's talking about drugs."

Kerry nearly laughed and said, "What?! Really? What sort?"

Mabel wanted this to be a serious talk. "Now Kerry, this is for all of you. I want to ask what you know about drugs?"

"What?" Hector said, smiling. "You mean weed? Ganga? Dope?"

Kerry added, smiling, "Reefer. Mary Jane."

"Poopy plant!" Fred shouted then broke down, giggling.

Hector rolled his eyes and said, "Poopy plant is not a name."

"No. I'm serious, kids. There are harder drugs than just weed."

"Momma said weed!" Fred said, breaking down and laughing. Hector and Kerry did too.

"Enough!" Mabel said, trying not to smile. "I mean it," she added sternly so that the boys weren't laughing outright anymore. Still, she didn't want to be too strict about it and didn't want to talk about Wade directly. "This is serious. There are harder drugs out there. Like cocaine, crack, that sort of thing."

"Why bring this up, Auntie?"

"Well. Like I said, there's some harder drugs in town than weed. And I... I want you all to know that you can talk to me if anyone ever tries to sell them to you. These drugs, they are not good drugs. They can hurt you. You can get addicted."

"What's addicted?" Fred asked, and while Hector rolled his eyes at his brother, it was clear he didn't really know what that meant either.

"It means you can't stop taking them. The drugs make you want to take more of them. And if you stop taking them, they cause you pain. Make you do things you don't want to. They can make you sick."

"So why take them?" Fred asked.

"Well," Mabel said, not sure how to say it. "They might make you feel good at first, but it turns on you and hurts your body. It can cause terrible pains. And… like I said, make you sick." She looked between the boys, who seemed as lost as ever, and since her explanation sounded lame even to her, she fell back to the popular saying of a big drug campaign by the First Lady of the White House. "So, if anyone asks you about drugs, just say no, okay?"

Kerry scoffed. "Really?! Just say no. That's it?"

"Well… yes," Mabel said. "What else are you supposed to say?"

"You talk about it. Like we're doing now. You tell people about it and not let it go unnoticed. People feel ashamed about it, but like you said, it's an addiction, so the best way to deal with it is to get it out in the open."

Mabel was taken aback at how wise Kerry sounded. "Do you know someone taking drugs?" she asked.

Hector and Fred were all ears now, getting to listen in on an adult conversation.

"No. Not here, but back in Seattle—" Kerry had never talked about her previous home life, so Mabel felt this was a bit of a breakthrough. "When was I was at home, I knew a girl on heroin."

"Did she get sick?" Fred asked.

"Kind of," Kerry replied. "She stopped going to

school. All the parents and teachers seemed to think it was some sort of a scandal, but it really wasn't. I wished the teachers had talked to us more about it, but they just avoided mentioning drugs and pretended it didn't happen. I thought that was wrong." Kerry looked at Mabel. "You're doing the right thing here, Auntie. It's not about just saying no. It's about talking. Being honest."

Kerry paused, looking pensive, and then bent over her breakfast, and started eating. Fred and Hector looked at each other, wide-eyed, and then started eating too.

Mabel looked over them all and felt that was enough for now. But she touched Kerry's hand, and they smiled at each other. Then Mabel got up and took out the Flintstone vitamins for Fred and Hector and set them down by their plates as always.

Fred started, shocked by the sight, and then said, seriously, "Momma! You're giving me drugs!"

Hector burst out laughing, and so did Kerry. Fred looked at them all confused, and then Mabel, trying not to laugh, explained to Fred this wasn't the drugs she was talking about. Fred didn't seem convinced but ate the vitamin anyway. Then Hector ran off, repeating, "Momma's giving drugs! Momma's giving drugs!" Fred quickly ran after him, shouting the same thing, and the morning routine turned to chaos.

Mabel resignedly picked up the plates and was going to clean up when Kerry stopped her with a serious look, which caught Mabel's attention.

"Auntie, I mean it. The best thing for you to do is what you just did. Just keep talking to them about drugs. That's all you need to. Don't stop." Then Kerry kissed

Mabel on the cheek and left to finish getting ready.

Surprised but pleased, Mabel got back to cleaning the dishes, feeling good about her talk even though she knew her message had not gotten through to the boys.

But it got her thinking about Winston again. How he was still stuck in prison, and while she couldn't do more about the drugs in town right now, she could at least focus back on his case. Three suspects were left on her list, and after finishing a waitressing shift this afternoon, she'd get back to them. Then, later on, she'd check in on Winston's lawyer too.

Maybe he'd had better luck.

CHAPTER 25

After the kids went to bed early, Mabel settled into a comfy chair in her den, rubbing her feet after a long day, and thought of how Bill used to do that for her and how good he was. Then she gazed out the window toward the mountain and wondered if he was up there tonight, looking up at the stars. He had a rental place in town but spent most of his time camped out on Dead Man's Peak. As an expert geologist and prospector, he knew that mountain like the back of his hand and had discovered and kept secret a few gemstone beds, whose gems were highly sought after by collectors, so he was doing fine for money and helped out when he could. He was a good man and a romantic, and she missed him.

But sitting here alone was doing no good, so she reached for the business card of Winston's lawyer, Lavi

D. Arronson. Time to follow up, she thought, hoping Arronson had progressed farther than she had. Pulling the kitchen phone with its long cord into the den, she sat down and dialed, figuring she'd be leaving a message on his office answering machine this late.

The phone rang twice when a voice came on the line. "Arronson."

"Oh," Mabel said, impressed he worked late. "I didn't expect to catch you at the office."

Arronson paused. "I work from home. Who is this?"

"It's Mabel Davison."

No response.

Had he forgotten me? "I talked to you after Winston's arraignment."

"Which one?"

"Winston Washington. Blue River. The murder?"

"Oh, oh, yes. Mr. Washington's case. Yes. I'm on it."

Mabel brightened. "What's new?"

"What do you mean?"

"What have you found out about the other suspects?"

"What other suspects?"

Mabel's high hopes faded fast. "I told you. The black truck. The second semen sample. Any leads on your end?"

"Uh." Arronson sounded confused. "I haven't... I mean, I don't follow. This is the Blue River case, right? You're the detective on it?"

Mabel passed over the detective part and got straight to the point. "Have you done anything on the case?"

"Yes, quite a bit," he said, and she felt relieved. "The prosecutor is interested in a deal. Manslaughter, eight to ten years, chance of parole in six."

Mabel nearly dropped the phone. "But he's innocent!"

"Mr. Washington wants this over with, and it's a good deal. If this goes to trial and he loses, he could be in prison for twenty years."

"I don't think you understand me. Why should he go to jail at all? We're here to help him. Aren't you looking at alternate options, other suspects, that sort of thing?"

"That's your job. Not mine."

Mabel started with a, "Well, Luv," but she didn't say it like she usually did — more like she growled it out. "I have been following up on some leads. I have been tracking down owners of black trucks who work at the sawmill. One even sic'd his dog on me. And so I've got three left, and I'm following up with that."

"Well, that's all interesting, but I need more than that. With no prelim now, if we go to trial, we'd need solid evidence to get him free. Otherwise, he loses."

"So *do* something," Mabel cried out in frustration. "Help me out here."

Arronson sounded confused. "I am doing something. I am getting him out of prison in six years with good behavior."

Mabel was getting angry, and the momma bear tone was creeping into her voice. "I don't think you understand the importance of this. That boy shouldn't go to jail at all. At. All. Don't you agree?" Arronson stayed silent, so Mabel pressed on. "Who are you to give up on a client—"

Arronson began to interject, but Mabel cut him off. "Don't you interrupt me! You are a public defender.

That's a sacred trust to a poor boy who has no one else in the world but you to defend him. An innocent child will spend six years of his life in jail with a record because you took the easy route. All you care about is making a deal and wiping your hands of this case. When did you lose your ideals, Mr. Public Defender? You defend people! So when did you stop caring about the people you're helping?! Dear me, I need you to *not* make deals, but to make sure we have the evidence needed to save him. This is unconscionable. This is… ugh!"

"Okay, okay," Arronson said, sounding worn down. "You made your point."

"You're darn sure I made my point," Mabel emphasized. "You're better than this…" She looked back to read his first name on the card. "What would your mother say about this, Lavi?" Mabel had never seen a name like that before, and it threw her. "What does your name mean anyway?"

Arronson hesitated and answered as if he was embarrassed. "Lion. It means lion in Hebrew."

Mabel sat up, excited. "Yes. You are a lion, Lavi! This is your chance to shine. You can save this boy if you try. We can save him!"

"Oh, all right then." Arronson's voice had a hint of a tired smile, as if Mabel's speech had sparked something inside him. "I'll look into it. What do you have?"

"I need you to look more into the case files, Lavi. Make sure there isn't something we missed. I don't have access to those."

"But you're the lead detective on the case."

Mabel hesitated and decided only to share part of the

truth. "No, I'm not. I'm just concerned he's not getting a fair deal. But these two men should be looked into — Don Sigmundson and Lee Wallach. Both are white supremacists and linked to a drug ring out here — real nefarious types. I'm going to find if they have alibis for the night of the murder. Then I'll track down a third, a Cole Smithson."

"Can you get DNA?"

"Uh, what's that?"

"It's a new test being developed. It's much better than the standard blood and protein serology tests." Mabel was lost but didn't interrupt him to ask. "I know a lawyer on the team that used it earlier this year in Florida. Get some biological material, anything they touched or drank out of is fine. But don't contaminate it with your hands — wear gloves or use a tissue, put it in a paper bag, that sort of thing. I might be able to get this test done to see if it matches the semen sample. DNA is like a chemical fingerprint. Oh yeah, see if you can also get regular fingerprints from these guys. There are some fingerprints from the scene if I remember correctly that are not matched to Mr. Washington."

"Right on, Lavi," Mabel said. "That's what I needed. Okay, I'll get them."

"Also, you better do this quick. The trial date is just under a month, remember. These DNA tests will take some time."

"Oh, dear, okay. That's fast."

"The prosecutor is going to be angry if we take the deal off the table, so I doubt he'll support an extension. We need evidence, Mabel, solid evidence to link the murder to someone else. If the evidence doesn't hold up, he loses. If he loses, he gets twenty years."

Mabel paused, starting to comprehend the high stakes of what she was doing. Knowing she wasn't an investigator and was out of her league, she needed help. Consuela wasn't enough, so she prodded Lavi. "We're in this together, Lavi. You are the lion. You went into law to do good. Let's do good here."

"I'll do my part, but I need you to do yours. Tell me what you find out about their whereabouts that night and whether you can get DNA samples. Who's the lead investigator working with you on this?"

Mabel dodged his question by answering only, "Your mother will be proud, Lavi. I got to go." Then she hung up the phone quickly. Her hands were shaking a little as she pondered Winston's fate. Maybe Lavi was right to seek a deal because if she failed, Winston would be behind bars for the rest of his life. Mabel rested her head in her hand and looked out the bay window of her den. She couldn't see the stars anymore, only the dark gray of the mountain and the forest's darker blue edge through the shadow of her reflection.

She'd never looked so stressed.

CHAPTER 26

Monday, October 20

I n the morning, Mabel called Consuela, hoping she could help procure any lunchroom dishes used by Lee Wallach, Cole Smithson, or Don Sigmundson, but Consuela dashed that idea, "Darling, those boys don't like sitting with the suit-and-tie types. They eat their lunches by their stations out on the floor." With less than four weeks to trial, Mabel needed those samples ASAP. If she couldn't get them at the mill, she'd have to think of another way. Changing the topic, she got Consuela to check the timecards of the three remaining suspects — none of them had worked the night of the murder, though all three had been scheduled. Consuela also provided information about the shutdown procedures, including when maintenance crews were on site. But none worked that night either, something Mabel thought only an insider — and certainly not poor Winston — would know. The information gave Mabel confidence that she was on the right track.

To find out whether Don at least had an alibi, she wanted to talk to the girlfriend. But with a morning shift at the diner, she was overwhelmed: the diner, the motel, the boys, her niece, and now this detective work. She doubted she could sneak out after the breakfast rush like last time. The mine crews were flocking to her diner for breakfast, lunch, and dinner, and she was starting to get lineups — unheard of for her place.

Even if she could talk to Don's girlfriend, Mabel tried to imagine how that conversation might go. "Hey Barbara, did your boyfriend kill a girl?" Or, "Hey Barbara, what was Don doing the night of September 3rd?" Mabel was under no illusions about her abilities as an investigator. The girl could easily just tell her to go to where God ain't welcome, and that would be the end of it. There had to be another way, but what?

Kerry came down for breakfast, yawning and looking grouchy. Mabel had an idea, hoping Kerry wouldn't give too much sass about it. "Kerry, I need your help."

"What now?" Kerry slumped into her chair.

"Do you know Barbara at the grocer?"

"Ugh, who's Barbara?"

"Works at the grocer and is dating one of my suspects."

"Oh?" Kerry replied, instantly interested, but the conversation ground to a halt as the two boys ran down the steps, fighting, pushing, and poking each other. It took both Mabel and Kerry a couple of minutes to get them settled. Then Mabel took Kerry aside. "Barbara is the girlfriend of Don Sigmundson. I don't know if she'd talk to me, and I don't know how to approach her to see where Don was—" she lowered her voice to a whisper "—the night that Karen was killed."

"You want me to ask her then?"

"She's closer to your age, maybe eighteen or nineteen, and I was hoping you might be able to relate better."

"Why not. All the school kids walk to the grocer at lunch to get some extra food if they need it. I can walk over today and see if I can get any info from her. Which night again?"

"September 3rd. It was a Wednesday."

Kerry frowned. "Anything else going on that day? Anything earlier I mean. Nobody remembers dates like that."

Mabel was at a loss.

"Okay, doesn't matter," Kerry said, waving her off. "I'll think of something."

Mabel smiled with relief. "Thank you for doing this. This is very helpful."

"No problem," Kerry said. "I get to help my Auntie in like *totally investigating a crime*. I just can't wait to tell Lisa."

"Oh, don't say anything to her. I don't want the word out."

"Too late. We already know. We listened in when you and Lisa's mom were talking."

"You little scoundrels!"

Kerry laughed. "Remember, you owe me for this."

"Yes." Mabel gave in. "I owe you." Kerry beamed.

Hector overheard his mother and starting whining.

"Why does Kerry get owed? Why can't I?"

"Oh, Luv," Mabel said. "You don't even know what we're talking about."

"I want to be owed, too," Fred chimed in.

"Enough! Off you go," she said, swatting their bums to get them going. They repeatedly protested, "I want to be owed!" until Kerry stepped in.

"If you're good, I'll get you some candy for lunch."

Fred cheered. Hector was unimpressed. "I'm too old for candy."

"But you *like* Betty Stuttgart, right?"

Hector blushed, and Mabel's ears pricked up. This was a first, hearing her ten-year-old boy had a crush on a girl. But Betty was thirteen! "I might just introduce you if you're good," Kerry said.

Hector blushed even deeper, embarrassed by his mother's attention, but nodded slightly. Fred picked up on this and said, "Hector's got a girlfriend, Hector's got a girlfriend."

Hector punched Fred in the shoulder and then ran out toward the driveway with Fred chasing after him. The bus had arrived, so Kerry lugged all their school bags out. "Be good!" Mabel shouted after them, but the boys were already climbing into the bus. "Love ya!" she called, but only Kerry heard. She turned back, waved, and then got on the bus. And though the morning ended in chaos, Mabel's heart swelled with love and pride at how they were finally pulling together as a family.

CHAPTER 27

Kerry and Lisa were talking and giggling as they lazed their way over to the grocer at lunch. They had become fast friends after Kerry had arrived in Blue River six months ago, and they spent the entire end of term and summer together. With Lisa never having had a girlfriend her age, it was a revelation to have Kerry in town, and even more so for Kerry, but in a different way. When Kerry came to Blue River, she wasn't looking for friendship and wanted to return to Seattle and be with her old friends. But now, thanks to Lisa, she didn't hate this place so much. And, truth be told, more and more, she even liked it. Lisa was a blast, and Hector and Fred, though a real pain sometimes, could also be fun.

Even more surprising, Lisa was not as tomboyish and bookish as the friends Kerry once gravitated to. Lisa loved makeup and was preparing to go to beauty school. Kerry picked up tips on using eyeliner and blush and taking better care of nails by merely being around her. And thanks to Lisa, Kerry was even starting to like it — though she preferred most days to go without. In return, Kerry tutored Lisa in math, and while Lisa couldn't believe a girl could be so good at it, Kerry loved it, in part because of her dad.

As they walked on, Lisa started to tell a joke. But Kerry only half-listened, reflecting instead on her father and wondering again if she were somehow to blame for his suicide. That maybe she wasn't good enough for him, and maybe that's why he did it. While Mabel kept reassuring her by saying, "Both parents loved you dearly, child," Kerry wasn't sure. Still, Mabel was a godsend. Kerry had learned more about her parent's hopes, dreams, and fears from Mabel than she had ever known or suspected at home. Now, she felt she could relate more to her parents after their death than when they were alive, and that hurt because she'd missed her chance.

When Lisa finished her punch line, Kerry smiled. Lisa was always good at pulling her out of her dark moods.

The village grocer and gas station were coming up on the corner of one of Blue River's few 'downtown' streets. A young, tattooed man with a shaved head was filling up his car with gas. Lisa and Kerry tensed, expecting the usual catcalling from a bored skinhead working one of Larson's farms stopping into town for gas and the hope of something more.

"Hey, ladies! Why don't you come for a drive? I'll show you around."

Lisa shook her head as they walked past.

"A couple of lesbians, uh?" the guy said, laughing like they would appreciate the joke. "I like those too."

"Get out of here, loser."

"Ahhh," he pouted. "Don't be stuck up like that. Don't go. Come on. You want some weed? I got something extra special too. Hey! I'm bored as fuck around here. Come back!"

Lisa and Kerry exchanged uncomfortable looks and didn't open up again until they walked under the grocery eaves and went inside.

Barbara was loitering behind the counter, filing her nails, looking bored. Kerry remembered her from the July fourth fireworks on the beach because wow, what a night that was. Mabel had built it up for days. "Oh, dear, you'll love it. Folks up here blast fireworks like their God-given right to spray-shoot machine guns. Bam, bam, bam, boom!" Kerry hadn't believed it because, until then, Blue River had been a total bust. But the fourth of July eventually came, and with hands pressed tightly to her ears, she'd watched wide-eyed a full twenty minutes of booms and bursts of light, far, far brighter than the night's backdrop of vibrant stars, and she had been wowed.

Yet, even that moment of awe hadn't lasted. While Kerry had left early because of the boys' bedtime, Lisa had stayed on and later told her about the aftermath. After the families had left the party, the bored, single men and women who worked at the mine or at Larson's farms had gotten drunk and fought and worse. Their chaos left the beach strewn with empty beer bottles, cigarette butts, and the odd used condom. Lisa's mom had organized a community cleanup, which Mabel and Kerry helped at, that filled bags and bags with garbage.

Lisa linked her arms with Kerry and pulled her towards the beauty supplies. She selected a lipstick and then guided Kerry back to the counter.

Barbara was still filing her nails and chewing bubblegum.

"Oh, what's your color?" Lisa asked, nodding at her hands.

Barbara blew a giant bubble, which she popped back into her mouth. "Lavender red," she replied.

"Ohhh, nice," Lisa said. "You got great nails. Can I see?"

Barbara laid her hands on the counter, fingers spread wide, pleased by the compliment.

Lisa gasped. "Oh, I'm so jealous. Look at this, Kerry." Kerry obliged, leaning over to take a look but not sure what she was admiring. "Gorgeous cuticles. Do you get manicures often, or is this all you?"

Barbara smacked a bubble back in her mouth and leaned forward, engaged now. She couldn't help but wiggle in her seat and smile. "It's me."

Lisa examined her hair now. "Wow! I love your hair too. Is that a professional perm?"

Barbara touched her hair and shook her curls. That's when both Kerry and Lisa saw a thin bruise high on her forehead and gaped at it. Barbara frowned and looked embarrassed, quickly fixing her hair to hide the bruise. Then she pulled away from the girls, moving around some papers behind the counter.

"My last boyfriend hit me too," Lisa said. "I get it. Men can be such jerks."

Kerry shot around in surprise as Barbara glanced back, embarrassed. She didn't say anything, so Lisa reached out to hold Barbara's hands.

"Who's your man?" Lisa asked her.

"I doubt you know him. He works out at the mill."

"My George did, too," Lisa said, proudly. "He was five years older than me."

Kerry was shocked and a little impressed, and maybe even a little jealous. She did the math and figured that Lisa had been dating a twenty-one-year-old man. She didn't think you could date boys older than your age.

"He was nice, at first," Lisa continued. "But he got jealous at times. You?"

"Sometimes," Barbara said, fiddling with her hair. Then she added with a sad smile, "Not very romantic, either."

Lisa rolled her eyes. "*Ughhh, tell me* about it. Cheap dates, all around. You end up on Smithson Island?" Barbara blushed in response, and they both giggled. Smithson Island was one of the make-out points for young and old alike. It was up near the new mine, accessed by a gravel road through the forest, a small island at the end of a large lake with a short wooden bridge from a beach shore. The waters were crystal clear and blue and reflected in a perfect mirror both the mountain and forest during the day and the moon and stars at night. It was common to have roaring fires in fire pits on the island or on the lake's beach, and many a young woman and man had lost their virginity at this spot.

"Do you know George? My old boyfriend?"

Barbara thought about it then shook her head. "Maybe's he's gone. I don't know him."

"Yeah, probably is," Lisa said with a laugh. "He certainly hasn't called me lately. Does your boyfriend work the night shifts? Those are the worst."

"Some nights, yeah. It's not great. He works a lot. And we have a trailer out on one of Larson's properties too. He manages one of the farms and Larson's pretty particular."

"He's a Larson man too?" Lisa asked, impressed, which threw Kerry, not knowing if this were part of an act or what Lisa really felt.

Barbara nodded and then sized up Lisa. "You know, there's some cute guys out at the farm. A girl like you might fit in."

Lisa asked, "Really?" And then twirled around, laughing.

Barbara giggled with her and then confided, "We're thinking of getting married too."

"Oh," Lisa said, sounding a little taken aback. Then she came out of it. "Congratulations! The mill's a good job for a husband."

"Yeah, I think so," Barbara said, proudly.

Lisa looked around and then lowered her voice. "Can your future husband score us some weed?"

Kerry gaped at Lisa, half-expecting Sheriff Dan to come in and arrest them all.

Barbara focused on Lisa and smiled. "Sure. Come out to the farm, and we can cut you some. You know Parker's

Ridge?" Lisa nodded. "It's the second left down the road. Go about a mile in. You can't miss it. There are a few trailers out there."

Lisa winked. "Gotcha. I'll do that."

Then Lisa and Barbara settled in to talk about boyfriends some more. But since Kerry hadn't even kissed a guy yet, she felt embarrassed, like a third wheel, and drifted from the conversation.

Then she heard Lisa ask what they had come in for and that brought her back. "Hey, was your boyfriend working the night that girl died at the mill?"

Barbara frowned and then shook her head. "Nah. Said he'd worked his shift that night, but I found out later that the mill was closed for maintenance. I think he went to the peelers instead."

"Ugh, Curt's Strip Club," Lisa said. "George did the same. How did you find out?"

"He came home late, stunk of beer, cuts on his knuckles, that sort of thing. Dummy said he got injured on shift. But you know how it is. Then we got into a fight about it, and eventually I just dropped it."

"Yeah, totally. Boyfriends are idiots." Lisa said, but this time neither laughed. "Well," Lisa added, moving back. "It's time we got back." She looked at Kerry and nodded her head in the direction of the schoolhouse. "Nice talking to you, Barbara. Maybe I'll see you at the farm."

Barbara brightened. "Sure thing. Anytime. I'll introduce you to some of the boys."

Lisa led the way out with Kerry trailing behind, somewhat unsettled. She had learned more about Lisa in the last ten minutes than she had since arriving in Blue River. It seemed Lisa was a lot more complicated — and more adult — than Kerry had realized.

Lisa put her arm around Kerry's shoulder and shook her out of it. "You heard that?" she said. "About the cuts on his hands. About how he lied about going to work. Barbara's boyfriend doesn't have much of an alibi, does he? Him lying and all. Let's run over to my place, and you can call Mabel. She's probably dying to know."

Kerry agreed, but she had more on her mind. "Hey, uh," she said. "I didn't know you dated an older boy."

Lisa laughed, then blushed. "I don't really want to talk about it. He broke my heart."

"When did it happen?"

"Last year. He left after we uh…" Lisa hesitated and looked embarrassed. "He left after he took me to Smithson Island. He said he loved me." She looked pained. "I guess he didn't."

"So after… He just dropped you? After he said he loved you?" Lisa nodded, her eyes tearing up. "Ughhh," Kerry said, determined now more than ever to get out of Blue River. "Men *are* jerks." She pulled her friend into a bear hug like one of Mabel's good ones. Lisa pushed her off playfully, and then they ran to Lisa's house to call Mabel before the one PM school bell.

CHAPTER 28

Tuesday, October 21

Energized by Kerry's tip from the previous day, Mabel plotted her next move. Knowing that at least one of her suspects might have visited Curt's stripper bar, Mabel thought it best to ask Curt in person. After getting Sally organized for the nine AM breakfast shift, she got in the car and drove over, thinking of what she would ask him. Like Mabel, Curt worked non-stop and spent most of his time running his bar. While they shared some of the same clientele — the construction crews, sawmill workers, and truckers of the region — only families and tourists dined at Mabel's, and only Larson's men ate at Curt's. And while Mabel prided herself on her cooking, Curt augmented his cheap four-dollar breakfast with a morning strip show. Curt had told her once that he used the morning show to try out his new strippers; if they did well, they graduated to the night show, where the tips were better.

She'd learned a lot about the strip club business from Curt. Most strip clubs around the region allowed clients to throw coins or yell insults at the girls, but Curt would have none of that. For all his faults, Curt considered his place as a kind of rural Gentlemen's Club, and, as the only strip bar for fifty miles, the patrons toed the line. If a Larson man acted up, the man got banned. And a ban meant a sentence of extreme boredom out on the various grow-ops, and even worse, exclusion from hanging out with Larson's uppers, who had their 'management' meetings at Curt's over beers — though Larson himself rarely showed up. He preferred being the lord of his own trailer compound, which had a sinister reputation with the strippers.

Thus, to Mabel, the strip club seemed the least of the town's many vices. The bar was in a two-level nondescript building with blackout windows and a reinforced steel front door that looked like it had survived a war. The morning was bright and sunny, but you wouldn't know it walking in. With the door open, what little light filtered in behind Mabel blinded the men at tables nearby and highlighted how seamy and run-down the place was. Once the door closed, the peeling paint and stained floors disappeared in the dim light, and the club seemed somewhat respectable again. Several men, a few she recognized from her diner, were scattered around the room. Most were either finishing their breakfasts or staring blankly at a naked woman dancing on a pole. The music wasn't as loud as it was at night, which Mabel guessed was a courtesy to those who hadn't yet had their second cup of coffee.

"Mabel!"

Mabel smiled and sat down on a stool as Curt swept the bar clean in front of her. While she didn't approve of these clubs and felt somewhat alien to the place, Curt had a kind heart and treated his women well.

"You want a water?" he asked.

Mabel nodded, and Curt fetched her one. Curt was roughly fifty, on his second wife —a former stripper like his first — and had five kids, mostly grown now, except for the two-year-old who'd come along with his second marriage. He wore a loose silk shirt unbuttoned at the neck, had thick, wavy hair with no hint of gray, and a lazy charm that served him well. He was a chain smoker, who almost always had a cigarette dangling from his mouth, as he did now. Although Curt's place was still independent as far as Mabel knew, his bar was a personal hangout for Larson's men and any State Police on Larson's payroll. Although Sheriff Dan wasn't on Larson's payroll yet, Dan showed up on occasion as he and Curt were hunting buddies. Larson tolerated Dan and there seemed to be an unspoken agreement — if Larson's men weren't bothered, neither he nor his men would bother the town. While this arrangement had served folks well as Larson formed his empire, now that Larson was the undisputed king of the drug trade in the region, his protection of local folks was slipping. Not enough to cause an uproar, not yet. Profits were still good, and families were taken care of, but more and more Larson didn't punish his men acting up as he once did, and fear was creeping in. Even

Curt looked a little older and more strained than the last time she'd seen him.

Curt brought her water. "What can I do for you? Business good?"

Mabel sipped the water, ice cold, which she approved of as any good waitress would. "The mine is bringing in a lot of crews to the diner. My motel is booked solid for the next six months at least, and I'm starting to think I need to hire more."

Curt nodded. "Me too. I'm bringing a couple of new girls in to maybe do another show. You know Lacey is my main waitress," Curt said, referring to his new wife. "But Candy's a server too now and not a pole girl no more."

Mabel turned around to glance at Candy, who was taking an order nearby. "She's pregnant again, right?"

"Yep, second child."

"Same boyfriend?"

"Nope. New one. Works at the mine. And now that she's working tables, she gets benefits too — I cover that," he said proudly. "Candy's Nana babysits while she works, and will watch the next one once she pops."

"Nice to see her settle down a bit. I hope the guy treats her right."

"Seems so. Actually, he's more of an office type, a scrawny one-hundred-pound thing that wears these wire-rimmed, coke-bottle glasses and seems kind of respectable. A nice, polite guy. Guess he also asked for her hand in marriage, but she told him no, not yet, not just 'cause of a baby on the way." He shrugged and took a drag on the cigarette. "Candy's a tough girl. She'll figure it out."

Mabel raised her eyebrows and said nothing more. Candy was twenty-three years old.

"Got a question for you," Mabel said, ending the small talk. "It's about the night Karen Thompson was murdered." That got Curt's attention quick. "I heard a few of the sawmill crew ended up here, and I'm wondering if you recall who." Mabel didn't say her suspects' names right off, hoping Curt would mention them natural like.

Curt turned serious and glanced around before he whispered, "I can't be talking about any of the Larson boys."

"So some of Larson's men were here that night?"

"When are they ain't? But you know as well as I, most of Larson's boys these days are staffing the sawmill shifts now because he wants them to have respectable jobs for their probation officers."

Mabel had heard the same rumor that Larson owned most of the sawmill. While Consuela hadn't confirmed it, she said her manager didn't seem to be the boss anymore and that some of the long-standing workers, especially those of color, had been losing their jobs to Larson's white men.

"I really do need this information."

Curt leaned on the bar casually for appearances but still whispered, "What for? You got trouble with Larson now?"

"Someone does. I can't say who in particular. I promise I won't mention where I got the information from."

Curt stubbed out his cigarette and nodded. "You

know I like you. But folks asking questions don't go over well in this town. Be careful what you're doing. It's—"

A waitress came by, and Curt stopped talking.

"Hiya, Mabel!"

"Hi, Candy!"

"What are you doing here? I haven't seen you show up before. What's up?"

Curt spoke up for Mabel. "She's doing us a courtesy."

Mabel smiled and nodded. "Congrats on the little one. Are you four or five months along?"

Candy smiled and patted her stomach. "Twenty weeks in and sick as a dog. This one is a handful, so I suspect a girl."

"Why don't you and your Nana swing by my house for a dinner one night?" Mabel asked. "My treat. I'd love to see you both again, plus your little one, Sam — such a sweet thing."

Candy put her arm around Mabel's shoulders. "Thanks, babe. Sam's growing like a weed, nearly two years old."

"Heard you have a new boyfriend too."

Candy blushed. "Yeah, Kelvin. He's an accountant at the mine. Sweet man."

"Would he come too? He's welcome for dinner."

Candy hesitated then beamed. "He'd like that. Thank you."

Curt interrupted. "Maybe you two can talk waitressing at that dinner too, and Mabel'll give you some tips. You're messing up your orders some."

Candy gave him a fierce look before she squeezed Mabel's shoulder. "We'll talk," she said and left.

Mabel watched her go before turning back. "I always liked her — good in school."

Curt picked up a new cigarette and a lighter. "Smart girl. Hard life. That's the Blue River way, I guess."

"Speaking of hard lives, was Petar here that night?"

Curt held the cigarette to the flame for a few seconds, thinking, before he crisped its end and took a puff. "Petar? Yeah, sure. Came in with the manager and a few boys, I think, after a trip to Edmonston and back. Stayed for a few, left at closing."

"You don't mind answering about him."

"He ain't a Larson boy."

"Like Don Sigmundson?"

Curt squinted before he took another puff of the cigarette. He blew out the smoke, reached over, and turned up the stereo on the bar to drown out his whisper. "He's someone I can't talk about."

Mabel felt the tension and followed Curt's gaze to the other men in the bar. Most were still staring at the pole girl doing her thing. Candy was at a table near the stage, serving a group of men. But as Mabel turned back to Curt, she felt the hairs rise on her neck like they were being watched, and so she leaned in and whispered, "Was he here that night?"

Curt frowned in response. "Briefly. Came early and left early with another. He had a few beers and then bought some off-sales for later. He was a little rowdy."

"He got into a fight here?" Mabel recalled what Kerry had said about cuts and bruises on Don's hands.

"Nope. Not here. If he had got into a fight, it wasn't on my property. Is that what this is about? He beat up someone you know?"

"Someone did. That's why I'm asking."

Curt frowned. "Larson's getting tougher now. I'm hearing stories."

"Is he coming after your place?"

"No. Not yet. But I don't want that to change."

Mabel nodded, feeling bad for Curt. Since most of his regular business was from Larson's men, he needed to comply. Like Sarah had said before, she, at least, had the construction workers, truckers, and tourists, and none of Larson's men bothered to visit her diner, being more of a family place and all.

Mabel got up and said, "Thanks for this. I better get going."

Curt reached over to stop her. "Be careful, Mabel. I hear things. Larson is asking about you. Don't make yourself a target. Whatever you're doing, don't stir things up."

Although his eyes were showing concern, it was still a kind of threat. It meant her business was at stake. But she wouldn't budge, not for this. "A girl was murdered, Curt. And I'm not the one who broke the peace here."

CHAPTER 29

With Don Sigmundson moving up to suspect number one, Mabel drove back to the diner and worked the rest of the morning shift with Sally. Then she went home to clean her messy pantry, which she had been putting off for months. An hour in, she found a full bottle of whiskey at the bottom. It stopped her cold, bringing her back to the dark days when Bill stashed bottles throughout the house. It was a while since she'd found one, as she'd done a hard clean after kicking Bill out. She set the bottle aside, a little depressed. Then Consuela phoned, with more bad news. She couldn't get a DNA sample from the lunchroom as Don was off for two weeks. With Winston's trial coming up fast, Mabel needed another way. Looking at the whiskey bottle gave her an idea.

A few semi-trucks swept past before she pulled out on the highway, reminding her of all the truck drivers she'd served over the years. She always made a point of asking them to watch their speed around the towns, not just for their sakes, but for the kids' as well. Accidents on these highways were rare but almost always fatal — at least according to Dan. He saw most of the grisly ones. It had hardened him up some, so when even *he* had trouble describing Karen Thompson's murder, it reinforced to Mabel how cruel the killer must be. "I don't know how you do it," she'd told Dan one night. "Seeing all those accident victims, let alone the murder." Fortunately for Blue River, murder was rare, with Karen being the only one in recent memory — if you didn't count Larson's men getting killed in some drug shoot-out in another county. None of those drugs battles had occurred in Blue River proper just yet, but times were changing.

Mabel followed Lisa's directions and made her way to Parker's Ridge and the farm where Don lived, with its collection of trailers and camper vans parked in a gravel lot on the edge of a forested slope. A small community of Larson's men lived out here, tending to one of several farms in the area. She pulled up to find a dozen or so empty, weathered lawn chairs around a big firepit. Only two guys were hanging out beside it, smoking and drinking beer. As Mabel watched, unimpressed, one of the skinheads drained a can and crumpled it against his forehead before tossing it into the cold firepit with the rest of the trash.

Mabel got out and made her way over. The men's glances at her waitress uniform and her canvas shoulder bag made her feel decidedly out of place on a marijuana farm run by skinheads.

"Either of you, Don Sigmundson?" she asked.

The two men glanced at each other and smirked but didn't reply. She focused on the younger one who'd been poking the ashes with a stick — he didn't look so angry.

"I'm looking for him."

They returned to their conversation, ignoring her.

"*Excuse* me," Mabel said. "That was rude, young man. I asked you a question."

The young guy finally turned to her. "Don ain't here."

"Where is he then?"

The older, angrier skinhead whispered something crude, and both laughed. The young guy then pointed his stick to a field through the woods. "Out back," he said to Mabel.

"I'd like to talk to him."

The young guy glanced at the older one for more direction, but the older man just belched loudly and grabbed another beer.

The young guy shrugged. "Sure. I'll get him." And then left.

The remaining skinhead belched loudly again, which Mabel took as a sign of disrespect. She glared at him.

The skinhead glared right back at her. "You got a problem?"

"I got a problem with trash who don't sit up for a woman and show her some respect."

The older skinhead downed his second beer before he tossed it into the ash pit with the others. Then he lifted the side of his shirt, making sure she could see the hidden pistol underneath.

Mabel rolled her eyes but then looked elsewhere, decidedly more nervous now. She was almost glad to see the young guy returning with a second fellow she assumed was Don Sigmundson.

The new man said, "Hey, lady. You looking for some weed?"

The men snickered. Mabel didn't. As per her plan, she put on a mock cheery tone, but it didn't quite come out that way with the way things were going. "I'm with the July fourth organizing committee, and we wanted to give you your unclaimed prize."

"That was months ago. I don't remember no prize."

"I know," she said, pressing on with her ruse. "But if you don't come to get the prize, we deliver it. We're honest folk around here."

"Honest folk, huh?" Don chuckled with the boys. "Okay, Mabel, is it? What's the prize?"

Mabel was shocked they knew her name until she remembered she'd foolishly kept her nametag on. Get it together, she warned herself. She pulled out a slate with a carbon paper credit slip and pieces of paper clipped to it. "You just need to sign here," she said and handed him the carbon slip and a pen and observed to see where he put his fingertips. He got some of the dry ink on his hand and tried to wipe it off on the paper, just like she wanted. She stopped herself from smiling that her plan was working. Once he signed it, he handed it back, and she was careful not to mar his prints with her own.

"So? What's the prize?" he asked.

"I need to see some ID too."

All three men found this funny. "ID?" Don said, laughing. "For a county fair prize?"

Mabel nodded, trying to look sincere.

Don made a funny face to the skinhead by the fire, and they both chuckled. "Okay," he said with mock respect. "My ID is in my trailer. Let's go get it then, ma'am." The other two chuckled in a way that made Mabel even more nervous, but she was determined to see this through.

She followed him to one of the trailers, outside of which were two chairs and a small side table that had a used cigarette tin, a few empty beer cans, and a plastic flower in a vase on it. The last touch was likely his girlfriend, Barbara's. As Don went into the trailer, Mabel hung back, took a tissue, and used it to grab a beer can and a cigarette butt carefully and put them in her bag. Next, she took out an envelope with one hundred dollars in it, and unsheathed the bottle of whiskey that she'd brought. When Don came back, he exchanged his ID for the whiskey and envelope. She wrote down his driver's license information and then gave it back to him while he hollered out to his friends, holding the bottle as the real prize.

"You should've told me it was whiskey and a Benjamin note," he said to her, happy now. "I'd have got my girl come and get it sooner. But then again, a good-looking woman like yourself, maybe you should come by more often."

Mabel resisted rolling her eyes, wanting to get out of here as quickly as she could. The other two men strolled up, and Don handed over the whiskey and said, "I'll get a couple of glasses."

The older, angrier-looking skinhead edged closer to Mabel, giving her a more appreciative once over. "If I'd known you're bringing some booze, I might have been nicer."

His unwashed smell repelled her, and she covered her nose in disgust.

The skinhead took offense and turned mean again. "Don't be a bitch about it."

His coarseness made her feel even more vulnerable, and she wanted to get away as fast as she could from these dangerous men.

She turned to go, and the skinhead called out from behind. "Maybe we'll stop by your diner tonight, *Mabel.* I'd like a spicy dish like you. Maybe you can serve it up to me, nice and fine. Just the way I like it, uh?" He laughed coarsely, but his voice had an undertone that made the threat real.

Mabel did not look back, mad and scared as she was, and then the men laughed again, likely at some joke at her expense. As she drove away, she resisted stepping on the gas, not wanting to look like she was running away, but her breathing came out in gasps, and her hands shook terribly.

CHAPTER 30

After the kids had finished their homework, they broke out the cards, and all four of them started playing at the kitchen table.

"Go fish," Mabel said to Fred, who groaned and then picked up a card. He jumped up excited and showed everyone a nine and then smacked down another nine. "Match!"

Hector grimaced. "No fair. You always get the cards."

Fred continued his turn by examining the backs of everyone's raised cards like he had X-ray vision and took his time to decide like he always did.

"Hurry it up," Hector grumbled as Kerry turned to Mabel and asked, "How did it go today?"

Mabel answered, cryptically, sensitive to the boys, "You mean with the farm?"

Kerry nodded, equally cagey.

"Oh, fine. Got what I needed."

"The, uh…" Kerry said, knowingly.

Mabel nodded.

"What are you talking about?" Hector said. "Is it about that dead girl in town?"

"Hector! Your brother!" Mabel said.

Fred turned pale. "There's a *dead girl here*!?"

"No!" Both Kerry and Mabel spoke together.

"No," Mabel repeated. "Hector's just talking about a girl that…" Mabel struggled to answer.

"Passed away," said Kerry, and Mabel nodded like that was the right way to say it.

"Was murdered," Hector said, scaring Fred even further.

"Hector!" Mabel said. "Watch it."

"He's taking forever," Hector pleaded. "We're going to be here all night."

"Is she a ghost now?"

"No, Fred," Kerry said, touching his hand. "There are no ghosts."

"Can you sleep with me tonight? For protection?" Fred asked Kerry, and she nodded while Hector just rolled his eyes.

Mabel stifled an "aw," putting her hand to her own heart, touched that her family was starting to get along, until Hector punched his brother and pleaded, with as much exasperation as he could muster, "*Please*, pick a card! It's taking *forev*—"

A loud bang and a shattering sound of glass frightened all of them.

Kerry and Mabel stood up in surprise.

The boys rushed to the den to find a web of cracks around a small round hole in their front windowpane.

Fred ran to touch it—

Mabel screamed, "Fred! No!"

She reached to pull him back and then clawed at Hector and Kerry to get down.

Another bang, more glass breaking.

Another bullet slammed into the far wall. The kids screamed. Mabel pushed them back into the kitchen and down onto the floor. She knocked the phone off its holder, scooped it off the floor, and immediately dialed the Sheriff.

It took several rings before Sheriff Dan came on the line. Mabel pleaded. "Dan! Hurry! There are gunshots. People are firing at us!" Mabel shared the details in a rush and then hung up, and with Dan on his way, Mabel crawled back to the den to peek out the broken window.

A car engine revved loudly, the tires spinning a donut loop into the gravel driveway, its blinding high-beams shining into the living room while the men in the car laughed and whooped it up. Mabel violently motioned Kerry and the terrified boys back. Then a series of lights went on in the motel, and several guests emerged from their rooms. The car tore off onto the highway with the men inside still laughing and hollering as it disappeared around the dark bend.

Several of the motel guests came into the parking lot, and one ran up to Mabel's front door. "You all right in there?"

Mabel made her way to the front door and opened it,

shaking. "Carlos! Did you see who it was?"

"I couldn't make it out," Carlos said. "Did they fire a weapon at your home? And with kids inside?! Those sons-a-bitches," he growled. Then he noticed Kerry and the terrified boys staring out from the kitchen. "Oh, pardon for cussing, Mabel."

"No, sons of bitches is right," Mabel replied. "Carlos, go rally your men outside."

Mabel then went back to the kitchen and told Kerry, "Take the boys upstairs."

Kerry nodded, white-faced, as Hector asked, "Mom, can I come with you?"

Mabel held his face gently and said, "No. Stay with Kerry." Then she whispered in his ear. "Protect the family. I need a strong man up there."

Hector wiped away his tears and nodded with pride. She grabbed her boys and Kerry at once and they hugged each other very tightly, and though Fred was still crying, Mabel said, "I love you all. Now go." And then Kerry and Hector guided the terrified Fred up.

Mabel watched them go all the way into Kerry's bedroom and shut the door, then closed her eyes, feeling ill from how close the bullets had come, and with her motel guests milling about outside, she steeled herself to address them and went out on the porch.

"Boys!" Her commanding voice silenced the dull chatter of the men. "Some of Larson's men did this. I think I know the ones. Can you do me a favor? Protect my ch-children." Her voice cracked from raw emotion, but Mabel kept her back straight.

Several men immediately offered to park their trucks

in front of her house. Carlos even said he would spend the night in his truck to keep watch.

Mabel thanked them all and left Carlos to organize things. And though Dan was on his way, he wasn't enough. The State Police needed to get involved — not only with the shooting but also with the drugs out on Don Sigmundson's farm.

If Larson wanted a fight, she thought, he got one. She went back to the kitchen and dialed the phone.

"911 Emergency," a woman answered.

"I'm reporting a shooting at my home," Mabel said, nearly losing her composure. "They smashed a window, and my kids were almost shot. I'm also reporting who did it — a man named Don Sigmundson and his cronies living out near Parker's Ridge. They run a drug farm, too. Yes… I'm aware. You better bring a number of officers in. I know one of the thugs is armed. Yes, I'll stay on the line."

Sheriff Dan's cruiser, with its red and blue lights flashing in the night, barreled down the highway toward her home. When he drove in, her motel guests blocked his path, forcing him to stop at a distance.

The operator came back on the line, and Mabel answered a few more questions and gave the farm's address. Then she hung up and went to talk to Dan.

"Dan! Those skinheads shot up my house. With my children inside!"

"Why did they target you?" Dan asked, lumbering up breathless and looking as grim as Mabel had ever seen. Rarely did Larson's men target regular citizens, which allowed Dan to look the other way when Larson went after other gangs or rival dealers. This would change all that. "What's going on?"

"I went over to one of Larson's farms today," Mabel said. "To get evidence. And I got it."

"Jesus!" The Sheriff wiped the sweat off his forehead. "Mabel, are you nuts?! These guys don't fool around."

"Neither do I."

"Really?" Dan asked rhetorically, getting worked up. "Really?! You're putting your life in danger for that Winston boy. He's not worth it!"

"Yes, he is!" Mabel said, equally as vehement. "And if you don't see all the harm Larson is doing, I'm going to take care of it myself."

"Oh, my God! Listen to you. And what about your kids? If he comes here again…"

Mabel folded her arms, defiant. But his words scared her.

Dan sensed it and tried to reason with her. "For God's sakes, Mabel. They shot at your house with your kids inside. That's how serious they are. Just leave it be." Then he looked around at the mine crews milling about in the dark. Mabel could tell the wheels were turning in his mind like he was trying to figure out how to bring back the truce between Larson's gang and the community. "Now look," Dan said. "Here's what is going to happen. I'm going to talk to Larson. Tonight. I'm going to tell him you're going to drop this thing with Winston and targeting his boys as suspects. I think he'll listen. He knows if he takes it too far, it's going to get too big and—"

"I already took care of it," Mabel interrupted him. "I

called the State Police, and they're going to come out and arrest Don Sigmundson and his gang. They're the ones that did this."

Dan dug his fingertips into his temples like he was trying to stop a raging headache. "Oh, Jesus. You called the Staties?"

Mabel nodded.

"Those Staties—" He paused, trying to control his anger and disbelief. "You know some of them officers are on Larson's payroll, right? You didn't give your name, did you?"

"Well, I... Yes."

The Sheriff screwed his eyes shut before glaring at her. "Jesus. Now Larson will know you reported one of his farms. Don't you understand? He'll be furious. This isn't some game."

"This isn't a game for me, Dan. He came after my kids."

"He'll do worse than that—" Dan stopped talking to tamp down his anger and think things through. "Okay. The Staties are going to take some time getting out here. You go inside and let me handle this."

"His men shot bullets into my house, Dan!" Mabel pleaded, near tears.

"I know. I'm going to do my best to straighten this out, but you've got to drop this Winston thing. Go inside, and I'll take care of it."

Mabel went, but she wasn't too happy about it, and in no way would she let Dan decide what she could or couldn't do. As she marched up her porch steps, her resolve hardened; if neither the State Police nor Dan would do something about it, she would. With one last card to play, she went to the kitchen and dialed a number.

The phone rang nearly eight times before it was answered. "Arronson," he said, sounding tired.

"It's Mabel," she said. "I've got some news for you."

To her surprise, Lavi's voice was suddenly furious. "I don't care. I thought you were some detective. Now I learn you're just some waitress who owns a diner and motel in Blue River. Do you know I could get in trouble with the State Bar for sharing sensitive information on a case?! I don't care what you heard or what you know, you've put me in a really bad spot."

"You just hold up yourself, *Lavi*," she said sternly. If Lavi expected she'd fold, he was dead wrong. "First of all, I did not say that I was a detective. That was on you. Second, you have not been doing your client any favors trying to make an innocent man plead a deal. And third, I have been out gathering evidence and got those DNA samples that you and those priceless detectives should have done, and now my house has been shot up by some skinheads."

"What?!"

"Yes," Mabel went on. "And one of those skinheads is Don Sigmundson, and that's who I think murdered Karen." Then she went on to describe why she suspected him and the threat made at the farm. "Now that I've called the State Police, they'll go over to his camper and search for evidence, maybe find the knife that was used. And now you'll have a new suspect thanks to me. There!"

After a moment of silence, the irritation was back in Lavi's voice. "Mabel, none of that is admissible. Even if the police go over to his farm and look for the weapon that shot your house, they can't simply do a blanket search related to the Karen Thompson murder. They can only get a specific warrant on what is probable. Any self-respecting judge would toss it out. At best, you can get him for shooting up your house, but the murder angle is pushing it." He sighed. "I should have stuck with the deal."

"But I have the evidence."

"I just told you! The police can't use anything they find."

"No, I got it before."

Then she explained her ruse about the draw prize.

Lavi heard her out. When he spoke, his voice was quiet. "You got all that?" Another pause, then: "When can you get that to me?"

"I can drive it up tomorrow morning, first thing."

"Okay, I can use that. But you need to do something for me. You can't be a witness on this case who's trying to solve a crime. That'll get me disbarred." He thought about it some more. "Here's what you do. Get a PI license."

"A what?"

"You heard me. I know someone who owns a registry, and he owes me some favors. Come up to Seattle tomorrow. He'll register you with a private investigator's license. It'll be temporary but good enough. How much do you charge?"

"What? I don't understand?"

"You need a PI license, and I need to pay you."

"But I don't need money. I have my own business."

"That's not the point," Lavi said. "I have to pay you to be legitimate. Does two hundred a week sound fair?"

"I-I-I don't know."

"Well, it isn't. It's cheap," Lavi said. "I'll make it three hundred. Most of the good ones charge that. You need to invoice me as well."

"Oh, dear," Mabel said. "I don't know what you mean."

"It means you are now officially a private detective under my employment. I can now share information with you relevant to the case. Any information you collect can be collected and processed through my office. So bring those samples to me and get that license and start getting as much additional information as you can about Don and any other characters and send it my way. The trial begins in three weeks, and we need to get moving on this. Any questions?

Mabel held her hand to her forehead, her head spinning with all that had happened tonight.

"Good," Lavi continued. "Now, you go look after your family. And Mabel?"

"Yes?" she asked weakly.

"Welcome to the private detective business."

CHAPTER 31

Thursday, October 23

Two days later, the State Police had just finished up their interview with Mabel, and while she had the politeness to serve them pie and coffee, she was furious. The State Police had not even shown up at the Larson farm till early this morning without a warrant. And without it, they couldn't search the farm, or so they told her. Mabel thought it was all BS, but she held her tongue. She respected the law, and they were its representatives and should be afforded some courtesy and a slice of pie.

When they left, the house was quiet. The kids were all at school, and its emptiness made her reflect again on how close they'd been to getting shot or killed. The silence reminded her of what it was like taking Kerry back to her dead parents' place after her mom's funeral. How all the life it once had was gone and would never come back — no laughter, tears, yelling, nothing. A home is meant to be full of sound. It meant your family was there and thriving. This emptiness she did not like.

Through the taped, bullet-scarred window, she watched Sheriff Dan's cruiser pull in. Though everyone knew who was ultimately responsible for the drive-by shooting, Dan had made no arrests.

She hadn't expected much from him but wished he would have done more. It was time someone stood up to Larson, so she would tear a strip off Dan again to get him to do it.

She went out to the porch and waited for him to get out, waving once to Carlos sitting in his truck, keeping watch over her place. For the past two days, Carlos' mine crews had been taking shifts parked in front of Mabel's house and yard. None of Larson's men had returned, though there'd been at least one suspicious vehicle loitering on the far side of the highway. When Carlos went to confront the driver, it had pulled away. If Larson's men were thinking of returning, they had these construction workers to deal with now. As she had told Sally, "Arming a man with a gun ain't enough to give a coward courage."

When Dan got out, he didn't walk up immediately but instead opened his cruiser's back door to let a young boy out. It was Hector — a glum, embarrassed Hector, by the looks of it. Mabel's heart fell. Hector had his arms crossed and moved only when Dan directed him to. As they drew close, Dan tipped his hat to Mabel and propelled Hector toward her.

Dan said to the boy, "You got something to say to

your ma?"

Hector stood mute, angry, and scared.

"Speak up," Dan prompted as Mabel added just as sternly, "The Sheriff asked you a question."

Hector whispered, "I got in trouble." He fidgeted a bit, then continued. "And I broke a window."

"You broke *several* windows. And you shot up some mailboxes too," Dan said.

"What!?"

Dan nodded to Mabel. "The Hudgens boys reported their gun stolen. Said Hector took it. Shot up some mailboxes. Then they saw him throw rocks at a neighbor's window. Broke three panes. A couple of other homes too."

"That's a lie!" Hector shouted.

Mabel dragged him closer by the collar. "Don't you dare say the Sheriff is lying!"

Hector burst into tears and sobbed, "No. Not him. Isaiah and Jacob. They told me to break the windows. And they gave me that gun to shoot those boxes!"

Mabel's heart ached for her son at the thought of Frank using his boys to make an example of Hector. "Are you hurt?" she asked, patting him down. "You're not hurt, are you?"

Hector shook his head, wiping away tears, and so Mabel pulled him in for a hug and whispered into the top of his head, "We're going to be talking about this. Those Hudgens boys are not good for you."

Hector started to cry. "I know. They're liars. They told me to do it."

Mabel kept rubbing his back gently and then looked

over at the Sheriff, who glanced away. She eased down on one knee to look into the face of her scared, hurt little boy, and give him a soft smile.

"You're not mad?"

Mabel wiped his cheeks. "No. I am not mad. Not at you. But we are going to talk about what you did. You shouldn't hang out with those Hudgens boys in the first place, and doing what they ask of you is just plain foolishness. You're not a follower, son. You are a leader. But they took advantage of you, that I'm sure." She kissed him on the forehead. "You go into the kitchen, so I can talk to the Sheriff. But don't think you got off just now. There is going to be punishment for breaking windows. We're going to have to pay those families back and apologize."

"Ahhh, mom," Hector pleaded.

"This is a moment to remember, Hector. You did wrong, and you're going to have to do right again. Now git." She tapped his bottom to get him going. She glanced at Dan and then stood up straight. Sadness, anger, and guilt coursed through her at once. She had a diner shift to get back to, but it looked like she would have to cancel it.

"I warned ya," Dan said. "I hate to say it, but I warned ya."

"I know you did. But they're coming after my kids now."

Dan examined her before he took off his hat and slapped it against his leg. "I talked to Larson."

"When? Before those Hudgens boys did this? You know they didn't think of it themselves. That was Frank. Or even Larson."

"Talked to Frank too. He wants charges laid."

Mabel scoffed. But when the Sherriff didn't react, it scared her. She asked, "But you're not going to. Are you?"

The Sheriff grimaced before he put his hat back on. "No, Mabel. I'm not going to charge your boy. I told Frank to give it up. Said you're going to pay for it all."

"Thank you, Dan," Mabel mouthed, tears of shame and relief coming to her eyes.

"Look," Dan relented. "I agree with you. You and I both know who's doing this. Larson is right pissed because you're putting his operation at risk. Keep this damn foolishness up, and you won't be no civilian to his drug business no more. You'll be a thorn in his side. You don't want that. You're hurtin' his profits."

"He's destroying this community."

"No. He's invested a lot in this community. Owns part of the mill, most of the farms, the gas station. He employs a lot of people here — good families who need the paychecks. Besides most of the—" He stopped, glanced around, and then whispered the rest "—drugs he makes he sells in the big cities, not here. And from what I can tell, he hasn't moved too much into the harder stuff either, which is good for all of us."

"Did you just hear yourself talk?!" Mabel said, furious. "You're the law. And you're turning a blind eye to his drug dealings?!"

Dan growled back, "I'm trying to protect our community. You think one person can stop a man like Larson? He's got the Staties in his back pocket." He rubbed the back of his head to calm himself down and almost pleaded with her. "Look. It's not easy here, Mabel. Sometimes it's only me between you folks and him. You need to know that I'm trying here."

"I know what you're trying to do," Mabel said, sighing. "I know you're well-meaning." Then she broke down with emotion. "And I know what you just did for Hector."

She came down the steps and gave him a hug.

"You can't be hugging no sheriff," he protested but didn't resist too strongly and then, in the end, gave her a little hug back. "Mabel, you need to look after your motel and diner, and your kids. You're a pillar of this community. Someone special here. I don't want to lose you. I made sure Larson knows that. But I can't keep stopping him if you get into his business. I warned him I'd also stop turning a blind eye if he goes after civilians, but you get into his business, you're not a civilian. Get it?"

Mabel nodded, gathering her emotions as she started to think it through. Dan could only do so much. She needed to go directly to the boss instead. She needed to talk to Larson — in person. Looking at Dan now, she felt sorry for him. He wasn't brave, he wasn't ambitious, but he was still a good man, and she appreciated him.

"I'll tell you what I'm going to do," she said. "I'm going to make this window and mailbox thing right. We'll pay for all damages and apologize. Then I'm going to make sure Hector doesn't spend any time with those Hudgens kids. Good?"

"And you've got to put this Winston thing to rest."

"I'm not going to lie to you. You need allies, Dan,"

she said. "You've been taking this on alone for too long."

Dan's voice broke as he said, "I do my best."

Mabel ended the conversation. "You coming Thursday to do your paperwork?"

"If you'll have me."

She smiled. "Of course. An extra scoop of ice cream on your pie? For your troubles?"

Dan stood straighter and hitched up his pants with one hand as he adjusted his hat. He seemed like a new man now that he thought Mabel was going to back down, so Mabel didn't tell him otherwise.

"You're the best," Dan said.

"I know," she said and smiled back.

Dan got back into his car, and she watched him go, waving to him out of respect before he drove up the highway. Then she looked in the direction of Larson's compound, and her hot mood turned ice cold.

CHAPTER 32

Saturday, October 25

Mabel spent the morning with Hector apologizing to the families, arranging to repair the damages, and handing out pies. She had raided her freezer and almost emptied her stock, but she wanted to make things right. The families had a friendly, "Boys will be boys" attitude to the situation, but that wasn't the reputation she wanted in Blue River. The one positive of the morning was that on the drive, between apologies, Hector had talked about a lot of things — how he was glad his Dad wasn't around but still missed him, his loneliness at school with only the Hudgens' kids being his age, his dislike of schoolwork. It was a series of good mother-and-son moments, which made Mabel regret not having made an effort to spend more one-on-one time with him. Hector knew now without a doubt that his so-called friends had betrayed him, and he was probably going to be a lot lonelier for it. So Mabel knew she needed to step up. She needed to work less and spend more time with Hector, Fred, and Kerry. Once this murder case was done, she told herself, she'd ask Sally to take more shifts so she could spend it at home.

But not today. Today she asked Kerry to watch the boys at Lisa's house, and after dropping Hector off, she drove on alone, steeling herself for what she was going to do next.

Confront Larson.

To tamp down her growing anxiety, she put an unlit cigarette to her lips and let her mind wander. She thought of Winston's trial coming up fast, too fast. The day after the shooting, Mabel had handed over the spent beer can, cigarette butts, and prints to Lavi's assistant, Janice. She worried that the DNA tests might take weeks to process in the lab, it being so new, but Janice assured her Lavi was on it and said, "He's more energized now." Maybe he just needed a kick in the pants, Mabel thought.

Another man who needed a kick in the pants was her husband. While Bill was a softy at heart, respectful and knew how to treat a woman, drinking had made him mean, prematurely grayed his hair, and aged his face older than his fifty-six years — though at least the rigors of the prospecting business kept his body energetic and strong.

And while he'd stopped his drinking finally, he was just too set in his ways. That's why relationships are so complicated, she thought — no one is ever so bad or so good; there are always shades of gray. And while most folks around here are good, for whatever reason, they go down the wrong path, or get complacent or fall into harmful patterns, and what makes them decent or good somehow gets forgotten. It's like Pete and Sarah. When did they buy into Larson's hate? And why let him get away with selling drugs to their son?

Maybe this mine will change things, she thought, driving past it. At least working at the mill or joining Larson's gang won't be the only option for Blue River's kids. But maybe I'm just all rosy-eyed about it. Maybe leaving is the only answer for the young — unless someone steps up.

After twenty minutes, she pulled off the highway and drove down the long straightaway to Larson's compound. For all his money, his complex was nothing more than a wooded acreage with a series of interconnected trailers and a single industrial-looking building. He was married but had no kids. His wife kept to herself, looking beaten down and unkempt when she showed up in town. Mabel worried about her.

The gravel parking lot was filled with cars and trucks, but no black ones. A dilapidated bus was parked on one end, piles of dry wood and spent metal rods stacked at the other, with various trails of plastic waste and crumpled beer cans leading into the woods in-between. If Larson were trying to destroy his own land, she thought, he was doing a good job of it.

She parked opposite two skinhead guards near the front door of the trailer complex. These two had a more professional air, watching every move she made.

She let out a long, slow breath.

She tried walking past them to knock on the door, but

one of the men halted her by lifting his palm and shaking his head. "You're in the wrong place," he said. It wasn't a question.

"I'm here to speak to Larson."

"He expecting you?"

Mabel shook her head.

"Then get along. You're definitely in the wrong place," he said, pointing back to her car. "You should have kept driving on the highway."

Mabel wanted to turn and leave but then thought of her kids and what she had steeled herself to do. To stop herself from running, she made it final.

"I'm the one who called the police about the Sigmundson farm."

That caught his attention. He examined her with a sense of disbelief and wonder and then nodded at his partner, who got up and walked into the house. While waiting, the guard kept his gaze on her, but she merely turned away to prepare for what was to come.

The door finally opened, and the second guard gestured for her to follow him inside. The hall had doors leading to stark offices on either side, dirty and well-trodden industrial floors, and walls plastered in posters advertising concerts of punk rock bands with white power ties and slogans. While most of the concert dates were in the past, they were still relatively recent, and represented most of the communities around Blue River — Larson's influence was spreading.

The place felt evil.

The skinhead led her to a door at the end of the dark hall. He walked in first then stepped aside.

Larson was sitting behind a desk. He had the eyes of a wolf, a heavily pitted face, and a receding, wispy hairline. A girl who reminded Mabel of Karen was sitting on his lap. Another older man was leaning against a bookshelf. He looked like a biker, with his leather vest and long, gray ponytail. There were no windows in here, which, when coupled with the harsh glare of industrial lights above, made it feel like an animal's cage.

Larson eased the girl off his knee, and Mabel got a closer look at her as she left. She was about eighteen, if that, with tattoos and face rings — and downcast eyes. Mabel wondered if she were a runaway here against her will.

Mabel had been keeping her hands together to prevent them from shaking, but seeing the young woman, practically a helpless child, in the man's lap, awoke a mother's fury in her.

"Was that your daughter?" she asked, throwing disgust at him.

Larson grinned and then swiveled in his chair to face his partner, who chuckled in return. Then Larson returned a mocking gaze to Mabel. "So you are the busybody interfering in my honest business."

Mabel snorted at the word 'honest.'

"Well?" Larson prodded, his voice both soft and menacing.

"Some of your gang shot at my house," Mabel said. "I've got kids."

Larson glanced over at his partner, and the older man spoke up and asked Mabel, "Are you wearing a wire?"

"A what?"

The older man asked the skinhead who'd brought her in. "She been checked?"

The man shook his head.

"Check her."

The skinhead moved to pat Mabel down, and she protested, "Hey! Git your hands off me!"

Larson growled, "I need to know you're not wearing a wire."

Mabel did not want to be touched, feeling horribly vulnerable, but finally relented. The man patting her down was a professional, yet his touch made her feel violated and exposed.

The man shook his head at Larson.

Larson nodded and then said her name, relishing every syllable, "Mabel Davison." He turned to his partner. "This woman has cost me some business."

Mabel felt her chest constrict. This was starting badly, but she kept on. "I want my children protected."

"In exchange for…?" the older man asked.

"That's it."

The older man kept speaking. "You going to get into our business again?"

"What do you mean?"

"You called the cops on one of our farms."

"They shot up my home. They deserve to go to prison."

"That's not how we see it. You came to them first. Why did you go?"

Mabel had no answer — she didn't want to admit it was to collect evidence on his men. So, she replied with a question. "What do you know about Karen Thompson

— the girl that got murdered at the mill?"

The old man said, "We know that Winston kid got caught. Why do you care? You stopped our boys from having some fun at the Sheriffs and punishing that n—"

"Don't you dare say it trash!"

The old man growled back. "You got some nerve."

Larson held up his hand for silence and then turned to Mabel. "That ain't your business."

"It is now. The boy the police have charged is innocent."

Larson examined her up and down. "And exactly what do you think happened?"

Mabel's mind was racing, wondering what these two knew about the murder. She thought of the girl that had left the room, how she reminded her of Karen. Did these men prey on young girls from the highway, too? Were these the killers?

"What do you know about Karen?" she asked back, ignoring his question.

"There are lots of city girls that travel the highways," Larson said. "They're runaways looking for a new daddy. They should go back home. I tell them that. But if they persist, I take them in like any good Christian."

Mabel scoffed. "What do you know about being a Christian? Wicked things are going on with your drugs, your farms. You pervert God's word to take in these naïve girls and angry boys and use them for your own gain. How dare you talk about God?"

"Don't you talk like that," the older man growled at Mabel.

Mabel ignored him and kept her gaze on Larson. "Did

you know her?" she asked. "Did she come here?"

Larson's humor came back, and he softly chuckled. "This is what I'm going to do," he said and leaned forward. "You're not a threat to me, and so I'll forgive you for what you've done until now. But now you're on watch. I've been good to this community, but maybe I've been too good. I'll let you decide. You say you care about this place? You care about those kids? Then stay out of my business. For all of your sakes." He directed the older man to escort her out.

"You don't own me," Mabel said.

Larson's humor left him as his eyes bore into hers. She shifted as she stood there, feeling the power of his gaze. But thinking of her kids kept her standing proud and prevented her from running away or backing down. After a long moment, he seemed to sense that she would not give in.

"No," Larson replied finally to her. "But I own everyone else." He turned to the older man and said, "Get her out of here, Eric." Then he zeroed in on her. "You've been warned."

As the older man bullied her out the door with his bulk, Mabel warned, "If you dare harm any child, mine, or others, you'll regret it. I'm not afraid of you."

It was not until she was well into the hall when Larson warned her back, "Be careful now. I know where you live."

CHAPTER 33

Driving home from Larson's, Mabel didn't know what she had accomplished. Whether or not Larson or one of his cronies killed Karen, Mabel had made herself more of a target, and that scared her. That man had an army and wasn't afraid of pulling a trigger, so what was she doing acting like a detective and putting her family at risk?

Mabel didn't have an answer. Except that Karen's parents needed to know the truth, Winston needed to be free, and Mabel couldn't simply turn a blind eye to the drugs anymore. Evil was right here in Blue River. It wasn't just a distant concept to talk about in Sunday service. And if she continued to turn a blind eye like her community, the evil would grow stronger and infect her children. Someone had to put a stop to Larson.

As she parked in front of her house, a large man loomed up on her porch. Oh, Lord, what now? Mabel thought, her fear rising again.

Then she felt a thrill.

It was her Bill.

He was wearing a muscle shirt and khaki pants, hair looking whiter than usual against tan muscles. He looked damn fine. She wondered what he was doing here since Kerry and the boys wouldn't be home for hours.

When she got out of the car and walked up the steps, her breathing hitched. She needed to put her hand to her chest. Bill looked so earnest and contrite that her defenses were down before she knew it. Moving quickly, he crossed the porch and took her in his arms. Mabel resisted, but his familiar embrace was comforting, and he smelled so good. From the horror she felt at the Larson farm to being here with someone who was good and kind and treated women right, he overwhelmed her.

Bill looked in her eyes. "I miss you."

Mabel half-heartedly pulled away, but then he kissed her, and she closed her eyes and felt it deeply. She pulled him closer, then leaned to whisper into his ear, "Get in."

Bill looked shocked, comically so.

"Hurry, before I change my mind," she laughed, then opened the door. "It's not locked," she said, leading him upstairs.

An hour later, lying beside each other in bed, Mabel felt settled, and so did Bill, though he seemed almost too at ease, which bothered her a little. She wanted him back but certainly hadn't forgiven him yet.

"When do the boys get home?" Bill asked, lighting a

cigarette, which Mabel had always disapproved of.

She turned the clock towards her. "In two hours."

"It'll be good to see the boys," he said.

His confidence bothered her, not wanting Hector and Fred to be put through the hell of seeing their dad if nothing had changed.

"Did you stop the drinking yet?

Bill took his time answering, taking a deep drag off his cigarette. "Yep," he said.

"That's good to hear. But why come back now?"

"Because you, Mabel, are the light of my life. I've missed you."

Mabel blushed. "And the kids?"

"I miss my kids. It's good to be back."

"Where were you?"

"Prospecting. Caught a few good ones that I might be selling at the Minneapolis trade show coming up end of the month."

Mabel frowned because travel was hard on him, and he tended to drink more when he was away.

"Are you going to keep off the booze?"

Bill's brow creased. He looked over and said, "I'm off it. I made a pledge."

"So, you're trying to change?"

"I have."

Mabel breathed a sigh of relief. She reached out and touched Bill's arm. "I'm so glad you came."

"How about you? How are things going here? One of your motel guests came up to me after I drove up. Questioned who I was when I sat on your porch. This guy Carlos didn't believe I was your husband at first." He sounded a little jealous. "You don't mention me or what?"

"Sorry fool like you?" she asked, then smiled to take away any sting, and he chuckled, and his jealousy was gone. He had too much confidence to be jealous for long.

Putting his arm around her, she rested her head against his chest. After a few puffs of his cigarette, he said, "Heard about what happened. If I'd have been here, I'd have given those skinheads a beating, gun or no gun."

"I know you would. How did you hear?"

"The Sheriff."

Mabel's brow creased, not liking that.

He took the last drag of his cigarette before he got up and headed to the bathroom.

She asked after him, "Dan talked to you?"

After he flushed the toilet, he said, "Told me about Hector too."

"So, you came because Dan asked you to?"

"I came because you need me. I'm here to help."

"I don't need any help. You know I can take care of myself."

"I know, but these guys are serious, and you need a man in the house to protect you and the boys. Look at Hector. That boy needs more discipline."

"What do you know what he needs? Those Hudgens kids put him up to it."

"No son of mine follows other people's orders. He needs to learn to think for himself. Be a leader."

Mabel leaned up on her elbow. "Now, Bill. You know I didn't like how you were treating those kids. That mine—" Bill started, and Mabel realized the subject was still a tender one "—got you mad. And that mine's here to stay, and I've got a motel full of construction workers building it. Can you handle that?"

Bill sat down on the edge of the bed and put on his t-shirt. "You asked me to stop drinking, and I stopped. Don't ask me to not care about that mine. I do, and I can't help it."

"It gets you angry, Bill."

"Of course, it does."

"But you treat the kids way too hard when you're angry."

"And you're too soft on them. Tough men are threatening this home. How can you stand up to them alone? Let me do it."

Mabel didn't like where this was going. Sure, threats had been made from Frank Hudgens, from Petar, and now from Larson, but she handled them, and whatever Dan thought, she didn't need Bill for protection.

"I've been working and doing my best with the kids since you've been gone. I've handled things as best I can."

"Yes, because you kicked me out."

"Because you were too hard on the kids."

"Look, you are a kind-hearted soul, and I love that about you, but this is a tough, man's world. Those boys need to know it."

"They do know it!" Mabel said. "Your boys know it. Hector is hurting because he has no friends."

"Then he shouldn't have been following them like a lamb in the first place. He needs to be his own man."

"That's the problem. He's trying to be, but he's just a

boy. He needs a stable presence."

"Then let me come back! I miss you all," he pleaded, his voice breaking. "You asked me to stop drinking. I stopped drinking. What else do you want?"

She started to regret letting him in the home but kept her voice gentle as she began getting dressed. "I know you're trying. Getting off the booze is a start — a very good start. But there's so much more. You need to tell Fred and Hector that you love them, and you're sorry. Those boys need to hear that."

Bill sat there for a moment and then sighed heavily. He started to put on his jeans as he said, "My dad didn't coddle me or say he loved me. I didn't get no special treatment. My boys need to learn this world is hard. Those boys need to be made into men, too, like my dad did for me."

"Those boys need love."

"They got you."

"They need more — from you. I need more too, Bill. For the kids."

"Ugh! I don't know what you want. You ask me to stop drinking, and I stopped. But I am who I am, and how do I change that?"

"That's it," Mabel shot back. "I need *you* to change."

She glared at him from across the room, not wanting to put her kids through this fighting again. If Bill was going to come back, it had to be better than this.

Bill looked at her for a long moment, and then his gaze shifted and fell. He put on his boots. "I suppose nothing's changed between us."

Mabel softened, wanting him to stay. But it was not

enough, she needed more.

After another long silence, Bill nodded, went to the door, and then hesitated, glancing back but not looking into her eyes. "Tell them... I dropped by. Tell them... well, you know." Then he left.

He stamped down the stairs and out the front door, but she didn't follow him. She collapsed on the bed, still warm and smelling of him, and had a good cry. Then she wiped her cheeks dry, stripped the top sheets off the bed, and went downstairs to put them in the wash.

CHAPTER 34

Friday, October 31

Friday morning, a few days after Bill had left, Mabel was simultaneously talking to Lavi on the phone while baking cookies for a Halloween kids' party later that night. And with only two weeks left to Winston's trial, the news about the fingerprints wasn't good.

"It's not a match."

She fiddled with the long phone cord and peeked inside the oven. "Are you sure?" she asked, followed by a muttered "shoot!" when Lavi confirmed it. "Well, what about the DNA sample?"

"There's no point."

"You've got to try."

"I know, but the test would take at least another week, maybe two, and we don't have enough reason to ask the judge to delay the trial. He'll think we're desperate and

HEART OF A RUNAWAY GIRL

fishing for options."

"Well, we are," Mabel said.

Lavi laughed. "Yes, but the judge can't know that. If we're going into this, I need to be strong and confident in our direction, or he'll dismiss all of my arguments."

"What about Larson? That girl? She looked exactly like Karen."

Lavi sighed. "That's not going to cut it."

"Did you talk to your DEA friends?" Mabel asked. She'd told Lavi about the drug operation and how the State Police had messed things up.

"Mabel, you can't be taking on a drug lord as well. We need to focus here."

Mabel reluctantly came back to the case. "I guess I'm just disappointed because I thought for sure the fingerprints would come back positive."

"I know, but who else is on your list? There's Lee Wallach, Cole Smithson, and now Larson, or someone connected to him."

"Lee's connected to him."

"Okay, focus on Lee then. Same thing, get his fingerprints, DNA, and find out if he has an alibi."

Mabel pressed her fingers into an aching temple, having no idea how she was going to do that, but she said only, "Yes, I'll get it."

"Good," Lavi said. "I'm going to reach out to the prosecutor as well. Float the idea of a deal."

Mabel's mouth opened to protest but then thought of where they were at and stayed quiet.

"Don't worry. I'm not going to take it just yet," Lavi said, reading into her silence. "I'm just saying that we

227

need one of the other suspects to come through. Fastest is fingerprints. Then we get a delay for the DNA."

"Delay for the DNA," Mabel repeated, trying to convince herself this was possible. "Okay, Luv."

"If you do that, I'll help you with Larson and get the DEA agent to contact you," Lavi said, then hung up.

Mabel rubbed her forehead to ease the ache until she smelled the burning cookies. "Oh no!" The cookies were black and smoking, so she used a towel to grab a tray and burned a finger pulling the tray out. She turned on the faucet and soaked her finger. Then pounded her fist on the countertop as the tears came, but the pain was not why she was crying. She felt like a failure because she needed to get to Lee but did not know how.

The flushing water soothed her finger and she looked over at the uncooked cookie dough.

Then she had an idea.

Within the hour, she had packed fresh-baked, Halloween-themed cookies into a basket, put on her Halloween costume for the day — the pink-haired pop star, *Jem*, from a popular kids' TV cartoon Fred watched — and was on her way to the mill. When she entered the front office decorated with hanging skeletons and *Friday the Thirteenth* horror masks, Consuela purred, "Ha ha, perfect." Consuela was dressed up too, like Madonna from an MTV music video.

Mabel smiled. "Love yours too, dear."

The office was empty except for the two of them, rare for here, so Mabel got right down to business. "Don Sigmundson came up short, Luv."

"Oh, the fingerprints didn't match?!" Consuela said. "I

thought it was him because he sure doesn't treat his girlfriend proper. I can tell you that."

"I know. So now I'm on to Lee Wallach or Cole Smithson."

Consuela frowned. "Lee's also one of the new boys I don't like." And then she explained how Lee had been hired only six months ago as part of a new crew replacing the seasoned regulars, and most of these were not as good at their jobs as the men they'd replaced. But the mill was running three shifts for the lumber needs of one and even the laziest worker like Lee could scrape by without causing too much of a bottleneck. Consuela couldn't understand it. How could a mill operate so poorly yet still be a money-maker? Management was debating in whispers whether this was becoming a money-laundering operation for Larson. But so far, Consuela didn't know for sure. "And that boy is a really angry guy, I can tell you that," she said about Lee. "Almost got into a fight with Jim Brown on the conveyor. And for nothing much at all, really."

Mabel shook her head in disgust. "Probably because he's black, dear." Consuela nodded. Then Mabel added, "I need the same as what I needed from Don. This DNA evidence, and don't ask me what that's all about. Mainly, I just need something he touched, so some lab tests of some sort can be done on it. Does Lee Wallach leave a lunch in the kitchen I could sample?"

"No," Consuela said. "Never."

"Does he drink coffee? Maybe raids the cookie counter?"

"He rarely comes into the office. A bit of a loner. But

if he hangs out with anyone, it's with his fellow skinheads out on the mill floor."

Mabel put her basket of cookies down on the counter. "Okay, it's like I thought. I'm going to have to go out to him. Do you have an extra coffee thermos and a pushcart?"

Consuela nodded.

"Let's get the coffee going. I have an idea."

After taking Consuela's mandatory worksite safety briefing, Mabel pushed a Halloween-decorated cart with coffee and cookies out into the mill where crews were hauling and stacking massive logs. Inside the building, each log was hoisted onto a conveyor and then violently sheared with a large saw. Lee Wallach worked the conveyor by himself.

Mabel recognized the area where Karen Thompson had been found, broken and abused, from the crime scene photos Mabel had seen. Her resolve hardened to what she had to do: spout racist filth to get on Lee's right side. Larson drew men like Lee in by perverting the grace and righteousness of religion to do wrong in God's name. These boys were probably looking for a savior, and they'd found one in Larson, who promised money, women, wealth, and purpose. Larson suckered these boys in like the false prophets of Ezekiel's days, and she was about to turn their hate against them.

But to be tactical, she didn't approach Lee right away. Instead, she chose a few men nearby — a couple of skinheads — to serve coffee and cookies to before getting them to sign a petition. The men admired her simple costume — probably because it showed off her ample cleavage. She kept her eye on Lee, who was watching what was going on. Only a few logs were running through the mill right now, and the men could afford to be distracted. Jim Brown approached, but Mabel waved him off, pointed to Lee, and pushed the cart over to him.

Lee was leaning against the conveyer, using the tip of an oversized knife to clean his dirty nails, and she wondered if it was just for show. He had a sallow, scrawny complexion, but there was an intensity to his deep-set blue eyes that promised no pushover.

"Good morning," she said, with a false cheeriness. "I've brought some Halloween cookies and coffee for the boys."

He ignored her until she added, "A gift from Larson."

Lee glanced up, and his rude mouth formed a thin smirk. "Well, then, I guess I'll have one."

She poured the coffee and forced the next words out of her mouth. "I can't believe Larson lets him work here," she said, nodding to Jim Brown in the distance.

Lee took a bite of the cookie. "Yeah. I don't get it."

"It won't be for long," Mabel said. "I got something I want you to sign. It's a petition I'm giving to Larson, so men like the Jim Browns ain't allowed to work here no more."

"'Bout time," he said. "Sure, I'll sign." He wiped his hands on his pants and took the clipboard and Mabel pointed out where to sign so his prints would be the only ones on the page.

"Do you have a girlfriend?" Mabel asked, hoping it didn't sound too practiced.

Lee spat to the side and shook his head.

"I can't believe some of our women date those kind," she added, nodding to where Jim Brown was working.

"Beats me."

"You know the girl murdered? She was dating one of them. Died over there, I heard." Mabel pointed in the distance where her body had been found, but Lee didn't look.

He examined Mabel but didn't say anything. Mabel wondered if he was getting suspicious. He'd finished the cookie, so she took his napkin. "More coffee?" she asked, then poured it before he answered, feeling his gaze still on her. She carried on. "When the shift, uh, shut down that night cause of the break, did you, uh, head over to Curt's too? With the rest of the crew? I heard a few had went."

Lee sipped his coffee as he stared at her. When he finished it, he handed it back and then finally broke the disconcerting silence. "Why ask about her?"

"Who, hon?" Mabel asked absently, using a fresh tissue to take his used coffee cup and place it carefully away from the others.

"Karen."

Bingo, Mabel thought, but kept acting casual. "No reason," she said. "She deserved what she got for dating out of her race. Especially with good guys like you around." Her skin crawled, hearing herself speak like that.

"Hey, you're the woman Larson warned us about."

"Ha ha, why would he do that, dear?" Mabel asked, nervous but trying not to show it.

"You're the woman who went to the farm."

232

"I don't know what you're talking about."

Lee grabbed her arm with one hand. "You own the diner. You're the waitress. I recognize you now."

"You're hurting me."

He was up close to her now. "You lying bitch," he said, touching the tip of his knife to Mabel's arm. "You women," he said, disgusted. "You're all the same." Then he released her.

Mabel rubbed her arm, and they stared at each other until Jim Brown shouted over to Lee, "Get ready, I got a log for ya."

Lee waved off the man as he kept glaring at Mabel. "Be seeing you," he said, then added, "Shame about Winston. He sold a lot of weed for us. But what do you expect from a guy like him."

He knows Winston! Mabel thought.

"Was he here?" she asked.

Lee smirked then shrugged. "Got work to do."

"Was he here?" she asked again.

He ignored her by moving towards the log on the far end of the conveyor.

Mabel wanted to chase after him and question him further about Winston, but the realization that Winston knew Lee and this mill had rocked her, and she got the cart moving and didn't look back until she'd reached Consuela's office.

"You okay, darling?" Consuela asked. "You look pale."

Mabel nodded. "I got what I needed," she said, showing Consuela the coffee cup and the signed petition.

"Wow," Consuela said. "Can't see what all that is for.

But you don't sound too happy about it. Did Lee tell you anything useful?"

Mabel thought about whether Winston had lied to her and had known the sawmill all along. "I don't know."

"I'm sorry to hear that, dear. Because that night, most of the boys went to Curt's so…" Consuela's words trailed off as her eyes flashed with some kind of insight, and then without another word, headed into the office, leaving Mabel to pack the evidence into bags and label them carefully. Consuela returned with one of the Mexican maintenance men. "This is Manuel," Consuela said. "He was at Curt's that night."

Manuel was a family man with two kids. He blushed. "Beg pardon. I'm sorry for going to those places, but that's where my boss goes."

Mabel stopped packing and briefly touched his arm. "Oh, don't worry about that. Curt's my friend. So, was Lee Wallach there that night?"

Manuel glanced around. Since Larson bought the mill, men like Jim and Manuel seemed to lose their jobs, only to be replaced by Larson's gang members. Consuela prodded. "We won't tell. Was Lee there?"

"Yes. But he left early — he told the boss he had a date."

"A date?" Mabel asked, not expecting that. "Who?"

Manuel shrugged. "He don't talk to me. I don't talk to him. Is that all? I got work to do."

He was clearly uncomfortable being asked these questions, so Mabel thanked him, and he left.

She turned to Consuela, who said, "I've never seen a girl wait in the office for Lee. He brought no one to the summer barbecue, either. You want to see if he's got an alibi for that night, right?" Mabel nodded. "What if Lee was going to see Karen?"

Mabel frowned. "But Karen was with Winston."

"You said the black truck was parked in your lot, right? Just waiting? Was Lee a customer that night?"

"Him? No. And I wouldn't want him as a customer either."

"Was Karen expecting someone that night?"

Mabel shook her head. "Winston told me what they were talking about. She wasn't seeing anyone. But..." She paused. "He did say Karen thought she was being followed."

"I wouldn't put it past a character like Lee to be watching a woman."

Mabel nodded slowly. "You mind if I use a phone? I'm going to call Winston's lawyer about this."

"Sure, Luv. Use the phone in the side office there. You'll get some privacy."

Mabel went over to the office, shut the door, and dialed the lawyer's number.

"Lavi, it's Mabel."

"You know only my mother calls me Lavi," he admonished gently.

"I like it. It suits you. Now let me finish. I got the samples for Lee."

"Lee Wallach? Already?" His voice brightened. "That's good work."

"You better believe it," Mabel said, then described both what had just happened and her and Consuela's suspicions about Lee, but nothing about what Lee had told her about Winston just yet — she had to think about that first.

"It'll be great to know who his date was that night."

"I know. I'll find out somehow."

"Well then, I've got news for you," Lavi said. She heard him flipping through files as he explained, "I got a hold of Lee Wallach's record."

"And?" Mabel's hopes went up.

"Nothing criminal." Mabel deflated, but Lavi wasn't done. "But it turns out he grew up in Seattle, not too far from the Thompson family."

"Dear, lead with that, would ya?! That's a connection. Have you found a confirmed link between the two? Have you talked to the parents?"

"Well, Mabel. I was hoping you could."

Mabel hesitated, thinking about the grieving couple. "What's their address?"

He told her, and she wrote it down, all the while thinking of all she had to do for tomorrow: ask Sally to take the Saturday shift, organize dinner, leave a reminder note for Kerry to cook it, drive to Seattle in the afternoon, talk to Karen's parents, get back to have dinner with Fred and Hector and let Kerry take the car to see her friends. My God, that's a lot, she thought. In the meantime, Lavi had been talking to her, and she missed it. "What, sorry, dear?" she asked, flustered.

He laughed. "I said a lot, but essentially I meant good work. You're putting my other detectives to shame."

"Oh!" she said, embarrassed. She wanted to deflect the praise as she usually did with any compliment, but her friends had been calling her on it, so she just said,

"Thanks, Luv."

"Trust me. You've earned it," Lavi said, and hung up.

Mabel didn't think so, reflecting upon her conversation with Lee. She then thanked Consuela and left the office, deep in thought. As she drove off, Lee Wallach was at the warehouse door watching her, and she wondered again if Winston had lied to her — about whether he had known about the mill all along.

CHAPTER 35

When Mabel returned to the diner, which had been plastered in Halloween-themed decorations of monsters and skeletons, it was chaos. Irate customers were waiting to pay at the counter. Sally, wearing a skeleton outfit, was crying in the kitchen while Kevin, dressed as a pirate, was consoling her.

"What's going on?!"

"Oh, Mabel," Sally said between sobs. "It's Sarah."

Mabel's hand flew to her heart. "Is she all right?"

"No. It's… her son — Wade. He's… he's dead!"

Mabel froze, shocked, then teared up. Sally, still crying, rushed over for a hug.

"I'll take care of the diner," Kevin said, and then went to the front, grabbing an apron and leaving Sally and Mabel alone crying together.

"How did it happen?" Mabel asked, finally pulling away.

Sally blew her nose with a tissue, then handed the box to Mabel. Mabel took one and dabbed at own her eyes, as Sally said, "It was an overdose."

"Oh my God, no!"

"Yes. I heard from Beatrice just before you came. Pete had found Wade unconscious in his trailer yesterday morning. They had just come back from a treatment center the day before. Pete rushed him to the hospital, but it was already too late. I had no idea."

Mabel winced, picturing the burned tinfoil, the spoon, the lighter, and Wade's manic behavior. Finally, she admitted, "I did. I found Wade in his trailer on drugs a few weeks back. I took him to Sarah's, but she already knew and—"

"How terrible!"

Mabel nodded. Tears stopped her from going on; she wished she could have done more.

Dabbing at her cheeks, Sally asked, "Should I get the girls together?"

Mabel reached out to touch her arm and nodded. Knowing how hard it was for grieving families to take care of themselves, Mabel had a group who did their best to make it easier for families in need by cooking a week's worth of dinners and dropping them off.

"I'll call Patty and Angelica to come by," Sally added, leaving Mabel alone in the kitchen.

Mabel bowed her head and prayed for Sarah and Pete and the strength to help them. Then she slowly put on her apron and started preparing the meals.

Later that afternoon, with the help of Sally, Angelica, and Patty, a week's worth of dinners and lunches and trays of muffins were prepared and loaded into Mabel's station wagon. After changing to regular clothes, she drove her friends to Sarah and Pete's. It was a solemn drive, each sharing a story about Wade, born in Blue River, schooled there, and now to be buried in its cemetery. Since the town's preacher had died from cancer last summer, the preacher in Edmonston would have to do the service, so the funeral would not likely be for another week or two, at the earliest.

Although Mabel knew Sarah the best, she talked the least on the journey over, holding in a terrible secret — that Sarah and Pete knew Larson's men supplied the drugs Wade had overdosed on. Though she suspected Sarah and Pete must hate Larson now and would have nothing to do with him, it was all too late for Wade, and for the horrible damage done by Larson to the hundreds, if not thousands, of families like Sarah and Pete's, who had family members using the harder drugs Larson was manufacturing, distributing and selling.

Sarah and Pete's farmhouse, a half-mile past the roadside trailer complex Wade had lived in, appeared so isolated and forlorn, only accentuating the loss the parents must be feeling. The gravel parking lot was full of cars and trucks. Mabel was surprised, not realizing how many friends Sarah and Pete had.

But as she parked at the end of the long line of vehicles, a crowd of young skinheads spilled out the front door, and behind them Larson himself. The women gasped. The skinheads made their way down to the cars, laughing and ribbing each other, then got in, except for one who held a car door open for Larson. But Larson remained on the porch, surveying his domain, then lit a cigarette, taking a long drag.

Pete came out next, looking stricken and worn, and waited till he had Larson's attention. Larson put one hand on Pete's shoulder and said something to Pete like he was bucking the man up. Pete, with his head down, just nodded. Then he shook Larson's hand.

"What nerve!" Mabel cried. "Pete should be throwing Larson off his porch rather than showing him any respect!"

Larson strode down the steps, head held high like he hadn't a care in the world, infuriating Mabel even more. She moved to get out and tear a strip off him, but Sally held her back.

"Mabel! Don't go out there!"

"Do you see that filth!?"

"That's Larson!" Patty said, deeply afraid. "You can't go out there."

"It was his drugs that killed Wade. I saw one of those skinheads give Wade drugs. It was Larson's men, all right. And I told Sarah—"

"Really?!" Sally gasped. "Did Sarah know?"

"And Pete still shook his hand?" Patty added, shocked.

"It's not their fault — Larson's to blame," Mabel added quickly, but the damage was done, the secret was out, and she immediately regretted it.

Larson got into the car and was driven away, and Mabel could have sworn Larson had seen her and smiled, disgusting her.

With the lot now emptied, all three women got out, and as Mabel opened the trunk, she said, "I didn't mean to tell you that Sarah and Pete knew. I know how tough it must be for them. Please don't say anything."

Sally nodded, and Patty put her arm around Mabel. "Don't worry. We understand."

Mabel teared up. "I just feel so bad for them." The other two put their arms around her shoulders, and they stood there for a moment, side by side, solemnly thinking of the couple. Then Mabel opened the trunk, and they each picked up a tray of food.

Pete came over to help. He appeared even more wan and distraught. "I see you brought food," he said, his voice breaking.

Mabel nodded, tearing up with him. "I'm so sorry for your loss."

Pete broke down, and the three women consoled him until he could regain some composure.

"Larson just left," he said, wiping his face.

Mabel's anger at Larson overcame her sympathy. "What did that animal want?"

"To talk business."

"Did he apologize, at least?" Mabel spit out.

Pete shook his head, staring at Larson's car merging onto the highway in the distance, then he started to sob again. "Oh my son," he cried.

The women tried soothing him, and as they did, Mabel's anger at Larson finally gave way to grief for Pete. He was inconsolable now, so Sally and Patty led him back to the house. The cold food in her hands seemed an empty gesture now. A week's worth of meals was not enough for this family to get over the shock, let alone horror of this loss, if they ever could.

Mabel solemnly walked into the house, and they went back and forth to the car bringing the rest of the trays. Sarah did not appear, and Pete just sat there in a chair, half in shock, but thanked them when they were done. Then all three women made their goodbyes and left.

Mabel felt terrible. Terrible, they had to deal with Larson and all his evil. Sarah and Pete had suffered under his domain, were still suffering, and would suffer again. It was clear Larson had come here to protect his business interests: he owned them; he owned the rest of the town.

While driving away, Mabel looked back and glimpsed Sarah, stone-faced, in the upper story window. Mabel waved, but Sarah did not, a forlorn prisoner to her grief — and to Larson's reign.

CHAPTER 36

Saturday, November 1

The next morning, Mabel spent the ninety-minute drive to Seattle thinking over what she would say to another set of grieving parents — Isabelle and Jack Thompson. She half-expected they might slam the door in her face. After all, Mabel was advocating for a person charged with killing their daughter. They were probably looking forward to closure with the upcoming trial, and now she was going to upend their world.

Recalling the parents had dressed as though they were middle-class, their neighborhood was anything but, with its wailing police sirens and boarded-up properties. She had to stop several times to get directions before she finally made it to the Thompson home, which was nicer than most.

A few kids played on the street. A lone dog barked in

the distance.

Mabel got out, a tin of fresh-baked cookies in her hands, and noticed every detail — the frayed welcome mat, the wreath on the door made of wilted flowers, the lawn overgrown and weedy. While the parents might have kept the grass trim at one time, their everyday world must have come to a full stop after Karen was murdered; any chores thereafter must have seemed meaningless. Already overwhelmed by emotions herself, she couldn't imagine what Isabelle and Jack felt.

She knocked on the door and heard movement inside. It took longer than expected, but the door finally opened. Karen's mother, Isabelle, looked older and frailer than previously, with dark puffy bags under her eyes.

Mabel said, "I'm sorry to bother you. But my name is Mabel Davison. We met before."

The mother's forehead creased into a frown, yet she was polite. "Yes, I remember. You were the waitress in Blue River."

Mabel nodded. "I, um, I wanted to follow up with you. I have… some questions."

Isabelle didn't seem to hear. "They let us bury our daughter. Finally."

Mabel instinctively reached out to touch the other woman's arm. "I'm so sorry for your loss."

Isabelle nodded, near tears, but didn't say anything.

Mabel extended the tin of cookies, which felt so inadequate after the shock of Isabelle's divulgence. "I wanted to bake something nice for you. For you and your husband."

"Thank you," Isabelle said, and her politeness got the

better of her grief. "Would you like to come in for some tea?"

Mabel thanked her and stepped in, noticing right away a heavy, unsettling silence hanging over everything inside, amplifying any noise to an unnatural disturbance. She removed her shoes though Isabelle said there no need. Mabel wanted to show respect.

The mother led Mabel into a barren, dusty kitchen, and Mabel wondered if they were eating. Isabelle seemed frail and was moving slowly, filling the kettle and putting it on to boil. She asked what type of tea Mabel liked, and Mabel took the opportunity to cross the room and touch Isabelle's shoulders in a comforting gesture while she picked a teabag from the selection. Isabelle leaned into Mabel's touch briefly before they sat down on either side of the table.

Only a ticking clock and the gurgling kettle broke the kitchen's stillness.

Isabelle glanced at the clock, so Mabel got right to it. "I'm so sorry for your loss."

The mother nodded slightly but didn't say anything.

"May I ask you questions about your daughter now?"

Isabelle dropped her gaze to a set of prayer beads in her hands and moved them one by one. "The detectives talked to us a few weeks back," she said, frowning. "We are a good family, you know."

Mabel tried to soothe her. "I can see that."

Isabelle started to tear up as she added, "Those detectives. They don't know what it's like to be a mother. To bury a child."

Mabel felt the twist of Isabelle's pain. "I have two

boys myself. And my niece lives with us. Kerry is around Karen's age, and I can't imagine what you're going through."

"Make sure you hug them."

Mabel nodded and blinked back tears, thinking her own tears weren't worth a grieving mother's.

"I didn't hug my daughter," Isabelle went on. "The last time she run out. We... had gotten into a fight. And now she's gone. She was a good girl."

"I know," Mabel said softly. "That's why I'm here."

The women locked eyes for a moment until the kettle shrilled, startling Mabel but not Isabelle. Isabelle got up slowly to turn off the stove and went about making tea. Her hands were frail and delicate but had a strength to them as she poured the tea into two cups, then she smiled slightly. "I remember you poured my coffee the last time."

Mabel was surprised she remembered, and it seemed like a peace offering of sorts. "I've been thinking of you," Mabel said. "Ever since you and your husband came by my diner. And I think of Karen, too. Often."

Isabelle's hand touched Mabel's. "Thank you," she said. "Now, tell me. What questions do you have?"

Mabel breathed out, and everything she had prepared to say went out the door, and she spoke from her heart. "The detectives say they caught the boy that killed your daughter, but I think they've arrested the wrong man. I'm here to ask you questions about other suspects." Mabel paused to gauge Isabelle's reaction.

The unnaturally loud sound of the ticking clock filled the silence between them. Isabelle's expression flickered from sadness to anger to pain. Mabel wondered if she was going to ask her to leave.

But when Isabelle finally spoke, her voice, starting in the barest of whispers, grew stronger as she carried on. "I… I got Karen's effects after she passed — the detectives had dropped them off. And there was this poem in her purse from that boy, Winston. A love poem. So I thought maybe it was a crime of passion, that maybe this Winston killed her over a stupid lover's quarrel. I don't know. But then I think of what was done to her… it was a real beast that did that to her." She sighed and glanced down at the beads in her hands. "Now, you think it's someone else?" Mabel nodded but did not interrupt. "So, who? Who hurt my girl?"

"I think…" she started to say and then stopped, uncertain. At least she could test the names to see if Isabelle recognized them. "I think it could be one of several men. A Cole Smithson, a Don Sigmundson, a Lee Wallach and—"

The mother started. "I know that name."

Mabel leaned forward. "Yes, Lee works at the mill where… it happened. He has a black truck, too." Then she realized that there were details of the investigation that Isabelle would not know, so she explained. "After Karen had a fight with Winston, she took a ride with someone in a black truck, but the detectives didn't really follow up that lead. I did. I found out who owned most of the black trucks in town, and three of them worked in the sawmill. Including Lee Wallach. I spoke to him yesterday."

The mother nodded, pointing a frail finger out the

window. "He used to live a few blocks down. He knew Karen. They played together when they were kids."

"He didn't tell me that," Mabel said. "He made it seem like he didn't really know her."

"Oh no, he definitely knew her. He was a delicate boy, thin and a bit of a loner. But my Karen liked to take in the awkward boys."

"Yes, well, he's now hooked up with a group of white racists. The man who leads them preys on weak boys who should know better."

The mother frowned. "That doesn't sound like him. As you can see, our neighborhood has all types. He had friends of color growing up."

Mabel hadn't considered Lee's racism to be a more recent thing. "He had black friends?"

The mother nodded. "So did Karen. Karen didn't care about the color of one's skin. If I remember correctly, that boy shadowed her like a lovesick puppy until his parents moved him away. He hasn't been around for several years."

"So, Karen would know him to see him?"

The mother nodded.

"Did Karen mention anything about him? Did they keep in touch? Is there anything about this boy Lee that you can recall?"

Isabelle seemed frozen in her chair as she considered it but suddenly nodded and got up. Beckoning Mabel to follow, she walked down a hall lined with family photos of happier times. Then she opened the door into Karen's bedroom. Karen was only sixteen when she was killed, but the room seemed frozen in time to that of a twelve-year-old or earlier, reflecting a younger, more innocent age. The well-used *Cabbage Patch* dolls on the shelves and the faded *She Ra Princess of Power* bedspread didn't reflect her teenage troubles. It wasn't surprising then, Mabel thought, that her mother had been shocked by her use of drugs.

Isabelle walked to the table and picked up a book. It was like a diary or a calendar, with a lot of writing inside. Mabel sat down beside Isabelle, who flipped through pages until she found the one she was looking for. The calendar page was dated several months ago and read, 'Call Lee.' Mabel felt a thrill that this was something important. "When did Karen leave?"

"A few days later," Isabelle said. "I didn't think this was anything important." She flipped through the other pages, tearing up. "Karen wrote down all her get-togethers with friends in here until she left. I was surprised she left this. But I think she wanted to put her whole life behind her." Then Isabelle broke down and sobbed.

Mabel reached out and hugged her until the sobs passed, and she regained some of her composure. "I'm sorry," she whispered. "I'm just an old fool."

Mabel squeezed. "No, you are a wonderful woman. I imagine your daughter thought the same." Isabelle shook her head, so Mabel went on. "The 'hope' tattoo proves it. She was going to come back to you."

Isabelle wiped the tears from her cheeks. "How do you know?"

"I looked into her eyes," Mabel said. "I have a gift. I can read people."

"So you think Lee Wallach did this?" Isabelle asked.

Isabelle and Mabel locked eyes. Mabel replied, "There's something about Lee that bothers me, and I'm going to find out about him, one way or another."

Isabelle placed her daughter's journal into Mabel's hands and folded her own hands on top of Mabel's as if it were atop a bible and squeezed hard. "You find this man that killed my daughter," she said. "Promise me this."

Mabel cleared her throat and nodded. Then she vowed, "I won't stop until I do. I promise you."

CHAPTER 37

Saturday, November 1 to Sunday, November 2

Mabel left Karen's house and made her way to a payphone at a local gas station to call Lavi and share the news. Lavi then arranged for his assistant to meet Mabel the next morning in Tacoma to hand over Karen's diary and Lee Wallach's fingerprint and DNA samples. He thought her evidence credible enough to get a delay to the trial's start even if Lee Wallach wasn't the one. As promised, Lavi had talked to a DEA agent, who had agreed to meet Mabel at her diner to discuss Larson. Lavi said the agent, named Tyrone Jackson, knew the Larson case well.

With those two pieces of good news, Mabel was too excited to sleep in the next day. Bright and early, she called Lavi's contact at the DEA and left a message on his machine. Now Mabel had only two things left on her

Sunday to-do list: pick up stock and supplies at the distributer in Tacoma and hand over the potential evidence to Lavi's assistant.

Due to the number of supplies needed, she'd borrowed the cook's van to do it all in one trip. She liked to be efficient that way.

A semi-trailer blew past her on the highway, startling her at first and then spurring her on; she was tired of being left behind. She put an unlit cigarette to her lips, floored the accelerator, took the rising grade with speed, and passed the semi near the top of the hill — what a thrill! The semi eventually passed her again on the downgrade, but it didn't matter. She'd had her fun.

She leaned back in her seat, unlit cigarette in hand, and noticed how swollen and unkept her hands were when once they'd been so thin and long with perfect nails. And though she'd be surprised to learn that most folks still considered her a stunner, it didn't really matter to her, not anymore. The soft light in the rear-view mirror highlighted her emerging wrinkles and stray gray hairs, and she considered them well earned.

An hour later, she'd arrived at the meeting spot. A relatively new, fancy coffee chain out of Seattle that sold mostly coffee beans, had the same name as Fred's favorite sci-fi TV character, and had a mermaid figure as a logo — go figure, Mabel thought. She sipped her coffee but didn't think it compared to her own. Lavi's assistant, Janice, was already on her second cup. In her early fifties, Janice was older than Mabel, and was dressed like the admin assistant she was — in a nice tailored suit. Mabel's evidence was in a box beside Janice, next to her purchase of roasted coffee beans.

Janice was doing most of the talking, mainly asking questions about Blue River, but when she finally took a breather to sip her coffee, Mabel asked one of her own. "So how is Lavi doing?"

Janice finished the sip and said, "I never really think of him as Lavi. It's always Mr. Arronson. Only you and his mother call him that. Have you met her, his mother?" Mabel shook her head. "Typical old Jewish lady. Dresses nice, hard on her son. Good gal. Keeps him on his toes. Which I guess you do too." She patted the box. "I must say, I haven't seen Mr. Arronson so engaged in a case in years. Normally, he's making excuses about why he's going to lose, but I think this case has been good for him. He's trying again, which is nice to see. How did you do it?"

"I don't know. I just told him he would be a better man for trying."

"That's it?"

Mabel paused her sip and then smiled wryly. "Well, I may have used my motherly charms on him too."

Janice laughed. "It worked. He's even trying these new-fangled DNA tests that a colleague of his published in some law magazine. They've only been used in Florida once and made a big splash. Expensive as all get out, but Mr. Arronson's set on it — paying extra for faster processing. Usually, our office is under budget by thousands, but he's spending it now."

"That's good to hear, Luv," Mabel said, happy Lavi was trying.

Janice nodded and then went silent and toyed with her

cup. She frowned, and her next question seemed to come out of nowhere. "What makes you think the boy is so innocent?"

"Winston?" Mabel paused. "I met him."

"I met him too. In fact, I deposed him actually — I took his original statement," she said, explaining it for Mabel, who didn't know what a deposition was. "It's a rare honest criminal who admits he's guilty from the start. And with him? I don't know. He has a long rap sheet. Drugs. Theft. He's not an innocent man. But guilty of murder?" She shrugged. "I've found working this job that most murders are committed by someone you know. Mr. Arronson has defended fathers, boyfriends, friends, women, all who killed loved ones — and almost all said they were innocent at first. It's a strange business being a defense attorney. It's about due process, he used to say. But he had a bad one once. Got a guy off who was guilty, and then the guy raped and killed another woman. That hit Mr. Arronson hard. He kept defending clients, but he lost his edge and didn't talk about due process anymore. So I don't know," she sighed. "It's nice to see him trying again, but I worry about him. If Winston isn't innocent…"

"What are you saying? You don't think he is?"

Janice tapped the box beside her. "What if all this evidence doesn't implicate a new suspect? What then?"

"We keep trying."

"What if there isn't another suspect?"

"What do you mean?"

"I've seen Mr. Arronson hit rock bottom before. I don't want to see him like that again."

"So you think Lavi should make a deal for Winston?"

Janice looked uncomfortable. "No. Not exactly. But I guess what I'm asking is how do you know he's innocent? What makes you so sure?"

"Well—" Mabel started but then asked herself how she really knew. Had she ever investigated a case before? All she had was her intuition. And what about Karen's mother and father, the people most traumatized by Karen's death? What if her hunch was wrong, and Winston was the killer? Mabel looked at Janice and said, "I promised Karen's mother. I promised her closure."

"Maybe she has it already, Mabel. Maybe Winston has been guilty all along."

"But I looked into his eyes."

Janice scrutinized Mabel. "Is that enough?"

Mabel touched her heart. "I think so."

"I hope to God you're right," Janice said. "For all their sakes."

Mabel remained silent, unsettled.

Then Janice made her goodbye and left.

Mabel spent the next hour in a daze, shopping for flats of frozen food and fresh vegetables worth hundreds. It took her longer than usual, distracted as she was, asking herself again and again, 'Was Winston really innocent?'

All she had were her instincts — no detective she, only a waitress in a small town in the middle of nowhere. She had no training, no special skills. All she did every day was serve people food and drinks and get to know them better. That was it. She was good at reading people, but she had no formal education beyond grade eleven. The police had already looked over all the evidence. She only had an idea a man was innocent, and no facts to back it up, not yet. And now it could be that the boy had lied to her all along.

She started the drive back to Blue River, with the day turning to dusk and the long shadows of the fading sun stretching out across the highway. But it was a long drive ahead — at least an hour at top speeds. The traffic eased once she had turned onto I-67 — the forest-lined highway that climbed up a tall ridge of Dead Man's Peak to fall on the other side to Blue River, the Long Lake, and beyond — making it a lonely road to Blue River and only a stopping point for most, and not a place to stay or visit long.

Mabel drove up the mountain's tallest ridge. At the top was a scenic view for tourists to gaze at the road descending in windy curves down the forest ridge to pass the new mine, and then her motel and diner and then on past Blue River. She had followed its longer track beyond to the coast once. Bill had taken her on a vacation before the kids were born. It was a fantastic trip, stopping at campgrounds, meeting new people, going for hikes, and spending time with each other. Hector was a result of that trip. She smiled, remembering how close she and Bill had been. He was often out in the field in some far-off country working as a geologist, and Mabel didn't really mind. Leaving it late to have kids had made people think they couldn't have any, but Mabel had just wanted to wait. She had a business to run and all. Now he was gone again, this time to Minneapolis, and likely he wouldn't be back till after its trade show — but she knew he would come back, he always did. And she'd always be there too, waiting for him. But if he still hadn't changed, she wouldn't let him stay long, not yet — well… maybe for an hour or two again, she thought, with a languorous smile.

But her boys needed a dad, more so than she needed a lover. She worried about them — well, mostly about Hector. At least Kerry's help was welcome, and while she was starting to do more around the house, she had also made it clear she was leaving as soon as she finished high school. Part of Mabel minded, part didn't, because she'd love Kerry to stay, but Kerry cared more about the larger world beyond a small town and needed to leave. Having suffered greatly from her parents' deaths, she needed more happiness in her life. She thought university might do that, though Mabel honestly couldn't advise her on it. Mabel had stopped schooling early to take care of the motel and diner after her dad had become sick, and her larger world was only Blue River. That was all she needed. Yet what was in Blue River for her kids once grown? For Fred, she had no worries. She expected university like Kerry. But for Hector? University wasn't really in the cards. The logging industry was dying, the mine only getting started. Yet what was the life of a miner for her eldest son, if that was what he was to become?

She didn't know. Only the hope it was a better life than one ruled by Larson.

She drove on.

With the man owning half the town already, she didn't want her sons to fall into his trap. If she could, she'd break up his empire in a heartbeat. But she wasn't so naïve. Even if she could somehow ever do that, that would devastate many families and likely gut this community. Those families supporting the drug trade now, like Sarah and Pete, weren't bad men and women. They'd just lost their way. Sarah and Pete hadn't seen the harm the harder drugs were doing to folks in Seattle or Tacoma, where Larson sold his, until it had affected their own son.

But even then, they kept supporting Larson.

She gripped the wheel tighter.

"The allure of money alters the morals of man." She recalled the words of Preacher Dave from a Sunday service long ago. And Larson had a lot of money.

She drove on.

She thought next of the girl sitting in Larson's lap that day, wondering whether she was another runaway that had run into the Larson gang and got stuck. She couldn't imagine she was there by choice, not anymore. At times, Mabel had caught herself searching for the girl in town. Hoping that she would find her and bring her back to the motel, to rescue her, if she wanted it. Because who knows what crimes Larson was hiding out there? He was into drugs, he was into abusing women, and he might be a murderer. Was Karen killed on Larson's orders? Was it a hate crime or about profits?

Mabel looked out at the darkening forest, the open, cheery wood of the day melting into the moodier, darker shades of night. She shivered, driving on, a little faster now.

But even in her current state of loneliness, and of fear of the unknowable darkness, she came back again and again to what Janice had said: "Was Winston innocent?"

She thought about Lavi helping a guilty man go free and then finding out the man had then raped and killed another poor soul. She made a face at how terrible it would feel, starting to understand why Lavi had lost his desire to defend indefensible crime.

And why was she defending Winston, really? Was it because he was black? Maybe after all this, it had been a crime of passion. Maybe he was guilty and she was the one blinded by his skin.

What if Janice was right? That question stayed in her mind for the rest of the drive.

Her motel and diner lights flashed bright and clear past the bend. It always brought a soft smile to her face to see them. A welcoming feeling at night, the neon lights, soft and comforting, advertised home. And while reasonably early for the evening, the mine crew's trucks were parked in front of her home like a blockade, making her feel safe and protected. She doubted Larson would pull another drive-by shooting here. If it happens, she thought, he'll get me on the road or in town. That made her turn ice cold, not for herself but out of anxiety for her children. Larson was not someone who cared about the innocent. If he now labeled her his enemy, she better make her kids more aware. She'd talk to them tonight. Tell them to be more careful and not to linger in town.

If this were to be a full-on war with Larson, she'd better be ready.

CHAPTER 38

When Mabel got back to the house, Kerry was sitting on the couch eating a *Hot Pocket*, with the synth sounds of Duran Duran's *A View to a Kill* escaping from the Walkman's headphones.

"Did you make dinner like I asked?" Mabel asked her.

Kerry lifted the headphones, and Mabel winced at the volume.

"Huh?" Kerry asked.

"Did you make dinner for the boys? I left a note."

"What note?"

"It was on the fridge. I made a vegetable lasagna. All you had to do was put it in the oven."

"Sorry. Didn't see it."

"What did the boys eat?"

"Hot Pockets," Kerry said, replacing her headphones.

"And, oh yeah, Halloween candy."

Mabel bit back a response. She went into the kitchen to confirm how Kerry could have missed the so-obvious note on the fridge, but it wasn't there. After a brief search, she found it under the table. She sighed, not able to get mad at anyone but herself. She rolled up her sleeves to clean the mess, thinking that at least the lab evidence was off to Lavi, and that was something — no matter what Janice had said.

After cleaning the dishes, she noticed another note in Kerry's handwriting on the table. It had a phone number and the word "emergency." Mabel went back into the den. "Who called?" she asked, but Kerry couldn't hear with the headphones on, so Mabel mimed at her to take them off and had to repeat the question once Kerry petulantly did so. "There's no name, and it says emergency," she added.

"I don't know, some girl who didn't want to leave her name," Kerry said. "Wants you to call her. Said it was urgent."

"You could have told me when I walked in," Mabel said, irritated.

"I left a note." Kerry pouted as she put her headphones back on.

Mabel growled, intending to give Kerry a talking to after she got off the call. She went back to the kitchen and dialed the number on the wall phone. Six rings in, she was about to hang up when a girl's timid voice came on the line. "Hello?"

"Hi. This is Mabel. You called me earlier?"

Silence.

"Hello?"

"Yes," said the girl meekly. "I have something to tell you." A pause. "That girl. Karen. I know who did it."

Mabel nearly dropped the phone. "Oh my gosh. Who is this?"

"I... I can't tell you."

"Then who did it, dear?"

"It was... I need to speak to you in person."

"Can't you tell me now? We can go to the police."

"No! No police," she said, panic in her voice. "I need to meet you somewhere."

"Well, why don't you come here? To the diner. It's safe. Lots of people around."

"No. You need to go to... where she died. To the sawmill."

Mabel was shocked. "Why there?"

The girl sounded muffled like she was talking away from the phone.

"I can't hear you, darling. Why there? The diner is much safer."

"Be there in ten minutes. Come alone." Then the line went dead.

Mabel looked at the phone, then redialed the number, but it just rang and rang. She put the receiver down, wondering if this was some crank call. She'd had a few of those in her time at the diner — asking for a Mr. I. M. Butts and Mrs. B.O. Stanks, that sort of thing — but this did not feel like a prank. The girl sounded scared to death, that's for sure. She looked at the time. It would take her ten minutes just to drive to the mill.

Mabel made a snap decision. She went into the other

room and sat down beside Kerry and gave her a look that meant business. "Take them off for a second, hon," she said, indicating the headphones. "Do you still want to see Lisa tonight?" Kerry nodded, breaking into a smile. "Then I need you to take the boys with you and drive me to the mill."

"Ugh, with the boys?! Why? I don't want to babysit when I see Lisa."

"It's an emergency."

"Okay, okay." Then she added, confused, "Wait. What? The mill? Why there?"

"That girl who called wants to meet me there alone."

"That sounds weird."

"I know. I'm going to call the Sheriff and ask him to meet me there. Then you can drive over to Lisa's place if you want. You don't have to wait."

"Yes!" Kerry said, pumping her fist, and got up quickly to run upstairs.

"But I've got to leave now!" Mabel shouted after her. "Don't take too long!"

Mabel called the Sheriff, but there was no answer, so she left a message on his machine to meet her there. Despite her plea to hurry, it still took Kerry five minutes to change and grab her things. By then, Mabel had the boys in the car. She started the engine as Kerry came tearing out of the house putting on her jacket and hefting her backpack. Then Kerry came up to the driver's side window hands held in mock prayer as she pleaded to drive. Mabel gave her a look, then nodded and got out of the car.

"Thanks, Auntie!" Kerry said sweetly, kissing her on

the cheek.

Mabel couldn't help but smile as she went around to the passenger side. "Book it, though," she said. "We're late."

"It's too hot back here," Hector pleaded from the back. "Can you open a window?"

Mabel cracked hers as they took off and breathed in the fresh forest air. Having been on the go all day, it was good to collect her wits before meeting this girl.

When they pulled up to the mill, only one other car was in the parking lot. The office lights were off, and only a few scattered dim security lights were on in the processing building, which had no walls and a peaked roof, and only the black profiles of vast machinery and tall stacks of lumber visible inside.

"You said she wanted to meet you at the mill, right?" Kerry said, now fully realizing the seriousness of it all. Mabel nodded. "You sure you want to go in there?"

Mabel tore her eyes from the scary darkness and put on a brave front for the kids. "No. But I called the Sheriff to meet me here so don't worry, dears, I'm only going to wait out by that car for Dan to show up."

"You sure?" Kerry asked, concerned. "This place seems pretty spooky."

"What? With all I've been through?" Mabel tried to laugh it off. "I don't seem to scare so easily anymore. Here—" She patted Kerry's arm. "Go to Lisa's, call the Sheriff, and tell him that he needs to pick me up right away. I'll be waiting outside. If this girl shows up, great, if not, I've only wasted some time. Deal?"

"If you say so," said Kerry, hesitant.

"Mom! Aren't you coming too?" Fred pleaded.

"Yeah, Mom!" Hector said. "I don't want to go to stupid Lisa's!"

Mabel turned around. "Boys! This is an emergency. Go to Consuela's, and I'll be there in no time. Make sure you listen to her and to your cousin too. And Kerry, don't you forget to call the Sheriff." Before Mabel had completely shut the door, she noticed their frightened little faces and added in a softer tone, "Be good. I love you."

The station wagon's tires kicked up dust and gravel as Mabel watched them turn onto the highway. The distant engine's sound faded under the chirping of crickets and the soft whistling of the wind through the logs and cutting machinery. A chain jangled lightly then went silent. She shivered and crossed her arms, but not just from the cold. Creepy *Friday the 13th Jason* horror hockey masks covered the office windows and the dark depths of the open-air warehouse were eerie.

The messy contents of the lone car offered no clues as to the identity of its owner. Mabel wondered if the girl's instructions, 'to meet where Karen had died,' actually meant inside the mill. She checked her watch. The Sheriff might be another twenty or thirty minutes. She felt foolish just standing there when the girl might be inside. Plus, she was getting more impatient — and colder — by the minute.

She moved closer and peered through the open entry leading to the processing facility.

"Hello?" she called out timidly.

Her soft voice disappeared into the darkness.

She huffed, a little angry for having come. She rechecked her watch. Ten minutes had passed alone. The Sheriff must be on his way by now, she thought. Feeling this was a waste of time, and wanting to get this over with, she decided to head in, check around quickly and then go back up to the road to wait for Dan.

Mabel stepped into the mill, which seemed far bigger and creepier at night. Her vision had trouble adjusting to the widely spaced, dim security lights, and the long, deep darkness between the machines and tall stacks of lumber. She got lost almost right away. After a few twists and turns, she eventually spotted the conveyor belt where she'd confronted Lee Wallach, and beyond that, the large sawing machine where Karen's broken, abused body had been found. A chill ran through her.

"Hello?" she called out weakly.

A chain rattled loudly by the conveyor.

A figure wearing a Halloween horror mask materialized.

"Oh dear Lord! You scared me, Luv!" Mabel said, her heart racing. "Come out in the light girl, and take off that horrid thing and let's talk."

The mask fell to the floor.

Lee Wallach grinned.

Mabel gasped, terrified, and backed up a step before another man's voice sounded behind her. "Got ya."

Mabel whirled around to see Don Sigmundson coming out of the darkness, a lecherous grin on his face. "I told you I was coming for you."

Lee Wallach stepped forward, a knife glinting in his hands.

"Don't you dare touch me!" she screamed, backing away, her breath coming in gasps until she bumped into something sharp and metal — the cutting machine.

Don laughed while Lee warned him, "We're taking too long. Let's get this done."

"Nah, we can take our time. Let's enjoy this."

Mabel looked between the two, her lungs screaming for breath. She tried to frighten them. "The Sheriff's outside!"

"We waited too long."

Don shook his head. "The bitch is lying. We would have heard him drive up."

Mabel glanced everywhere for a way out. She was blocked on either side except for a slight gap at the base of the machinery behind her.

The two men edged closer.

"That girl!" she cried out. "She knows I'm here."

Don laughed. "She does what I say, and no one will miss her."

"I've called the Sheriff! I've collected evidence on you. You're going to jail."

Lee swore and then growled at Don, "Let's get this done."

Don waved him off. "What evidence?" he asked Mabel. "What are you talking about?"

"Fingerprints. Lab samples. And Karen's diary — with Lee's name in it. It's all there. The lawyer has it."

"Which lawyer?" Don growled, eyes ablaze.

Mabel dived under the sawing machine, landing hard on a dirt floor covered in sharp woodchips and slivers. A rough hand grasped her leg. She screamed and kicked.

His grip eased, and she yanked it away just in time as the knife sunk into the dirt. Heavy smells of machine oil and pine suffocated her senses. She crawled deeper into the narrow passage, dark and claustrophobic under the machine, until she dragged herself out from underneath into a small open space where twin cutting blades violently sheared massive logs.

Trapped by the serrated steel, she heard footfalls around her. Then a flashlight beam blasted through a gap underneath at the far end, blinding her. It was Lee. He shouted in a rage, "Come out, bitch! You can't get away."

Still on all fours, Mabel shuddered, almost hyperventilating, and edged away. She turned toward her right, but a long sharp sawblade nearly cut her face, and she backed further underneath the machine.

"I got her!" Don called out and reached down from above. She dodged his grasp, then struggled to get away in the ever-narrowing space beneath the machinery. Frantic, she clawed at the wood chips and slivers to drag herself forward as something sharp nicked the back of her leg, drawing blood. She could hear the men climbing up and over the machinery as they hunted for her, but she changed directions to get away. Fighting back sobs to stay quiet, she dragged herself forward, in pain, terrified, and finally emerged out one side. Don and Lee were nowhere to be seen, but she could see the parking lot ahead in the distance. She scrambled out, got to her feet, and ran.

"There she is!"

Heavy footsteps sounded behind her. She screamed, then stumbled, but held her balance and kept running toward the parking lot, screaming as loud as she could, and — not believing her eyes — saw Dan's cruiser pulling in, red and blue emergency lights flashing, followed by her car with Kerry and Consuela inside.

Dan got out of his car with his gun drawn. "Freeze!" he yelled toward the sawmill as Mabel ran past him and straight into the arms of the two women.

"Freeze, dammit," shouted Dan, and the three looked back to see Lee, knife in hand.

"I'll shoot!"

Lee let the knife go and dropped down onto his knees, putting his hands behind his head, his eyes never leaving Mabel.

"You're hurt," came Consuela's voice from what seemed like a million miles away. "Are you all right?"

Covered in dirt, dust, and blood, Mabel started to feel the pain in the gash on her leg and where the splinters in her hands had dug deep. Cold and faint, she started shaking violently.

Consuela's voice came again. "Kerry, help me put her into the car."

As they guided her in, Mabel saw Dan putting handcuffs on Lee.

"There's two of them!" she called out.

Dan pulled Lee to his feet. He glanced back, but no one else was in sight. Mabel grabbed Consuela. "There's two of 'em. The other is Don." She shouted hysterically, "They're murderers!"

Kerry pulled Mabel in. "It's okay, Auntie, it's okay."

"Kerry," Consuela said again, "get Mabel in the car now and lock the doors."

Mabel shivered uncontrollably as Kerry wrapped a

blanket around her shoulders and sat close to keep her warm.

A sharp rap on the window. Mabel screamed.

It was Dan.

Kerry unlocked the door and Dan opened it. "You okay?" he asked Mabel. She nodded but couldn't speak. "You said there were two of them, right?"

Mabel stuttered. "D-don-on. Don-n Sigmund-son."

"Don Sigmundson," Dan repeated.

"And-d Lee... Lee... Wall-a-ch."

"I got him, Mabel. He's in the car. And we'll get Don, too."

Mabel closed her eyes and nodded, feeling faint. She sunk back exhausted into her seat and then rested her head onto Kerry's shoulder and burst into tears.

CHAPTER 39

Tuesday, November 4

Two days later, Mabel was resting in her den, feet up on pillows, a quilted comforter over her legs. The cut on her leg looked worse than it was but had still required stitches. The doctor had put a couple of stitches in her hands too, where the worst of the slivers had dug deep. Mabel was proving to be a terrible patient, worrying too much about all the work not getting done and getting grumpier by the second. And though Sally had stepped up to take her shifts at the diner and Consuela had dropped off pre-made dinners, it was Kerry — who'd taken time off school — who'd proven to be the biggest godsend.

The boys didn't know the full extent of what had happened, just that their mom had gotten hurt at the mill and needed time to get better. While Fred had accepted this explanation, Hector was suspicious. He'd hang around whenever someone showed up, eavesdropping to get the real story.

Dan's cruiser pulled up, and Dan got out with a wave at her. He'd been alternating with the State Police keeping watch outside since Don Sigmundson was still on the run, and they were worried he'd come for her again. Mabel almost wished he would. Between her protective customers and the police presence, if Don tried anything here, he would be caught pretty quick.

Dan opened the door and admonished her as he knocked the dust off his boots. "You should really lock this door."

"Just come in and mind your business."

Dan smiled, took off his cap, and rubbed his unruly hair. "Got some good news for ya," he said. "I know where Don Sigmundson is hiding out — in a remote trailer in back of one of them Larson's farms."

"That's great news!" Mabel said. Then after a pause, added, "So what are you doing talking to me? Go get him!"

Dan cleared his throat. "Well, them Staties are doing that. Sending two units over now."

Mabel crossed her arms. "Any of them working on Larson's team?"

Dan looked a little uncomfortable. "Some, but they're going to bring him in, I got assurances on that."

"Will they really bring him in?"

"Have to. This is murder."

"Bet they'll avoid the drugs on the farm."

Dan played with the brim of his hat before he nodded. "Thought I'd tell you the good news."

Mabel huffed. "I'd sleep better with Larson and his gang in prison too." She shook her head, looking out the window, not too happy how this was turning out. "So how do you know he's even there?"

"Well now," the Sheriff said, perking up. "Barbara — his girlfriend — called it in."

"I told ya, Dan! She's the one who called me that night and set me up."

"Well, about that… It couldn't be her because she was with her mom. So I don't know who made that phone call to you. But it sure wasn't her."

Mabel wrapped her shawl tighter around her. "Are you sure?"

He nodded. "Talked to both Barbara and her mom, together and separate. Barbara is plain furious — and, to be frank, she's pretty upset that her boyfriend was involved in Karen's murder, not to mention the attack on you. She passes her best wishes to you, by the way." Dan paused for a reaction, but when Mabel said nothing, he cleared his throat and continued. "Don had called her to bring him some food to his hideout, secret-like, and as soon as she got off the phone, she called me and told me where he was."

Mabel shifted in her seat. "Well, that girl who called me that night sure sounded scared. If it wasn't Barbara, which I don't quite believe, those two thugs threatened someone else. You better ask Lee or Don when you get them, cause a girl could be in trouble."

"Will do," Dan said. Then he cleared his throat again and nodded. "Well, I better be off then," he said and rose heavily to his feet. But before he left, he looked down and said, voice raw with emotion, "Mabel, I... I sure am glad you made it out of that mill. 'Cause I don't know what this community would do without you."

Mabel softened and reached out to grasp his hand and squeezed. "Dan, I owe you so much. Not just for me, but for helping with Hector. Thank you."

Dan blushed, stammered a quick, "no problem," and then lumbered out the door and down the steps.

Mabel watched Dan get in his car to take off and said, "Kerry, bring me the phone," and when Kerry dragged the phone over, she added, "And don't you listen, child."

Kerry shrugged, put on her headphones, and turned up her music.

Mabel dialed the number Lavi had given her.

It rang multiple times before a gruff voice answered. "Tyrone Jackson."

"Tyrone. The name is Mabel Davison in Blue River. I think Lavi Arronson spoke to you about me."

"Mabel! Nice talking to you. I hear you've been dealing with one of my star criminals — a Karl Larson. He's a tough character."

"Don't I know it," Mabel drawled out.

Tyrone laughed and said, "Mr. Arronson spoke very highly of you. Said you were one of his best investigators."

"Well, I... I don't know about that. But thank you."

"So, what can I do for you?"

"Are you going to follow the law when it comes to Larson?" Mabel asked, getting right to her point.

"That's a strange question."

"Not if you know that Larson has some influence on

the State Police. So if I tell you things, are you going to ignore them or act on them?"

"Ma'am, Larson has a lot to worry about from me. My team and I represent the whole northwest region, and I know the man well, trust me. Karl Larson is the number one a-hole on my shit list, pardon my language."

"Good," she said. "Because I know something you don't. The State Police are going to raid one of his farms to arrest a murderer, but they ain't going to do anything about the drugs."

"What murderer? I never heard about that!"

"Well, then that's a good thing we're talking, Luv." She told him about what she'd seen at the farm, how it was connected to a murder investigation, and how Larson and his skinheads were harvesting marijuana. "If the State Police don't see all the marijuana in the fields, they'd be blind."

"Okay, Mabel," Tyrone replied. "I'm very glad you called. Here is what I'm going to do. First, I'm going to get a search warrant and send my team out there as fast as I can."

That surprised her. "You will?"

"I've wanted to have a look at one of Larson's farms near Blue River for a while now, and I'm not giving up this chance."

Mabel felt a little faint, not used to being treated so seriously. "Well, that's good to hear."

"Second," Tyrone said. "I'm going to need you to make a witness statement. I can keep you off the record before the court date, but if it goes to court, you're going to have to go on the stand, and I'll be honest, Larson plays rough to witnesses. I don't want to sugarcoat it, but I will do everything in my power to keep you protected as a witness. Do you understand?"

Mabel pumped her fist in delight, ignoring the risk. She said wistfully, "Oh Tyrone, if you could help clean up this community, that would be fantastic."

"Well, let's not get ahead of ourselves here," he said, gruffly but with a touch of pride. "Raiding the farm is only the first step."

"Just get him, dear. You've got my full support."

"Then don't tell anyone about this call. Neither your Sheriff friend nor the State Police."

"My lips are sealed."

"I look forward to meeting you. Mr. Arronson, he, uh, may not have played you up enough," Tyrone said before he hung up.

Mabel danced in place on the couch, ecstatic. Kerry took off her headphones and smiled at her aunt's enthusiasm.

"What's going on, Auntie?"

"I can't say. But it looks like some good news is finally to come to this community."

"Because you talked to the DEA?"

Mabel's face fell. "So, you *have* been listening, you little scamp!"

Kerry smiled mischievously. "*Girl,* you need to learn a thing or two about teenagers." Then she crawled under the quilt beside Mabel and added, "But don't worry, I can keep your secrets."

CHAPTER 40

Friday, November 14

On the day of the trial, after getting the boys settled with Consuela, Kerry raced Mabel to the Seattle courthouse. They arrived just in time. The court was calling Winston's case.

Kerry guided Mabel to the last seats at the back of the courtroom. Mabel's leg was hurting, and her hands were still bandaged, but she felt a lot better with the stitches out. She scanned the courtroom packed with journalists. Lavi had warned her last week that this case was getting national media attention, but it hadn't sunk in until seeing this. She recalled that conversation as she watched Lavi now, in a perfectly pressed suit, standing tall at the defense table, getting ready for Winston to come out. "Mabel, you got it. It's good," Lavi had said over the phone. "While the fingerprint evidence was a wash, the different DNA pulls were a match. First, Lee Wallach's sem—um… you know… the sample of—"

"You can say it," Mabel had prompted. "The semen samples?"

Lavi had laughed nervously. "I can't say that to you anymore. But yes, that. It matched with a 99.8 percent probability it was him. Then the lab matched Don Sigmundson's DNA to the dried blood under Karen's nails. Isn't that great?"

Mabel had imagined instead what Karen must have gone through that night. The horror and terror that young girl must have faced. She didn't want to ruin his good mood during the call, so she had said only, "That's good it was a match, dear."

"Isn't it? And only the second time this has been done in the country, Mabel. It's a big thing. This will be in the textbooks, I bet. The first time this has been used on a case involving a rape and murder." Mabel wasn't too impressed by that, but Lavi was, and so she had just let him talk as her mind had drifted to what had happened since. Don Sigmundson was dead. Having armed himself inside a locked trailer on the remote drug farm, a standoff had ensued. But to the State Police's surprise, the DEA arrived in force to expand the operation to include a drug search.

During the ensuing three-hour standoff, Don asked for his girlfriend, Barbara, but the DEA negotiator wouldn't allow it, worried about her safety. Instead, she got on the bullhorn, pleading with her ex-boyfriend to turn himself in. Less than an hour later, Don had turned the gun on himself.

Mabel shook her head at all this violence. Then recalled the last thing Lavi told her. "Lee Wallach claimed to be an unwilling accomplice to the murder and that Don was its mastermind. No one believed him. I talked to my contact on the force, and he warned me that the charges might not stick — until your DNA evidence came in. When they confronted Lee with the new evidence, Lee broke down and admitted his guilt. Admitted everything, Mabel!"

Mabel had smiled with relief. "That's good, dear. I'm glad this is over with."

"I can't thank you enough. I really can't. It's made me believe in the law again."

Mabel perked up. "I can tell. I'm glad for you."

"And don't worry. I'm going to help you with that DEA case. I will." Larson had been furious about the raid. The DEA arrested several skinheads, including the one who'd flashed a gun at Mabel, and Larson had hired a high-priced lawyer to get them off.

"Yes, it's not the end for him, but at least it was the beginning of folks standing up to him and his gang," Mabel had said.

Now Winston's case was coming to an end, and here she was, a week later, back in the courtroom about to watch it happen.

Her thoughts stopped as the atmosphere in the courtroom turned electric. Winston was escorted through a side door, wearing a shirt and tie instead of a prisoner's orange jumpsuit.

He walked tentatively over to Lavi behind the bench and seemed overwhelmed by all the attention.

The bailiff called everyone to order, and the presiding judge took his seat. He put on his spectacles, then addressed the lawyers. "Mr. Arronson and Mr. Davis, I take it something very unusual happened between the arraignment and today."

Ted Davis, the prosecutor, replied first. "Yes, Your Honor. The defense has brought forward new evidence, and the State no longer believes Winston Washington committed the crime as charged."

The judge looked interested. "So, do you have another suspect?"

The prosecutor replied, "Yes, Your Honor. The evidence offered by the defense implicates a new suspect. Two of them, in fact, but one of them is now deceased. The prosecutor's office is currently preparing the new charges for the one remaining suspect."

"I take it you're sure this time?" the judge admonished the prosecutor.

A few people in the courthouse laughed out loud, and Mabel felt a thrill. She looked over at the prosecutor, whose shoulders sagged a little.

Kerry giggled and hugged Mabel as they looked on.

"Well, then," said the judge, turning to Winston. "Mr. Washington, do you understand that the charges against you have been dropped?"

Winston didn't respond until Lavi whispered in his ear. "Yes... yes, Your Honor," he stammered out.

"Excellent. The State, I am sure, will apologize for the manner of your incarceration."

Winston addressed the judge. "So I'm free to go?"

The judge nodded.

The bailiff started to speak, but shouts of joy from Winston's family and friends drowned out his voice. Lavi shook Winston's hand before family pulled the young man into their arms. The journalists stood up as one and with microphones and tape recorders in hand began to crowd around the defendant. Winston looked about as happy as Mabel had ever seen him.

Lavi pulled away from the group and then introduced himself to Kerry and said to her, "Your aunt is an extraordinary person."

Mabel blushed. "Thank you so much for what you did for that boy."

"It was all you, Mabel. You did it."

Mabel's emotions burst. The case was finished. She just laughed, not knowing what to do. Then she hugged Lavi, who, unused to such affection, awkwardly patted her shoulder in return.

When she released him, he asked her, "Are you sure you don't want to talk to the reporters? This is an exceptional case, getting lots of attention, as you can see."

Mabel shook her head, more than happy to go back to being a waitress. Winston was free, and that was enough for her. "You do it, Lavi."

"All right then," Lavi said. "But don't go far."

The bailiff called for everyone to clear the courtroom. Winston, surrounded by family, friends, and reporters, started to walk out through the press. "Don't you want to talk to him, Auntie?" Kerry asked her.

Mabel looked at Winston as he passed and then back at Kerry. "That's okay," Mabel said. "Let him enjoy his time with his family."

"But you did so much for him."

"It's not what you get for yourself that matters, dear. It's what you do for others."

"Oh, Auntie," Kerry said, taking her arm. "If you're not going to brag, I can at least teach you how to relax."

Mabel smiled and brought her in for a hug and a kiss on the top of her head. "I'm willing to learn, but I'm afraid I've got two boys about to be teenagers and won't have the time to relax. So how about this? Why don't you teach me how to deal with that?"

Kerry chuckled, "That I can do. I'm not leaving yet, I still got ten months before university."

"Then let's make the best of them."

CHAPTER 41

Sunday, November 16

Mabel was still sore from her leg injury and getting used to the physical routine of work again, but nothing would have stopped her from attending Wade's funeral. The service was held at the Blue River Community Hall down by the beach along Long Lake.

The Edmonston preacher's schedule delayed the funeral a week, and though he didn't know Wade personally, he did a fine job. Many folks from around the community had attended — and fortunately, none from Larson's gang.

After the service, the friends and family drove up the few blocks to the Blue River cemetery on the town's edge. The river flowed nearby, and though not yet frozen over, ice spun in its currents. It was a cold day with a thin blanket of snow covering the town, the trees, and the tops of gravestones. As the mourners gathered around the gravesite, their warm breath flashed into cold mists that sparkled in the sunshine. As if there were angels here, Mabel thought. She dabbed at her eyes and held her boys and Kerry close to feel their warmth. Then she imagined how tough it was for Sarah right now. Wade's spirit was no more, and his cold and lifeless body was about to be buried in a casket.

Sarah and Pete held a solemn vigil at the grave's head. While Sarah softly cried, Pete looked silently on, seeming to have aged years in the last week. His son had been his only child, and any hoped-for legacy Pete had wanted to pass on was being buried in front of him, the true legacy of his work with Larson. Mabel's heart reached out to them both.

As the preacher settled in at the front of the gravesite, Mabel thought about Dan's latest warning: Larson had threatened vengeance upon the person who had tipped off the DEA and sworn that the community would pay if the culprit didn't come forward. Although Dan warned Larson to leave it be, Larson was holding firm. And while Dan had not yet asked what Mabel's role was with the DEA, she wondered how long it would take Larson to figure it out — he was no fool.

"Let us pray," the preacher said, starting the service.

Mabel bowed her head and prayed.

CHAPTER 42

Sunday, November 30

Two weeks later, the Sheriff pulled up as Mabel was leaving her house to start her Sunday shift in the diner. The temperature had dipped below freezing, and she could see her breath. She gazed out over the forest to the snow-capped mountains and smelled the fresh scent of pine in the air, feeling good to be alive. She invited Dan to come back inside, but he hung back by his car. "Got to talk to you in private," he said.

Mabel gave him a strange look and let her front door swing closed.

Dan took off his hat and held it with two hands, respectful like. "Got word from the jail. Buster called," Dan said and then cleared his throat. "That Lee Wallach feller. He, um... had agreed to turn State's evidence against Larson."

Mabel was pleased by the news. "I really hope that doesn't affect Lee's sentence. He's being tried for Karen's murder."

"Well, about that…" Dan said, slapping his hat against his leg. "Something else about him. It's… well, somebody murdered Lee Wallach this morning. Another inmate. A skinhead."

Mabel gasped. "H-he's dead?"

The Sheriff nodded. "A Larson man got to him."

Mabel was stunned. She looked off at the mountain that only moments ago seemed so unchangeable, immovable, resolute, and yet that too was a lie. Snow and rain chipped away at its face every season, and someday all this land would be changed — like this case. Her troubled gaze fell to her shoes. Nothing was sensible about Lee Wallach's death. With Lee on trial, Karen's family might have learned why he had killed her, but now, they'd never know. She had no idea what God's plan was in all this.

Dan said, "I'm sorry. He deserved to go to trial for what he did to you."

"For what he did to Karen," Mabel corrected. "*Karen* was murdered."

"I know. But I didn't know her. I know you."

Mabel let it pass. He meant well.

Dan went on. "I talked to the Staties, and they don't know who tipped off the DEA and neither does Larson. But he's looking. And he's staying true to his threat."

Mabel remained silent.

Dan scrutinized her for a long moment and then seemed to struggle with what he was going to say, until finally, he asked, "Was that you? That got them involved?"

"I'm glad someone did it."

Dan stared at her for a moment and then nodded and put his hat back on. "Me, too."

Mabel blinked several times, not expecting that of Dan. "I thought that…"

"I know I ain't the best Sheriff, but I don't want to see the drugs around here no more than you do. It's not good for this community."

Mabel smiled. Dan was finally starting to come around.

"If you need anything, Mabel, just ask." He tipped his hat and backed up.

"Aren't you going to come into the diner?" Mabel asked. "You came all this way… you might as well get some pie."

The Sheriff hesitated then shook his head. "Nah, got a job to do," he said gruffly. Then he got into his cruiser and headed off on the highway to do his rounds.

CHAPTER 43

Tuesday, December 16

Mabel was talking to Kevin when the door chimed twice, signaling a customer's arrival. She looked over and gasped, thrilled to see who it was.

Above the door, the Christmas lights framed Winston in twinkling blue and white light, but he looked as lost as he had at the arraignment. She hadn't expected to see him again.

"Winston! So good to see you. Anywhere is fine, Luv."

He just stood there in his winter jacket, not meeting her eyes. "I ain't looking for something to eat. I'm here to talk to you." She waited till his brown eyes lifted, and she saw his pain. Without a word, she guided him to a booth in the back — the one where he'd sat with Karen all those months ago.

They sat down together, and he spread his hands wide

on the table and just stared at them. She reached out and said, "I'm so glad to see you."

Winston's eyes swam with regret. He cleared his throat and pulled his hands down and said, almost in a whisper, "I just wanted to thank you. For what you did. Mr. Arronson, my lawyer, told me."

Mabel was about to brush off the compliment, but since this was Winston, she said, "I'm not used to getting thanks, dear. I just… I think looking out for people is the right thing to do, and no thanks are needed."

He said slowly, "I heard you were almost killed by those two. And that's something I don't get. I lied to you about some things. So why did you put yourself in danger for me?"

"Because you didn't do it."

"But how could you know that?"

"I looked into your eyes," she said. But she could tell it wasn't enough for him, so she added, "I have a gift. I can read people."

Winston blinked several times and then looked down at his hands again and thought about what she said.

"You're a good person, Winston."

Winston winced. "No," he said. "I'm not. I was a drug dealer. I'm not good. And…" He paused, swallowing hard, and then added, with a sense of guilt and recrimination scarring his voice, "I didn't… I didn't even follow her that night. I… I didn't stop her from getting into that truck." He sighed. "I keep thinking about that night over and over again, and I wish I had done something different. But I didn't, and it's all my fault she's gone." He wiped his eyes to stem the flood of tears, but they only came down stronger. He glanced around, embarrassed.

Mabel tried to console him. "That's because you survived. You're feeling the guilt that all survivors face. It's not your fault."

"I should have done more," he replied, grasping the table's edge with both hands like he wanted to tear it off, but when he couldn't, his anger dissipated, and he sank back into the vinyl seat, defeated.

She reached out to touch him. "You did. You gave her hope."

Winston's tears came again, and he hung his head. Mabel moved into the seat beside him and gave him a long hug as he sobbed into her shoulder. She waited till he was spent, exhausted.

"So, what are you going to do now?" she asked gently.

Winston shrugged. "I'm done with that life I led. But I… I don't know what I'm going to do."

"Maybe you should go to school again? You're a smart man."

"I don't know about that. But I'm definitely getting as far away from here as I can."

His words saddened her. "Someday, this community is going to be whole again," she told him. "Larson and his gang won't always be around, and this will be a good community to live in again."

"Larson has a lot of powerful friends. I can't see that ever happening."

"He has a few enemies, too," she offered.

He shrugged, not believing someone could dethrone Larson. Then he grabbed a napkin and blew his nose.

"My mom is waiting for me in the car. I just wanted to talk to you before we leave for good."

"Oh, your mother's in the car!" Mabel was delighted to hear this. "Please, bring her in. I just baked an apple pie, and it smells delicious. I want you both to join me."

Winston cocked his head back. "Really?"

"Winston," Mabel said, "I want you and your mother to feel at home."

Winston shook his head. "Not in this community. My skin will never make me equal here."

Mabel recognized his truth, more aware than ever that she did not understand his view but needed to. "Someday, I hope, enough of us will understand," she said. "And there will be change."

CHAPTER 44

Saturday, January 10, 1987

A harsh winter carried on into the new year. Mabel's injuries had healed but her nights were troubled by a recurring nightmare that brought her back to the sawmill and her frantic escape from Lee and Don. Often, she'd wake up in panicky starts and suffer moments of wide-eyed terror before realizing she was safe in her own darkened bedroom. Then she would remind herself they were truly dead and tried to take some solace that Karen might now rest in peace.

It was late morning, and Mabel was working the counter of the diner when the phone rang. "It's for you," Kevin called out from the kitchen.

Assuming Sally was calling about taking another shift, Mabel picked up the phone and offered a cheery, "Hi, dear!"

The man on the line sputtered. "Oh, hi Mabel."

Mabel smiled and said, in her singsong voice, "Lavi! Good to hear from you. I thought my staff were calling me."

"Ha ha, no worries there. How are you doing?"

She looked around her diner, with her customers content and Fred and Hector doing their homework, and said, proudly, "Just fine."

"Good," he said. "Because I have a case for you."

Mabel scoffed. "Lavi, I'm done with all that. I've got lots of work to do."

"I know, Mabel. But it's about a girl. Sixteen and a runaway. But it's not the girl I'm representing, it's the mother. She attacked a police officer when he refused to believe her daughter was in trouble, and now she's frantic. She's a poor, single mother and hasn't got anyone to help her. If I can prove the police were negligent on this, it might help reduce her sentence some. But that's not why I'm calling. She wants her daughter back, and I can't help her there."

Mabel leaned against the counter for strength, saddened to hear about another girl in trouble. "I'm not an investigator, Lavi. There are better people than me out there."

"No, Mabel. You're my best," Lavi said. "I want you to take it."

Mabel struggled to decide.

"Mabel?" Lavi prompted. "Will you take it?"

Mabel opened her mouth to speak but then looked upon her children, with their heads down studying together, and they looked so beautiful. Her heart ached, and then she knew.

The End.

SNEAK PEEK OF MISSED ME (BOOK 2)

CHAPTER 1

Saturday, January 10, 1987

Mabel stretched the diner's phone cord to get a little privacy away from her customers. "Lavi," she whispered as loud as she dared, "I don't want to take the case."

"Why don't you just hear the details?" Lavi Arronson, a public defender in Seattle, pressed on. "I've got a client, Candy Johnson. She's a single mom, hardworking like you. But her sixteen-year-old daughter got into drugs and is now missing."

Mabel's hand fluttered to her heart as she automatically thought of a teen girl she had seen caught in the clutches of that racist Larson. She'd had a few run-ins with him in the past, the latest last fall, and wanted to wipe the stain of him out of Blue River — a mountain community home to a failing sawmill, a budding mine and thanks to Karl Larson, the largest drug operation in Washington State. But she hadn't seen the young girl since, and Mabel often found herself searching for any sign of her whenever she drove into town or past one of Larson's weed farms.

Lavi must have taken her silence as encouragement. "Candy went to the police with her concerns, and guess what happened?"

"They didn't believe her."

"They said addicts like her often run away and she'll be back. But Candy had talked to her daughter just before she disappeared, and the girl was afraid, Mabel. Two drug dealers, skinheads, might have abducted her, and she needs help."

The familiar clinking of coffee cups, the scraping of cutlery on plates, and the buzz of conversation like music turned her around. Her sons, Hector and Fred, and their cousin Kerry were doing homework at the diner counter. Kerry was tutoring a confused Hector in math, and Fred was reading a book — so sweet.

The last case had exhausted Mabel, not to mention nearly killed her. She couldn't do this. She needed more time with her family.

"Lavi—" she started, but he interrupted.

"Angela."

"What?"

"Her name is Angela. The daughter."

Mabel closed her eyes. She didn't want to know the girl's name. It would have been a lot easier if she hadn't known her name. Her mind flashed back to that teen girl at Larson's farm, with her face piercings and black lipstick, getting up from that pig's lap and pawing hands. And then the poor dear girl, blue eyes down and cheeks an embarrassed red, walked past with folded arms, and Mabel had thought of her ever since.

"Mabel?" Lavi prompted, a note of concern in his voice.

Mabel tore herself from her reverie and huffed, angrier at herself than with Lavi's manipulation. "I can't do this, Lavi. I am so busy here, and . . ." She sighed and then turned away from her children so they wouldn't overhear. "You said there was a file on her, a picture maybe?"

Lavi sounded confident again. "Of course. I'll have Janice drive them down to Blue River."

"It's an hour-and-a-half drive, dear!" Mabel said, not wanting Lavi's assistant, Janice, to make such a long trip. "I have my Friday Tacoma run for the diner. We can meet halfway, and I can pick it up then."

"I can't wait. The prosecutor wants prison time for resisting arrest. But if we can show a judge that her daughter was in real danger, a good one might give her a pass. Otherwise, as a repeat offender, she's facing some real time if convicted."

Mabel considered what she would do if one of her

kids had disappeared. Anything and everything. She shivered, not wanting to think about it but empathizing with this mother — a single mom, no less. Such a mama would do anything for her cubs.

Fred finished his milk at the counter, and Mabel instinctively moved over by stretching the phone cord farther and poured him another glass. He raised his head slightly, distracted from reading, and gave her a slight smile. She smiled in turn and lightly caressed his hair as he went back to his schoolwork. Then she thought about the girl trapped at Larson's.

"Where does the mother live?"

"Seattle."

Mabel frowned as she considered her hectic schedule. After tomorrow's winter festival, she was hoping to take Monday off as well — her first back-to-back day off in weeks; but she could do it then. "I'll come to you. In Seattle."

"You can meet the mother too," Lavi said.

"I'm not saying I'll take it; I'm just saying I'll have a look."

Lavi gave her Candy Johnson's address, and Mabel wrote it on her notepad underneath a trucker's order for a tuna melt and fries. Then she wrote down the mother's name, Candy, and the daughter's, Angela. A pretty name.

"You're the best, Mabel."

"Hmm," she said, not believing him. "I've got to run. I've orders to fill."

Lavi laughed. "I'm glad to hear it. Oh . . . before you go, how's your leg healing?"

Mabel winced, though it didn't hurt anymore. She had

a two-inch scar on her calf where a rapist-killer's knife had snicked deep and several scars on her hands from crawling through a sawmill to get away from him and his vile friend. She still had nightmares, though the two killers were now dead — one by suicide, one murdered in prison by members of his own gang. Larson's gang.

"It's fine, dear," Mabel said, not wanting to talk about it more. Then she lied — "I got to go. Kevin's calling" — and hung up.

She pressed her hand on the wall, trying to catch her breath as she relived the terror of that night. Then, as Fred looked up and asked, concerned, "You okay, Mama?" she forced her lips into a smile, nodded, and started gathering some dirty dishes. When she took them into the kitchen and placed them in the industrial sink, the cook — twenty-one-year-old, long-haired, tattooed Kevin — was too busy grilling burgers to notice. Her tears burst out, so she turned on the faucet to drown out the sound of her sobbing. She wasn't a detective, only a diner and motel owner and waitress, no matter what Lavi thought. But a mother had lost a child, and that horror overwhelmed her, as it would any mom.

End of Chapter 1 of Missed Me
(Book 2 of the Mabel Davison Series)

CONTINUE THIS EXCITING SERIES

Order on Amazon or my website www.trevorwiltzen.com

ABOUT THE AUTHOR

Trevor Wiltzen lives in a small big-city in the prairies called Edmonton, Alberta. When he is not working (or writing), he spends time with his wonderful wife, two beautiful boys, and their friendly dog Maggie.

GET YOUR MYSTERY NOW

Post your review of the Heart of the Runaway Girl on Amazon, Bookbub, and Goodreads today.

Visit my website www.trevorwiltzen.com for sneak peeks, free content, giveaways and the latest news on the series.

W

Manufactured by Amazon.ca
Bolton, ON